"A story of heartache and loss. A mother's struggle to right the wrongs of a crime against children that causes her to lose the love and respect of her own son. Written from the heart, this story may arouse your anger, and shock you in parts, but it will keep you reading as you experience hope, crave redemption and trust that there's a good outcome."

— Author Kitty Boyes, *The Arina Perry Series*

. . . . .

"This is a solid debut novel by a local Vermont author. It is thought provoking as well as heartfelt and heartbreaking. How far and how much would you be willing to lose in the face of right and wrong? One woman puts it to the test and personally I was on her side the entire way."

— Vicki Thornton, Blair Books & More (Chester, VT)

Rectified

Rectified

Pollyanna Porter

2021 / *Vermont*

Book Design by Jennifer Payne,
Words by Jen (Branford, CT)

Quote by Angelou, Maya. *Letter to My Daughter.* United States: Random House Publishing Group, 2008.

Printed in the USA

Library of Congress Control Number: 2020920100

ISBN: 978-0-578-78294-2

Copies of Rectified may be purchased
from online retailers or by visiting:

www.read-rectified.com

Dedication

To the memory of Bobbie Porter, my mother.
Thank you for the wonderful right.

and

To the educators and counselors I've traveled this
lifetime with, especially Christy, Moria and Steve.
Thank you for your endless dedication to
improving the lives of children.

"You may not control all the events
that happen to you, but you can
decide not to be reduced by them."

— Maya Angelou

Chapter 1
present

Sometimes when I wake in the middle of the night, or before dawn, too early to get up, I replay over what I saw. The boy and the man together, first at the building lot, then in the diner. I freeze the frames then try to align them again, as I did, shockingly that day, over my half-eaten eggs and toast. I wonder where or how the angles could have been different. Through the frame of a window as I watched, repulsed? Could I have stayed in the car, choosing to lean back in the driver's seat in anticipation, instead of hiking in? Or maybe in the Café, when the boy tied his shoe. What if I had sat at the counter, oblivious to everything but the Living Arts section of the newspaper? So many chances to miss the alignment, yet I didn't, and here I am. A handful of times, while in this kind of mental replay, I'll go further out and ask myself, *'What if I never told?'* I always come back to the inevitable, middle of the night, early morning surrender: *'I did tell and shit happened.'* I hope, more than anything, that my son, Michael, is okay. Despite me or because of me, this is my biggest take away. The jury is out on that.

On those difficult nights and early mornings, I invariably get a call to substitute teach. I'm still not quite comfortable in this coastal town of one month. I've got to be patient. I know this. I have staying power because there is no alternative for me right now. Two to three times a day, I wonder why my exodus and self-imposed exile had to be so drastic. From rolling hills and mountains to windswept docks, pounding surf and dense fog. From the known work day, with routines, schedules, expectations to the never known. But here I am, again, on one of those middle-of-the-night kind of mornings, answering my cell and getting up.

I am starting to adjust to my immediate surroundings in the rented loft above Robert's Tackle and Bait Shop, overlooking this small inlet. The Lincoln rocker, no longer at a fireplace, but near the large window facing the water. The maple dresser and handmade braided rug defining the area in the alcove of my bedroom, and the old bottle collection of different shapes, sizes, and colors placed on the wooden beams near the peaks above each end of the large, bright room. Everything else—my new, refurbished kitchen table and chairs, the bed and comforter, couch, coffee table, and other throw rugs—are newly purchased but blend in well. I only wish the gray skies and the smell of the sea were not so constant and so strong.

Land-locked for all of my forty-two years, I become unnerved every time I have to walk the wharf to get to my car in the semi-darkness. This morning I am down the stairs by 7:15 and off to a new school, for a fifth grade classroom I've never been in. I am glad the owner of the bait shop (is his name Robert?) is there and waves to me. My witness and possible rescuer should I fall overboard into the cold, dirty, dark, swirling water as it breaks onto the small jetty.

My Subaru is parked under the street lamp and is one of only two cars in the parking lot. Its new white Maine license plate is still a surprise to me when I see it. It's eerily foggy on this mid-October morning as I climb in and start the car.

I am heading to Morris Elementary, a school about twelve miles northwest of where I'm living now. I replay the directions I got from the school's secretary: "Go to the main office off of the Patterson Street side, come in, and we'll get you set up."

A strong yearning hits me as I turn onto Route 101. It's for my old classroom of sixteen years at Peddan Middle School in southern Vermont. I would just be arriving and turning on my classroom lights at this time, while calling out to other teachers as they passed by my door. The smell of coffee from the teacher's room would be strong and inviting. Gladys, our school secretary, would be rounding the corner of my wing with her hand weights and saying a cheery, "Good morning."

The sense of loss overwhelms me, but I don't dwell on it. I can't. Things happened and as I've said, the jury is still out. The real jury never did have to weigh in, but I bet those jurors had some strong thoughts before and after all this. It seems most everyone did. But the one person I care about, whose thoughts and forgiveness have yet to come, wants nothing to do with me. I can wait. Patience is a virtue.

I check my makeup in the rear-view mirror, not too much, not too little. I feel good this morning despite the intrusion of thoughts in the wee hours. I've gained some of the weight back that I lost over the last year, and I like the highlights the new place gave me. In fact, I liked the hair dresser a lot. She was fun and informative, giving me the lowdown of the area—best restaurants, best bars, best places to see the 'local color.' Donna towered over me by about six inches and eighty pounds. Her hair, piled high on

top of her head with bright blue streaks, was a little con-
cerning to me when I first entered the salon. But she
assured me she was the only anomaly.

"You're beautiful, honey. You'll make a splash in our
parts, believe me," she said as she showed me the choices of
highlight shades. I chose my usual color, but she overrode
me and pointed to one with caramel undertones. I yielded,
not quite sure, but not quite unsure either.

We were almost done when I smiled at her through the
mirror, taken aback by the new low lights.

"See, you're a vision for our sore eyes. Soon men up here
will be asking you for your number. Be picky, you can
afford it," she quipped as she gave me a hand mirror to see
the back.

"I'm surprised how much I really like it," I said. "And
Donna, I came here to kind of lay low, even disappear."

"Well honey, that isn't gonna happen, "she replied,
raising her eyebrows to the two older women in various
states of cut, perm and dye.

Today, driving north, I feel the weight of everything that
happened pressing down on me. I try to shake it off as I
drive into another day of a new school and the unknown.

Chapter 2
past

Apickup, coming up the icy pass, flipped and slid over into my lane, resting about thirty yards in front of me. I pumped my brakes, stopped, and put my flashers on. It was dark out, and at first I wasn't even sure what I had just seen. Immediately, a man started to climb out of the truck and I watched as he fell down, hard, sliding across the road. I stared and did nothing. I didn't dare get out or back up or drive to him. I was afraid of skidding off the road into the bank of trees to my right. I sat, with my legs shaking, the heater cooking, and my radio on. He made his way up to me and motioned to the passenger side. I gave a thumbs up—my mittens were on—and he climbed in. I quickly turned off the radio.

I sometimes try to remember how those first few moments went on that December morning, two years ago. I think we both were in a strange, suspended state.

Once he got in the car I said, "Hey, you okay? What should we...what should I do?" Looking at him, he seemed fine, but I couldn't tell for sure. He had a ball cap on, with sandy colored hair poking out, and a dark, close-cropped beard and mustache. His cheeks were red, his nose running. A bruise was forming on his left cheekbone. I looked down at his left hand; it was shaking and bleeding. He reached up to wipe his nose. I quickly reached into the center console and brought out a wad of Kleenexes. "Here," I said. All around us the snow was falling thick, but it was quiet inside the car.

Taking the Kleenexes, he replied, "Thanks," and wiped his nose, flexed his hand, and put another Kleenex on the cut. His coat, pants, and boots were covered in snow.

His voice was low, full of disbelief. "Wow, that was a surprise. Musta hit a real icy patch. Didn't expect that."

Just then another truck started to come up the pass, much slower, but it too started to slide and stopped just before the overturned truck. Between the upside-down pickup with its lights still on, this second stopped vehicle, and the heavy snow, Sutter's Gulf looked surreal, no longer a familiar place to me.

A man got out of the second truck and waved to me. I opened the car door and stood up, holding onto the door-frame for balance.

"He's okay, he's right here," I yelled across the stretch. "His hand is bleeding but I think that's it."

"Got road flares I'm putting out. Get him to the restaurant down the hill, call the state troopers." The man impressed me with his take-charge commands. My *teacher takes directions in an emergency* instincts kicked into gear.

I yelled, "Okay," and got back into the car. It was still pretty warm inside, but I thought my passenger looked colder. His face was drained of color, and he was visibly shivering. *What does shock look like?* I tried to remember. I turned the fan to the car heater up to high and reached over, in front of him, to make sure the vents on his side were all open. "Sorry, but you really need this," I said.

I also grabbed my lunch bag from the floor behind the passenger seat. I reached in and took out a water bottle. Unscrewing the cap, I handed it to him.

"Please, drink some water."

He took it, and drank.

The Gulf is a stretch of Vermont road outside of the ski town, Langdon. The road freezes up in the winter and can become treacherous driving. It's carved out of a mountain pass—rock ledges face drivers going north, while a steep bank of trees meet drivers in the southbound lane. For a distance of about five miles, the road gets little sun as it makes its way through the pass. Despite road crews' efforts, its steep angle and winding cut can become hazardous quickly, giving little warning of slippery conditions.

Every first snow storm, Gladys, from school, and I would joke about how the 'Sutter's Gulf Support Group' was now up and running. She and I were its only members. Our daily commute to and from school placed us smack in the Gulf twice a day, sometimes as early as 6:45 a.m., and later, on route home, about 4:00. It was not uncommon for us to seek each other out in school if something odd happened in the Gulf. Once, Gladys had to wait with a few other cars for a bull moose to mosey on across. "How it went up that bank remains a mystery to me," she said at the time. Another time, I saw three men on bicycles, decked out in colorful Speedo biking shorts and shirts, sipping from what looked like a champagne bottle on the shoulder of the northbound lane. I drove by, slowed down and gawked, thinking, *What the hell are you doing?* Shortly after, there was a blurb in the paper that the three were celebrating their 1,000-mile marker, commemorating a friend who died of cancer. Gladys and I were chicken-shit drivers in the pass during the winter, though speed demons any other time of the year.

I put the Subaru in low and crawled on down the Gulf until it leveled out. My wipers were on high; it was hard to see beyond the hood of the Subaru. Not far ahead, I could make out lights on the left side of the road. There were three, maybe four cars at the restaurant, The Chat and Chew, and I pulled in. It was a small, faded green diner. Not much to it, but I could see people inside. The snow was coming down harder, and the wind had picked up. Other than the second pickup, very little traffic, if any, had passed us in the span of about ten minutes.

I turned the car off and looked at the man. "Let's get you inside and see how you're doing, okay? I've got to call the state troopers. And you may need some medical attention. Can I call someone for you?"

He seemed a little better and smiled at me. It caught me by surprise; his smile was big, earnest, and he had straight, white teeth. His eyebrows, dark like his beard, were thick, a striking contrast to his lighter hair. The bruise from the fall was starting to give him a shiner. I remember thinking *cute guy* as I put my hood up, over my hat, ready to get out of the car.

"I don't think I dare call my wife and have her drive in this."

I nodded and we both went into the diner. Things picked up from there. It was evident that the people in The Chat and Chew knew him, and they quickly took over. They called the state troopers and I think a tow truck. He sat at the counter and someone gave him coffee, ice for his cheek, and a first aid kit. I was able to call school and tell Gladys I'd be late. I imagined the school buses would be in for a treacherous morning.

I also phoned Jeffrey, my husband, to tell him what had happened and that I was fine. He was in Boston, oblivious to the sudden snow squall in the pass.

I tried to get the man's attention before I left to wish him well, but he was on his cell. After school that day, on my drive back up the Gulf, I couldn't see any trace of where the truck had flipped. The Gulf was bare, the afternoon sun was trying to peak through, and the trees were snow laden and magnificent. I remember thinking that I'd done my good deed for the week, maybe even the month. I have since had many regrets—none of the actual good deed, but of what followed with him. And of course, Michael, always Michael.

The first time I saw my passenger again was sometime in January at the Langdon Food Co-op. I didn't recognize him at all. He was holding a little girl's hand. She was about four years old, wearing a bright pink knitted hat with matching mittens.

I heard the two of them conversing about which muffins they should buy. She was pleading with him. "I want the chocolate ones, Daddy, the chocolate."

He was trying to steer her towards the blueberry, but she was not having any of it.

I turned the corner and smiled at her, agreeing, "I'd pick those too."

The man suddenly stood up and looked at me, exclaiming, "Hey, I've been wanting to run into you!"

I looked behind me and then back again, at him. "Excuse me?"

"It's me, the guy you helped in the Gulf, in the pickup?"

I must have seemed like an imbecile because I just stood there, trying to figure him out. The man in front of me was hatless, tall, and he looked older, maybe almost my age. Then he smiled, and it was the same big smile with great teeth I'd notice that morning. *Yep, cute guy again,* I thought.

"Wow." I knew how dumb this sounded, but it was all I had and all I gave. I just stood there.

"Yeah, well, I want to thank you so much for helping me out," he replied, still looking at me while his daughter was reaching for one of the chocolate chip muffins on the counter. She yanked on his hand, but he kept staring at me. I continued to stand with a puzzled expression.

"I, um, well, you're welcome, but I really didn't do much or at least anything more than the next driver would have done."

For some reason, I was stumbling and embarrassed. I needed to get moving, but, like a fool, I quickly added, "I hope your truck's okay."

He laughed. "My truck? My truck was totaled. I'm lucky I didn't get hurt, other than a few cuts and bruises. Really, thank you. My wife thanks you too. I hope I didn't wreck your car with any blood or my boots or anything?"

"No, nothing." I smiled and looked down at his little girl, joyfully eating the muffin. Chocolate was smeared across her lips and on her pink mittens.

"Oh, no Emily, the mittens. Sweetie, Mommy is going to have a fit. That's why I wanted you to get the blueberry ones."

I leaned down to her and in a conspiratorial tone of voice said, "Well, chocolate is easier to wash out than blueberry stains. So, Emily—it is Emily, right?" She nodded. "You may have made the smarter choice than Dad." The child was definitely enjoying the muffin. After each bite she would look at how much was left.

The man smiled. "Hey, my name is Craig, Craig Portman, and, as you've figured out, this is Emily. And you are?"

At this, I reached out and shook his extended hand.

"Sara Clemens." Then I quickly corrected, "I mean Sara Scott, my goodness."

"Well, which is it, Clemens or Scott?" His smile was disarming. This whole exchange had proved daunting to me, his presence was commanding. I found it hard to keep up coherent dialogue on my part. *What is it about him?* I wondered. A bead of perspiration rolled down my back. The store was warm, and I was in full winter gear.

"It's Scott for sure." My face was burning.

"Well, nice to meet you." He smiled again. "It's your hat, I remembered your hat." I turned and left the store abruptly.

When I got to my car, I could not believe I had said my maiden name. I also hadn't even picked up the couple of items I needed. I sat in the car, hoping they would leave soon. And they did, walking to a truck, this one silver with an extended cab. I watched him, Craig-something-now, get a wipe from his dashboard, and lean into Emily in the backseat, wiping her face and hands, chatting the whole time. When he drove past me, I ducked down, scooping my hat off quickly, hoping he hadn't recognized me or my car.

As I turned to watch him drive out of the parking lot, I noticed a little sticker of a pink unicorn on the back window. I liked that. But, overall, I didn't like how stupid I felt. It was a new feeling and totally uncomfortable. I started up my Outback and looked down at my hat. It was a Norwegian winter hat, red and white with a star pattern. "I love this hat," I said out loud as I put it back on.

I told myself that that was that. But it wasn't. I kept going over this exchange in the Co-op, and then would imagine, in great detail, the ordeal of the morning accident. It was a loop that played over and over in my head. The reel, entitled "Craig" in my mind, would begin the minute I was in my car for the morning commute to school and then continue when I drove back home each afternoon. For eighteen miles I went over every detail, sometimes rewriting the dialogue to what I wish I had said. Sometimes imagining what I would have done instead. It was pointless and absurd, but there it played. I never changed anything profoundly, I just tweaked my part mostly, making me sound more with-it, even sophisticated at times. During all the other parts of my day and night, especially when I was with Jeffrey or around Michael, I tried to make sure the reel didn't permeate my thoughts. This proved difficult, and ultimately became impossible when we finally met again.

My husband, Jeffrey, and I were in our nineteenth year of marriage. We were on autopilot much of the time. We could finish each other's sentences, know what the other would order out at dinner, choose the same movie to watch, and, as Michael pointed out, use the same expressions when reprimanding him. "You even deliver it with the same exact cadence," he'd lament.

The Christmas before, I had given Jeffrey a blue tartan bathrobe only to unwrap my own tartan bathrobe from him. When Jeffrey was on a business trip and someone needed to know what he thought on a particular issue in Langdon, sometimes I'd fudge it, making up what I knew he would say from notes he kept in his office. Once, Jeffrey was quoted in the Langdon Shopper about a new sewage treatment plant proposal.

Reading the article and seeing his quote, he said, "I sound pretty smart. Funny, I don't remember the call."

I had looked over at him with my eyebrows raised. "They had a deadline, and when they called, I went into your office, and…"

"Thanks, babe." Smiling, he resumed his reading.

We signed each other's names on checks and credit cards, and laughed when our Edward Jones broker would not place a rather large 'sell order' without hearing from us both.

Dialing the broker's number, Jeffrey joked, "What's he think? One of us is going to abscond with all our money and leave town?"

We also knew each other well in the bedroom. I had been with two other men before my life with Jeffrey. Actually, they were boys: one Michael's present age, and the other a gangly sophomore in college who I dated for a total of forty-three days. The saying, *'He taught me everything I knew'* fit us as a couple, as Jeffrey was much more experienced than I was when we first met. Sometimes, especially in our earlier days when Michael was younger, I would do something 'new' to surprise Jeffrey. Once I wanted us to try edible massaging oil. I ordered some, in mango. Jeffrey had an immediate reaction and started to itch. He'd gotten up and run to the shower while I changed the sheets. Then Michael had awakened and we all ended up eating cheerios at the kitchen table in the middle of the night. When it back-fired like that he'd laugh, "Please, no more *Playgirl* articles." But when it pleased him, he'd whisper, "Now that was very, very good," and he'd pull me close, wanting to know what else the article or book had said. But it'd been awhile since I cared enough to surprise him.

There was a predictability in our marriage, a comfort-ableness that lent itself to stability and security. Was there ever an undercurrent of unhappiness? As Michael became more independent, I had fleeting thoughts: *Is this it?* I don't know how Jeffrey felt or if he had similar thoughts. We didn't discuss our marriage in these terms.

In recalling the exchange in the Co-op with Craig and his daughter, I wish things had stopped there. I've wondered if the predictability in my marriage was why I was so affected by the surprising and unpredictable way Craig Portman had looked at me that day. He had stared at me in a way that Jeffrey and I had stopped long ago. Or maybe we had never looked at each other like that.

One morning in late January, our coffee maker did not kick in. I am one of those people who needs a cup just to get going, so I left the house after declining Jeffrey's offer to run to the convenience store. In retrospect, it's another one of the many variables I play out that would have affected the outcome. I don't exactly remember when, or why, I decided that I'd get the coffee at The Chat and Chew. I'd never once stopped there before the accident in all the years of driving to work.

I pulled into the restaurant, narrowly focused on getting that big cup to drink for the rest of my commute to school. The bell of the door jingled as I entered and the warmth of the diner hit me. I went straight to the counter and did not notice the man sitting on the stool nearby until he reached over and gently pulled on my coat sleeve. I turned and there was Craig, smiling, the ball cap back on. It was a Boston Red Sox cap in faded blue. My heart missed a beat. I know it's a cliché, but it described perfectly the reaction I had.

"There's that beautiful hat again," he said, looking at me and smiling.

I reached up, touched my own hat, and looked at him, feeling as if something seismic was happening. I can only describe the feeling now as an attraction that was primal, beyond articulation. I hadn't felt this way for years, if ever, I recall.

I ordered my coffee black and as the woman started to pour it Craig called out to her, "Sheila, make it your best 'pour' of the morning and add it to my bill."

Sheila looked up at us both. She wasn't smiling, a look of concern across her face. It was as if she too was registering this moment.

I took the coffee from her and said, "Thank you." I turned and looked at Craig and lifted the coffee as if in a toast. "Thank you too." I didn't want to leave, but I had nothing else to say.

As I started to get into my car, I noticed the silver truck. Just then Craig came out, down the steps and over to my window. I rolled it down.

"Hey, I go north this time of day, and you go south. I work in Langdon, on The Mountain. Where you headed to?" he asked in the chilly air.

"I teach down at the middle school, in Peddan. And right now I'd better get going, or I'll be late." I didn't want to go. It was evident to me, but was it to him?

"Have a good day, Sara Clemens—correction Scott." Then hesitantly, he said, "Maybe, um, maybe we can meet up again sometime." He was looking at me now, intently, with no smile.

Something jolted me. Maybe I was emboldened by the better dialogue I'd been practicing in my head, or maybe it was the practice of teaching my students clarifying questions. Whatever it was I countered bluntly, "Craig, what's going on here? What are you saying to me?" How ballsy I was.

And how honestly he answered, "I think about you a lot. I mean a lot."

"Do you do this often?" I replied, harshly.

He countered in a strong, urgent voice, "Never."

I didn't know what else to say, and he appeared to be at a loss too. I put up my window and backed out, giving him a short wave of acknowledgment as I pulled out on to the highway. He remained standing there, motionless, watching me leave.

To say I was rocked by our exchange would be an understatement. Like when you google anything, and then start to see it in your Facebook feed, I started to imagine seeing Craig everywhere.

In actually googling him, I found out where he lived and drove past his modest house in the dark, winter dinner hours, sometimes even taking a detour and driving by on the way home from school. I watched for him in every silver truck that passed through Langdon. I searched Facebook for any posts associated with his name. I even combed over The Mountain website, looking at employees and their bios, hoping I could get as much information on him as possible. He may have been doing similar things, as I think I watched the pink unicorn sticker drive by my house slowly on the next two Saturday mornings.

But here's an interesting point: I avoided the Co-op at all times. I couldn't bear the thought of being drawn into this thing, whatever this thing was, with that precious little girl present. She had become my speed bump.

Still, at home, in the privacy of my own bed, I fantasized about him, and Jeffrey was the beneficiary. I would visualize his face, sandy hair, and beard. I was alive and sensitive to my own touch, something I had never fully explored in my sexual past. Jeffrey looked at me with curiosity on a few of those winter mornings as I surprised him by reaching over.

At one point he asked me to stop my sexual mutterings. "What's gotten into you?" he whispered and I replied, rather flippantly, "Don't you like it?"

Another evening, as Jeffrey came into the bathroom and reached for the floss, I closed the door, hands on the vanity, inviting him to me. Jeffrey didn't hesitate and came up from behind. I watched him in the mirror, again imagining a different face. He knew something was different, and I've wondered since, did he know it didn't involve him? He obliged me every time and our sex life was humming. I was insatiable. I was being primed for an affair, and I welcomed it.

Craig and my first time together was almost anticlimactic. I was coming out of the Rec Center on The Mountain with my friend Jeannie. We'd just walked the indoor track, and the cold air felt good after an hour of walking laps with hand weights. I noticed the pink unicorn immediately and stopped, my legs going weak.

Our cars were parked next to each other and Jeannie asked, "Hey, what's wrong?"

I turned back to the Rec Center entrance. "I left my water bottle inside. I'm going back in to get it."

Pointing, she replied, "No, you didn't silly, it's right in your hand."

"No, not this." I held up the Dasani. "I got a really nice one at Christmas and I'm pretty sure it's in their lost and found. I need to go back in and check. You go ahead." I was amazed how easily the lies, from this point on, rolled off my tongue.

"Ok, Sara, girl. Good walk tonight. Text me tomorrow."

As soon as she left the parking lot, I came out from my hiding spot in the lobby and walked over to the passenger side of Craig's truck. He reached over, opened the door, and, just like that, I was in.

"Hey." He looked at me and I closed the door.

"Hey, back," I replied.

"I'm not following you. I'm getting off work and happened to drive through and saw your car. I was hoping I'd see you." He gave me a tentative glance.

There was a pause. "I know your plate numbers," he added, looking straight at me now, no smile.

We sat and said nothing. Then he started up the truck and drove out of the lot. I wish I could say I was hesitant or contemplating this thoroughly with much trepidation, but the truth was that I was purring inside with anticipation and commitment. This was inevitable. I knew, without being told, that he was going to a place where we could have privacy.

In less than twenty minutes we were parked behind the local closed up grocery store, in back of the dumpster. Craig and I were kissing heavily. He told me he had imagined this and I felt good to him. I liked his voice up against my ear, and I smothered my face in his hair.

Again, I asked, this time in a whisper, "Have you done this before?"

And again, his adamant, urgent response, "Never."

He drove me back to the Rec Center. I got out and smiled as I closed the door.

I looked back at his truck when I reached my car. His window was down, and he waved to me.

Later, my lips were sore, my legs weak as I walked up onto our family porch. Lust is very different than love. I had no illusions, even then. I wanted lust.

When I woke up the next morning after the dumpster 'fire' with Craig, I laid in awe. How did I cross into this territory without so much as a thought as to what I was doing. Clearly, I wasn't thinking. A feeling of dread started to take hold of me.

Then, a trip to the bathroom to pee brought on a rather pleasant realization. I stood in front of the bathroom mirror and looked at my face. My long, dark hair was messy, my skin clear and pale, my lips puffy. But my dark brown eyes told a different story. They were lit up. "I'm alive," I whispered. I returned to my bed. I called in sick to school, yelled to Jeffrey that I didn't feel well and that he needed to take care of Michael, and closed my door.

When Jeffrey spoke from the landing outside our door, he asked, "Hey Sara, can I get you anything?"

I replied impatiently, "No, I need sleep."

Soon the house was quiet, and I relived the forty minutes in Craig's truck in thorough detail. With the early February sun streaming in, I folded myself into the big white comforter, on gray, cotton flannel sheets and fell asleep for hours.

W here was Michael in these early days of Craig and me? He was in his last year of school, having come off of a great soccer season with the Varsity team. He was immersed in the college application process with Jeffrey. The Common Application had been sent out, and we were all anticipating early acceptance letters.

Michael was definitely in love, and, I'm sure, in lust with Lexi (aren't all cute, naturally blond high school girls named some derivative of Lexi, Lexis, Alexis)? Together they were sweet and clearly devoted. I thought Lexi brought out the best in Michael, and she treated him with great adoration. It was reciprocated by Michael. I loved seeing this side of him, the sweet, tender side when he looked at her or grabbed her hand as she walked by.

Lexi had grown comfortable coming into our home with Michael, throwing off her sneakers or Uggs, getting her own snack and curling up in the den as we all watched *Game of Thrones*. They disappeared sometimes to Michael's bedroom but observed our one rule: No sex in the house (at least while we were there), and door always ajar. Sometimes, I would observe her running down the stairs and hurriedly saying goodnight to Jeffrey and me as her mother waited in the driveway. I'm sure she had her own moments of puffy lips and lit up eyes.

Lexi's mother, a divorced woman about ten years older than me, asked me the summer of their junior year if we could grab breakfast together. Marilyn voiced her concerns about the budding romance the minute I sat down.

She was the executive secretary to one of the owners of The Mountain and struck me as a kind of no nonsense, direct, organized, and very smart lady, and the mother of a sweet, wide-eyed girl with all the innocence of youth. Marilyn was one of those women who could pull off having a beautiful face framed in completely white hair.

"Well, Sara, we've got a case of love birds, don't we?" She smiled but carefully looked at me, gauging my own assessment and place as Michael's mother. I could see a little bit of Lexi in her, but I found Marilyn intimidating and I sat up straighter.

"Yes, I think Michael has fallen hard for your daughter, who I think is pretty wonderful. Are you concerned?" I asked, now nervously thinking she may not like Michael, or us, at all.

Marilyn looked at me carefully. "Here's what I think, Sara, and please understand, I am coming from that mother bear place. Lexi is smart and has to stay focused on school, then more school. She's wavering between nursing school, possibly becoming a physicians' assistant, or going even further. She's got the aptitude to do it. And the drive I think, or thought, until this handsome fella with the best soccer calves in town started knocking at our door."

I fumbled in my reply. "Well, I mean I don't think Michael plans to derail any of that, of course. He's just a kid too, and I'm sure he admires Lexi's brain and motivation."

Marilyn's laugh caught me off guard. "Oh, honey, I don't think that boy of yours admires that girl of mine's brain at all. I think they're both admiring the front and back end of what they're seeing of each other!"

I burst out laughing too and all the tension I had felt dissipated. We ordered our breakfast, Marilyn, a lumberjack's special while I chose the Greek omelet.

We didn't bring up the kids again until the end of the breakfast and Marilyn came right out and stated, without one bit of hesitancy or uncomfortableness, "I'm making Lexi an appointment to go on the pill. I'm not going to cross-examine her if they're already there, or ask if they're hoping to get there. Nor am I, in anyway, encouraging her, or them to do *it*." She made air quotes around the word. "I'm just going to tell her that this is what big girls do. I wanted you to know."

I looked at her and instantly thought how good she must be at her job, anticipating things those bigwigs need to know and figuring a plan on how to address it. I then thought of Michael and his awakening and what Jeffrey and he may have already discussed. They were close, and I was sure Jeffrey had done his 'fatherly talk.'

I thanked Marilyn and said I was paying for our breakfast. "After all, you just saved us both a boat load of money by being proactive."

She smiled and leaned in. "Do you know what the cost of medical school is? It's enough to shit bricks, honey, big ones."

I liked Marilyn and still do, to this day. She became one of the key players whose path I sometimes tumble down in my imaginings, of 'what if.' The last time we saw one another she squeezed my hand tight and told me Michael would be okay. I hoped she was right.

Chapter 3
present

I opened my car door in the parking lot of the new school, Morris Elementary. Sitting, I held the keys and reviewed all that had transpired in the span of seven hours. The fifth graders, mostly eleven-year-olds, were kind and considerate of me, volunteering to show me the way to their other classes, the cafeteria and most importantly, where to go in case of a fire drill. The other teachers in the upper elementary wing had smiled at me and checked in throughout the day.

Tami, the young secretary, had come down to the room at lunch and asked me to stop in to see the principal before leaving for the day. She looked concerned, and for a brief second, I wondered if I had done something wrong.

David Parks, the principal, extended his hand, and asked me to sit down. "I'll get right to it, the teacher you are subbing for, Mrs. O'Brien, has gone into premature labor this morning. I am not sure of the details, but I believe she will be out for a significant period of time. It's rather shaky as you can imagine. The baby, her first, if it arrives, will be about twenty-six, twenty-seven weeks. Although I'm told, most babies born at this stage make it."

"Oh wow, I'm sorry to hear this." I looked at him and waited.

"I'm asking if you'd be willing to take on the rest of the week in her classroom? And then beyond? I've heard great things about you today, from most everyone, including two of her students. A long-term spot would pay you per diem. With your experience and education, I am sure, it would be significantly more than sub pay."

"Of course, I can stay the week, and possibly beyond, if that's what you need. She must be a great teacher. Her classroom and students were wonderful today."

Standing up, Mr. Parks concluded our conversation. "Thank you. She's going to need a lot of support but knowing we've found a sub with your credentials will ease her worries and, frankly, mine too."

Turning the key in the ignition of the Subaru, I decided to drive down the longer, coastal route back to the loft. The afternoon light, playing on the water, cast shadows on the dunes; hues of green and yellow danced in the high reeds. It felt odd not to be in Langdon. Leaf peepers would be arriving this weekend and the town would be busy with tour buses and flatlanders' cars—a Vermont term for anyone who lived out-of-state.

As I neared my wharf, I passed the Wine and Cheese Shop and did a quick turn around and parked. Inside, I chose a good Chardonnay for the night to go with the scallops I had bought off the boat yesterday. I planned on sautéed scallops, brown rice, scallions, and a salad. Even though it was just 4:30, I wanted to drink, eat, and be in bed by 8:00. I was deep into binging *OA* on Netflix, but now I thought, *I'm a working girl again.*

I wished, more than anything, I could call Michael. The last time I tried, he picked up just long enough to hang up. Tonight, I held back and felt the start of something. I realized it was the familiar feeling that teaching brought me; purpose and direction. I laid out my school clothes on the bench at the foot of my bed. I slept soundly through the night.

Chapter 4

past

Jeffrey and I met years ago at Keene State. He was a graduate student in the Educational Leadership Program, and I was a senior, completing my course work for a BS in Elementary Education. I was also waiting for my student teaching assignment to begin. He was thirty-four, I was almost twenty-two.

We happened to go to the same movie at the Student Union when *Citizen Kane* was being shown one Sunday evening. We found ourselves getting up in the same aisle row as the lights came on. He looked at me and said, "Rosebud meant what?"

I wondered if he might be a professor. He was definitely older, with some gray, handsome and athletic.

"Is this a trick question?" I responded. We were two of about six people who had sat through the whole movie.

He asked me if I was into the old classics, and I told him the truth. "No, not really. I'm pretty sure there's a bat in the studio I'm renting, and I get nervous when it gets dark."

He looked at me and said, "I hate bats, my parents always have bats in their house. Tell you what, if we can get a tennis racket, I'll come get it."

I liked him right away.

We walked across the Quad to the Fitness Center. When the kid behind the desk asked Jeffrey where he was going with the badminton racket (all we could find), Jeffrey raised his eyebrows. The kid got the idea, and said, "Wipe it down good if you have to."

Jeffrey got the bat, but my place looked like a monumental struggle had ensued. It wasn't far from the truth.

We started to date, and I began my student teaching. He'd already taught high school social studies for eight years but was back on campus to get a second graduate degree, this one in hopes of becoming an educational consultant. He also had just been jilted. I think my maturity negated our age difference.

Jeffrey was kind and somewhat fragile during this time. It was my most serious relationship to date. My mother came to Keene for a weekend. She was impressed. "I like him Sara. He's got a good head on his shoulders, and he's got goals." I knew what she meant, and I agreed. I did not tell her that he'd been left at the altar. I did not want to dim her view of him. Besides, as our weeks grew into months, Jeffrey became stronger, coming out of a woefully hurt ego.

When I told Jeffrey I was pregnant, just after our six-month dating anniversary, his exact words were: "I'm okay with that. I'm ready to be a father."

His parents ran a resort in the Adirondacks in the summer and fall months and skimped by each winter. "It's either feast or famine," Mrs. Scott laughed to me the first time we met. It was famine time when we drove up through Speculator, grabbing two extra-large pizzas with all the fixings, en route to tell them they had a new grandchild on the way. I remember chaos and joy and Jeffrey smiling at me as the family rejoiced in the great room of their home, fire blazing and paper plates with pizza being passed about. "Getting married was a minor step on the way to becoming parents," his father had said. Later, that evening, under down quilts, we could see our breath as we made love, full of optimism for us and the little bean growing inside me.

We were married within three months (I was barely showing) and our mothers were thrilled as they stood next to each other, at the pale yellow, linen-covered table where we cut the wedding cake. My own mother had had a geriatric pregnancy at age thirty-eight, and I was her only child. Jeffrey, on the other hand, was from a big family of two girls and four boys, he being the oldest.

Jeffrey and I almost said no to two of his brothers when they invited us to go on a ski vacation to Langdon. Michael was ten weeks old. We were living in West Roxbury, just outside of Boston, while Jeffrey was taking a post graduate course in school leadership at Boston College. We were subletting an apartment that a friend of a friend of his sister Beth knew. His siblings and their connections always amazed me. It was like their family was one big, messy ball of string, and, at any time, if you were in want of something, all you had to do was unravel the string, roll it to the end, and somehow you'd have it or a way to get it. My family, on the other hand, had been just my mother, step-father and me. Our analogy was just the opposite: it was a roll of scotch tape, with small precise pieces cut to the exact length needed. I loved Jeffrey's family with their spontaneous nature and their welcoming arms.

The house his brothers—Ryan and Everett—were renting for a week was big, they assured us. It had plenty of room to accommodate three couples, Michael, and all our baby gear. Jeffrey was adamant that we go too. Actually, I was ready to get out of our third floor sublet and head to Vermont. Michael slept a lot—never through the night, but he was easy to pack up in the front carrier and get around.

The countryside, driving Route 2 then up I-91, was beautiful. Snow-covered fields gave way to snow-covered hills, then mountains. We stopped at a place called The Vermont Country Store just off the interstate. It was fun weaving in and around the aisles, taste testing the dips and crackers, cheese and sausage. Jeffrey took the longest time choosing what to put in his bag of penny candy while I drank a coke in an old-fashioned bottle taken out of a red cooler. We bought my star pattern Norwegian hat that day. After, I nursed Michael in the car while Jeffrey entertained me with stories from his childhood. I was happy with a new kind of contentment, of being a mother and on an adventure.

We loved Langdon. It was small and quaint without being pretentious or outrageously expensive. Its shops were varied all along Main Street, with a few cafés sprinkled in. I liked the house the brothers had rented. It was just off Main Street, an easy walk to downtown. I could stand outside the house and see The Mountain, even hear the snow guns at night while I was awake with Michael. The brothers gave us the biggest suite and for six nights I got to know the house's night noises well. During the day, they skied while I explored downtown, the town's library, and walked the neighborhood of old homes set back with large trees, Michael asleep in my front pack.

On one of the sunny, winter afternoons of walking, I passed a house with a girl, about eleven or twelve, building a snowman with two little boys. She wore a bright green winter coat and black snow pants. Her hair was light brown, freckles covered the bridge of her nose, and her cheeks were red. The two little boys were dressed exactly the same in red snowsuits, their hats and mittens colorful and matching.

At first, I thought they were twins, but soon saw that one was larger than the other. They were serious as they rolled the snow and patted down the three distinct mounds, making up the snowman's body. The girl was clearly babysitting and praised the two little brothers as they worked together. As I strolled by, I stopped and watched. *How much we're going to love Michael at their ages,* I thought. The girl looked up at me and smiled. I waved as I continued my walk, Michael sound asleep. As I reached the top of the street, I glanced up at the street sign, and said, out loud, "We like you Dunsmore Street." I adjusted Michael's hat to cover his ears.

We ate out each night in Langdon's many restaurants, Michael either sleeping or me discreetly nursing. Jeffrey, his brothers, and their girlfriends were in high spirits. The skiing conditions were fabulous. Afterwards, at the rental, they'd play cards, drink brandy or scotch, and smoke cigars on the back deck. Lights out was at 9:00 p.m. sharp to be ready to ski early each morning.

When it was time to head back to West Roxbury, I asked Jeffrey to drive down Dunsmore Street. He indulged me and I smiled when I passed the house with the rather dapper snowman out front.

"This is the kind of street I'd love to live on one day," I said. "Where Michael can learn to ride his bike, run through the back yards, and walk to school."

Jeffrey smiled. "I agree."

We passed the school, a big brick building with two floors and more large trees. I turned back to read its sign: 'PTA meeting Tuesday.' *So much awaits us,* I thought, *as this new, wonderful world of being parents unfolds for us.*

A year and a half later, early one spring morning, Jeffrey came to me, carrying his laptop. We were still in West Roxbury, this time in a first-floor apartment. Jeffrey's consulting business had started to take off. Both of us wanted to get settled and for me to start my teaching career. Our location would be dependent on where I taught. Jeffrey could work, fly, and consult from wherever our home was. Michael was ready to start to socialize; he'd be three by the fall and ready for preschool. We'd been going two days a week to a play group at the local Y. I had also started to substitute teach. It was time for me to have my own classroom.

Jeffrey showed me two notices. The first was for a sixth grade Language Arts teacher opening in Peddan, Vermont. "It's about eighteen miles from Langdon."

I looked up and smiled.

"And look." He quickly opened up a second window on his laptop. It was a house for sale in Langdon. The address was 18 Dunsmore Street. I didn't remember the house specifically, but I knew how much I had loved the whole feel of the street and Langdon. "Oh my gosh, Jeffrey. Really?"

He had picked up Michael, playing beside me on the living room floor and twirled him around. When he stopped, he sang out, "And we, beautiful mother of Michael, have an appointment to see it this Friday!"

We put an offer in on the house right after the realtor took us through it, pending the inspection. I applied and interviewed for the position in Peddan, and, with fingers crossed, got the teaching job. I called the Langdon Elementary kindergarten teacher and asked her for recommendations for a day care offering preschool. She referred me to a wonderful woman named Karen Duling. Her house, like ours, was big, old, and had a vegetable garden with a large St. Bernard puppy named Gus keeping watch. One whole wall of her kitchen was a chalk board; the day care children loved to stand at it and draw, learning their colors, shapes, and letters. Michael would be joining four other toddlers and one newborn. Karen mostly had teachers' children because, as she explained to me, she had her own children and wanted the same vacations free. She struck me as a caring, conscientious early childhood educator who knew how to speak to small children with respect and sincerity.

W ithin days of moving into 18 Dunsmore Street, I felt comfortable going off to exercise on my own. I had scouted out the different places to walk and settled on the large cemetery off Dickerson Street. I had seen people walking there, and the gates appeared to be open daily.

On my first morning I was walking down a row of headstones, and turned quickly onto a shaded path, and picked up my pace. I was pushing it a bit but it felt good, and I liked the quietness of the cemetery. It was cool this early summer morning, the air crisp.

From behind me I heard, "Don't want to scare you, I'm coming up on your right."

A woman, about my age, passed me, and waved. I liked her stride and admired her leggings. I followed her, thinking, *she's got a route staked out.*

The very next day I saw her again, coming out from the woods, just beyond the big "Robinson" family plot. She waved and smiled, then caught up to me.

"Hey, if ever you gotta go, like you can't wait, where I just came from is the perfect little place to pee. No poison ivy, and privacy. Heck, I should leave a roll of TP there, I use it enough!"

I laughed and said, "Thanks for the tip."

That day's outfit was colorful; a bright yellow windbreaker and tie-dye leggings. The lipstick she wore matched her wide headband. She moved on ahead.

The third morning I was in the Langdon Cemetery to power walk, I looked for her. Sure enough, there she was up in the Russian section; the distinct Russian orthodox crosses visible from my spot below. She saw me and waved. I slowed down. I was hoping to talk a little more with her.

"Hey, how are you?" I asked. We passed two big willow trees then stopped. A hearse was parked ahead and cars were driving in, lining up beyond the hearse. A fresh grave site appeared to be prepped and a man was placing flowers out near the gathering.

Whispering, the woman said, "I think we best turn around. Seems a little disrespectful if we walk by."

"I think you're right."

In perfect unison we turned and headed for the gate, on to the street.

We weren't more than twenty feet out of the cemetery when I tripped on the uneven sidewalk and went sprawling across the pavement, tearing my yoga pants and skinning my knee. I had buffered my fall with my hands, and now they were scraped and covered with small stones.

"Are you okay?" she asked as she helped me up. I was more embarrassed than hurt.

I felt foolish and replied, "I'm fine, just clumsy. I'm Sara, by the way."

"And I'm Jeannie. You may be the first person I have ever met who is equally as uncoordinated as me, or maybe, just maybe, a tad bit more." I started to laugh, then winced from the cut on my knee.

Jeannie walked me home to Dunsmore Street, discovering that this was my very first week as a new resident of Langdon. She met Jeffrey and three-year-old Michael on the porch. After I got washed up and a band-aid on my cut, Michael asked her if she liked his elephant. He held up a tattered gray stuffed elephant to her face.

Jeannie looked up at Jeffrey and me, clearly amused. "I sure do. Is he your friend?"

Michael nodded 'yes.' He then made a sad face and said something Jeannie couldn't quite make out.

Jeffrey laughed at Jeannie's puzzled expression. "I think he's trying to tell you that his little stuffie is his only friend right now since we are new and without friends. But we are optimistic."

Jeannie smiled at Michael, "Can I be your friend, too?"

Michael responded by solemnly shaking his head up and down again. As Jeannie and I sat on the porch and continued chatting, with two glasses of lemonade, he moved over, and climbed onto her lap. That was the start of our settling in, making friends and raising our son.

Jeffrey and I became fully vested in the Langdon community scene, especially any happenings centered around Michael. Jeffrey volunteered often to be an organizer, coach, or contact person for different functions and projects—as much as his educational consulting schedule allowed. Multiple events marked the calendar prominently displayed on our refrigerator. Jeffrey relished this, and I often sat amused, in the early evenings, after dinner, or on Saturday mornings when the phone rang.

"I understand your concerns, and I will see what I can do. Please, always feel free to call me. I want this to work out for you."

Walking back into the kitchen I would look up at Jeffrey, curious to know the latest issues on whatever committee he was serving on. Often, he would share the gist of these conversations.

"Helen Thompson is upset that the new playground rubber mulch was not the blue color she wanted."

"They make blue mulch? You've got to be kidding!" I shut my laptop in disbelief that this was even a possibility.

Jeffrey, eyebrows furled, replied, "It took us two full meetings with the eight committee members to decide on our final color. It's going to be cocoa brown. But the black rubber mulch was a close second. I didn't have the heart to tell Helen blue got zero votes."

He was as serious as if he had just told me a school district was debating which grading policy he'd presented to them for consideration.

Jeffrey would grab his date book and the phone, walk to his office or the den, always being kind and friendly to the parent or other involved community member on the line. For a man who stood at a podium with conference partici-pants numbering in the hundreds, he was equally at ease with the people of Langdon. He once spent hours plotting with the father of one of Michael's Cub Scout buddies on how best to remove a bevy of skunks living underneath the Rod and Gun Club where the Scouts met. The father, a school bus driver, and Jeffrey made a debacle of the whole thing, finally having to call in the local wildlife expert for help.

Many times, after a call, I'd hear Jeffrey yell out, "Come on Michael, we've got places to go and people to see!"

Standing up, with arms straight out, Michael would reply, "Ready for takeoff!"

And then they'd go. Jeffrey, grabbing Michael by the seat of his pants, his other hand scrunching up Michael's shirt in back, would fly him to the door after zooming by me for sloppy goodbye kisses.

"See ya later, Mommy!"

Upon their return home, Michael would run through the house to find me and tell me all about what the two of them had done and where they'd gone. He often brought me little trinkets—a feather, a bag of flower seeds, some colorful pen that was for sale at the counter, knowing I would love it.

"Here, Mommy, this is for you." He'd wrap his little arms around my neck for a hug, only to break away to find his father again.

Jeffrey and Michael were nowhere near my thoughts as I walked along Main Street in late April. It felt really good to be out, smelling spring, wearing just a sweat-shirt and blue jeans. The sidewalks were recently swept by a street cleaner and The Mountain was showing green, with just a smattering of white. I was walking at a pretty brisk pace.

My level of excitement at seeing Craig in minutes was high. Our usual communication was through texting, a simple time and place to meet and an item or object named with some kind of status. Like, *"Shutters done, Tuesday 7-Maple."* I would know Maple from a previous rendezvous. If, for some reason, something didn't work, I would text Craig back, *"Invoice needed first"* or *"Shipment delayed."*

But I was mostly freed up to meet him whenever he could get away. Often, he would end his shift on The Mountain early and we'd meet. As the days became longer and it stayed light out, we were running into new challenges and had to be extremely careful. Also, since he was in main-tenance and The Mountain was done for the season, his hours were drastically reduced.

On this April day, during my week off from school, I had received, *"Furnace needs air filter, 2-Dickerson and Whitcomb."* I was surprised at the time, but he knew I had the day free. I left the house, excited, and as I walked, I watched for his truck.

At Dickerson and Whitcomb, I took out my phone. It was 1:58. I pretended to be texting and Craig pulled up at the four way stop. I quickly jumped in and off we drove. As we headed east, out of town, Craig grabbed my hand and squeezed it. I put on his ball cap and sunglasses. I remember him putting in a Darius Rucker CD.

Soon he was pulled over, up a rugged logging road. We became oblivious to the world, and I think if anyone had knocked on the window right then, we wouldn't have cared or been able to stop ourselves.

After, Craig reached for a water bottle, still cold, from the floor of the back seat and handed it to me. I uncapped it and took a long sip, then passed it to him. He was always gentle and thoughtful towards me in these moments, asking, as he did now, "You okay?"

I looked at him and said, "I've never been better." I was completely satiated and spent. He nodded, then drank from the water.

From the middle of January to the end of April, I'd been consumed with the affair. I hoped my obsession didn't show to Michael, Jeffrey, or at school. I was unaware, though, of the changes happening to me. Overtly, I'd lost pounds on a frame that was never large to begin with. Jeannie, my walking buddy, pointed out my weight loss as we walked Carley Road the next evening, after my Dickerson and Whitcomb rendezvous with Craig.

"Look at your sweats, they're falling off you! You're not trying to lose, are you?" she asked as we walked in perfect harmony, swatting the black flies.

"No, no, I guess I've been so busy with school, and Michael, you know his college stuff, I haven't been eating well." My energy level was low.

That was so far from the truth. Michael and Lexi were getting acceptance letters and while I would congratulate them, it was hard for me to focus on what comments went with which letter. Thinking about Craig constantly, I felt disjointed and became confused about what Lexi said on the University of Vermont or Michael thought about Colby Sawyer College. Our evenings at the house, especially while eating dinner, were all about the pros and cons of each place. Jeffrey had taken time to research the programs the kids were interested in, and I'd watch his animated face as he told them what he'd read.

Once, during this stretch of time, Michael showed his exasperation with me because I had put Jeffrey's notes in our recycling bin. They looked gibberish to me; I hadn't bothered to read them. "What are you doing, Mom? Dad's got all our possibilities mapped out," he exclaimed as he put the papers back, neatly, on a clipboard on our kitchen table. I made sure not to touch them again.

Mid-week of this April break, I was in the kitchen, making a tossed salad with mesclun lettuce, bell peppers, and grape tomatoes. I was whisking a balsamic vinaigrette dressing—knowing Michael would not like my homemade dressing, I put aside a plate of undressed salad for him in the refrigerator.

"Dinner, guys. Now!" I called out. It had been raining most of the day. The daffodils were blooming, and light green shoots from our lilies and irises were clearly visible from the kitchen window.

Michael came in and opened the fridge. He brought out the ranch dressing and carried it to the table, sliding onto the bench seat, to the same spot he'd held for the past fifteen years.

"Lexi's coming over. Do we have Rocky Road, Mom?"

"Do we what, Michael?" Jeffrey asked as he came into the kitchen, smiling at me and taking his spot across from Michael. I walked over and placed a Pyrex dish of Shepherd's pie on a hot mat between the two of them.

"Please be careful, both of you. This dish is hot."

Glancing at the table I said, "Michael, you brought the dressing, but not the salad, you silly boy."

"Oops, sorry," Michael replied, already digging into a serving of the pie. Like Jeffrey, Michael was compact and strong, his leg and calf muscles works of sculptured art. He was dark-haired like both of us (before Jeffrey's premature gray), but his features were all mine. If I'd been a male, I'd look like Michael, or if Michael was a girl, he'd look just like me. Once Lexi and I had laughed at that until Michael became irritated with us.

Reaching for his salad in the refrigerator, I said, "Yes, we have Rocky Road."

"Great. Lexi should be here any minute. Dad, her mom wants you to take a look at her financial aid packages from Syracuse and Cornell. Marilyn thinks she knows which is the better one but said she'd really appreciate your assessment."

"Okay," Jeffrey said, helping himself to the vinai-grette-tossed salad.

Just then Lexi's beautiful face appeared at our kitchen door. I motioned for her to come in.

I felt the cold spring air behind her. Smiling, standing on the inside door mat, Lexi was dripping wet. She wore a long black raincoat with an oversized hood. "Hi guys! Oh, you're eating, I'm sorry."

"You're welcome to join us, honey. It's good to see you." I added, "You walked?"

Michael jumped up and helped Lexi out of the wet coat. "Isn't this your mother's? And didn't you wear it in the Spook House when you were that pathetic witch?"

Laughing, she reached up and placed the wet coat on the coat hook above the baseboard. In her hands, shielded from the rain, were two good sized folders. "Yes, it is and yes, I did. Mom's raincoat was perfect for getting these over here dry."

Lexi was striking in the way that naturally beautiful people are who have no idea just how naturally beautiful they are. She didn't need make up; I doubted if she'd ever had her blond hair colored or highlighted. Her features blended into a perfect combination of clarity and definition. What Lexi concentrated most on were her studies. Without being a social misfit, she was able to be brainy, sweet, and, I am sure, 'hot' to Michael and the boys in his class.

Michael moved to make room for Lexi at the table. "Thanks, love," she said.

Jeffrey looked up and smiled at me, this sweet moment registering on the both of us.

Taking us all in, Lexi commented, "The temperature is dropping. I'm surprised how chilly it's gotten. It may even spit some snow. But it feels really good in here."

I ate the salad and a little bit of the Shepherd's pie. I thought it was dry, but Jeffrey went for seconds and Michael for his usual thirds.

When Michael brought his fork up, he moved it over to Lexi. "Taste? It's really good." Lexi took a bite. "Yummy. That's good, Sara."

"Sweetie, grab Lexi a plate, okay?" I asked. And again, Michael got up quickly. I thought he was adorable in how he attended to her. Lexi smiled as he returned and set down the plate in front of her.

The kids started to talk about the scrimmage the girls' softball team had played the day before, and the fact that the boys' first baseball game was canceled due to the heavy rain. There was a new, budding maturity about them both. *One foot out the door,* I thought. *They already look like college freshmen.*

I started to clear the table. Lexi and Jeffrey were beginning to compare the papers from the folders she had brought. Heads bent, Jeffrey with his reading glasses on, Lexi focused on everything he was saying.

Michael got up and came over to me at the counter. "Mom, I'm going to get Lexi and Dad some ice cream. Do you want any?" I looked up at him and smiled. He wasn't usually this solicitous of me. But I could tell he was happy. The rain was coming down harder, and here we all were, his people, warm and dry. Feeling treasonous from my involvement with Craig, I reached out and touched his arm.

"No, honey, I'm good." I heard him going down the basement stairs to our freezer chest.

I stayed standing at the kitchen window, looking at all the signs of spring taking hold. But my mind went elsewhere. I replayed the recent ride up the logging road with Craig and felt the familiar stirrings. I didn't turn around when Michael came back into the kitchen. Instead, I remained staring out, wondering when I'd be with Craig again. I was hoping we could rendezvous soon in a place we could actually lay down. That was my wish, drenched in guilt, at this moment. As my beautiful son was scooping Rocky Road ice cream into three dishes, ready to sit down and talk financial aid packages, college towns, enrollment sizes, distances from home, and possibly distances from his girlfriend, I hoped to fuck my lover lying down.

Chapter 5

present

I was leaning against the hallway door of my new classroom, watching Mr. Parks walk away. The baby had
come an hour ago, a little boy. It was going to be some
time before the students had their teacher back.

Bethany, the paraeducator assigned to the room, was
sitting next to one little girl named Maddie. She seemed out
of sorts and I sat down next to her. Bethany got up and
motioned to the clock. I nodded. It was time for P.E.

Maddie had grown more anxious every day this week.
She had sidled up to me just this morning and said, "You're
nice, but I want to know what you done to Mrs. O'Brien?"

Now, looking down at her, I felt a familiar tug. She
carried the look of a child deeply rooted in poverty who
needed school to get out of the bleakness of her life at home.
She was small for the fifth grade with long, wavy, blond
hair, pulled back in one of those hair ties with a bow
attached. The bow was dirty and skewed to one side. She
had a thin face. She scrunched up her eyes a lot. I wondered
if she should be wearing glasses.

Over the course of my years teaching, I'd had similar students who needed us to survive or to make survival at least possible. Outside agencies now came into schools to provide much needed services for lower socio-economic families. Dentists, clinicians and pediatricians were among some of the professionals Peddan Middle School welcomed on a monthly basis.

"Maddie," I said as I leaned down to speak to her, "Mrs. O'Brien has had her baby and it's tiny. She needs to stay in the hospital with the baby for many days. I'm sorry, sweetheart."

Maddie, searching my face with her little eyes, was clearly not sure she should believe me. "Well, I want her back, and nobody, not even that baby brat, is gonna change that."

She quickly got up and ran out the door, to the gym. Glancing around the classroom, I understood what a big change this was going to be for Mrs. O'Brien's class and for me. Now, I would be doing all the lesson planning as well as parent contacts, report cards, possible professional development, and a host of other things. I welcomed this and vowed to work hard at it, but I knew it was going to be a difficult transition for Maddie and possibly other children.

Maddie was, as I suspected, terribly sad as the day went on. She expressed it by scowling at me when I was reading aloud to the class, and she got up repeatedly during math time to sit in the 'calming chair.' I watched her poke another student.

The school counselor, Marsha, came into the room during my lunch. "Well, welcome to Morris Elementary, I just heard."

I smiled. "Tough situation, but I'm glad I'll be here. Mr. Parks really didn't tell me much. Do you know any more about mom and baby?"

"Just that it's going to be a long haul, as you can imagine. I thought, if you're okay with it, that I'd take the last forty-five minutes of the day to tell the students and let them ask us questions. Would that be okay?"

"Yes, definitely. I did tell Maddie already. She was struggling. I need to give her space, but I want to let her know that I'm here for her."

Marsha nodded. "I've got some stress toys and fidgets to help alleviate some of her anxiety. I'll bring them this afternoon."

After the students were dismissed for the day, the school secretary called into the room to say Mr. O'Brien was here to retrieve some of Mrs. O'Brien's personal items. I told her I would help him gather the things.

Shortly after, a man arrived and stood in the doorway. He was holding a bundle of something. I got up quickly from the desk and came over. "Hi, I'm Sara Scott. I hope mom and baby are doing okay."

He stood, a little awkwardly and replied, "They're making their way, you know. I've got a list and it says where everything is. Do you mind if I go ahead?" He was handsome, his face wind-burned and lined. He was of average height, with dark auburn hair and hints of gray appearing at his temples. He wore a red flannel shirt with heavy Carhart pants and steel toed work boots. My guess was he was a carpenter or builder. I thought he was a bit old for a father having his first baby.

"I can help you if you'd like," I told him.

"That would be good. Before I forget, this goes to Maddie, it's her laundry. Kristin, that's Mrs. O'Brien, my sister-in-law, thinks she's probably more than due for clean socks and underwear." He looked down at his note and read, "Please ask Maddie to bring in her bundle." He looked up at me and smiled. "I think that's code for Maddie to switch these clean clothes out now for her dirty clothes and I'll be back to get that bundle."

I understood. Mrs. O'Brien did Maddie's laundry each week, and he wasn't her husband, but her brother-in-law. "Tell you what," I said, looking at him. "I live all by myself, and I've got a great set up with a stacked washer and dryer just off my kitchen. I can easily do Maddie's wash. Please, please tell Kristen not to worry. She has enough on her hands."

He nodded and replied, "I know that would be greatly appreciated. She and my brother are anticipating eighteen, twenty hours a day in the Prenatal Wing."

"Good, I mean that's not good, but good, as in check that off her list. Now, what else have we got?"

We took a few minutes to gather up sneakers in the closet, a fall coat, a cloth lunch bag, and a chain with a cross on it that was inside a seashell on her desk.

As he was leaving, he paused at the door. "So, you've got a nice set up...where are you living?"

I leaned forward, wondering why he was interested. "Yes, I do. It's a loft down in Bristol. Why do you ask?"

Smiling, he said, "I heard a teacher was renting the place. I designed and built it. Glad it suits you."

The very next Monday, Maddie plopped the bundle—now full of her dirty clothes—on my desk without so much as a word or comment. I tucked it under my cabinet. That night I washed it all, mostly socks and undies, a couple of under shirts, leggings, and four shirts that I already recognized she wore often. In the morning I showed her the bundle when the other students were occupied in choice time. She picked it up, opened it, and inhaled deeply.

She faked like she was going to throw up. "Nope, that won't do, makes me want to puke." She wouldn't take the bundle.

I wanted to say a few choice words to her, but I held my tongue. Later that day, in the staff room I was recounting to Marsha what Maddie had done. Her eyes grew wide and she said, "Oh my God, Kristen went through this too, exactly the way you're describing it. Wait, I'll be right back."

In a few minutes I could hear Marsha's distinct shuffle coming back down the hall. She returned, waving a small piece of paper triumphantly. "This is from Maddie's fourth grade teacher."

I read, "It's got to be Tide, Fresh Scent."

Marsha continued, "She got that from Maddie's third grade teacher, who by the way, has retired to Naples, Florida."

That night I rewashed everything in Maddie's bundle, including the actual drawstring bundle with detergent poured from a big, 64oz container of Tide, Fresh Scent. Like the morning before, I called Maddie over while everyone was engaged in activities of their choice. She picked it up, opened it, and inhaled deeply. A hint of a smile of satisfaction crossed her face, and the bundle disappeared next to a spot by her book bag.

As we were lining up for the class to go to lunch later that day, I felt a little hand reach in to take mine. Maddie looked up and said rather sweetly, which was clearly—up to this point—unrecognizable to me, "That sweater looks real good on you Mrs. Scott." And off we marched to sloppy joes and apple sauce. Maddie had me at that.

Chapter 6
past

The morning after our Shepard's pie dinner, I received a text. *"Mower blade sharpened, 4-B10."* I knew this was a construction site on The Mountain that was tied up in various building regulations, codes, all to do with environmental snags. We'd been near there before and I quickly texted back, *"Confirm, need tarp/blanket for blade."* Craig texted back a thumb's up emoji.

I went about my day in anticipation, taking a long, hot bath. I fantasized about our bodies finally and fully coming together as the water drained out of the tub, the bathroom holding the warmth and steam of the water.

Michael was participating in the Youth Rec t-ball program for most of the day, earning the last of his community service credits. Jeffrey had just left for Boston, to work as a consultant to the Dedham School District's professional development strand. He wouldn't be home till Saturday night.

I stood naked in front of the full-length mirror in our bedroom. My bum was red from the bath, my nipples erect from the cooler air once out of the sauna-like bathroom. I liked what I saw, even though I knew I shouldn't lose another pound. I turned this way and that, posing as sexually as I could, hoping for Craig to finally see me completely naked. Up to this point we'd had flashes of body parts, always with breathless appreciation but never long or lingering.

I remember grabbing the straight back chair from Michael's room and placing it in front of the mirror. I sat down and experimented with opening my legs to see what Craig would see. I then stood and turned, hands on my fanny, bending this way and that, looking back at the mirror to see what I looked like from every angle.

I quickly ran to the bathroom and put on makeup to be even more accurate in anticipating what Craig would see. I returned to the mirror and got back into the posing. My hair was long and draped to the side. I made several faces, hoping to convey wanton lust.

I heard the ding of a text come in and I went to retrieve my phone. I had left it down in the kitchen charging. Walking naked through the house, I felt bold and completely at ease. The text said, *"Blade ready-3."* I looked at the clock on the stove, it was 2:20. I texted, *"Confirm"* right back. I was thrilled we'd be meeting earlier than originally planned.

I ran back upstairs and got dressed with a strong sense of urgency for finally having a tryst worthy of its name.

Now, I don't even recognize that person, that woman who ran out the door to drive to a vacant construction site surrounded by big equipment, cleared trees, and a large blue tarp draped and anchored over a partially erected structure not more than ten minutes from her house. Who didn't even think of her marriage or her son, who acted solely on impulse and desire.

There was a back way to access the B10 lot that Craig had taken me to, and I felt my Outback could handle the terrain. That day, more than ever I was ready, because it was finally warm and I envisioned us in various positions, with time and privacy.

I stopped the car and got out. I could see the structure through the woods, not far, but I had to be careful maneuvering over the felled trees and vast roots. It was also muddy, and I watched my step. I knew I was early but anticipated getting the lay of the building so I could tell Craig where we should spread our blanket. I also thought I might greet him stark naked, re-enacting those earlier poses I'd practiced in detail.

I came out of the clearing and onto what looked to be the back deck of this large, half-erected mountain house. I thought it had the makings of being spacious and attractive, though it definitely lacked the view of many of the homes that bordered The Mountain. I understood that this—and the neighboring lots—were much lower in price and more affordable to upper middle-class families skiing here. I sat down and took off my hiking boots, thinking I shouldn't be bringing in globs of mud from outside. While there were no actual windows in the house yet, just window frames, I knew Craig and I would finally have the privacy we craved.

As I put my Keens off to the side and started to get up, I thought I heard a noise. It wasn't loud, but it sounded strange, almost like whimpering. I ducked down and listened. It was either a hurt animal or possibly a person, I couldn't tell. I crawled over to the window frame and looked up and in. There stood an old man, not very tall and with a bulging stomach, leaning against the rough-cut wall, naked from the waist down. His pants and boxers were in a pool at the base of his feet, and his hands were cupped behind the head of a teenage boy who looked to be about eighteen, moving back and forth, in full fellatio. He was breathing hard, eyes closed, whimpering, "Not yet, not yet." The boy's head was moving faster and faster as the man was nearing ejaculation.

I quickly dropped from the window, scurried over to my boots, grabbed them, and took off running for the woods. Once there, behind a large birch tree, I threw up all over its trunk. It was mostly egg from my morning breakfast. I started to cry, and it was difficult for me to keep my balance and put my boots back on. My socks were wet, but I didn't care. I didn't tie either shoe. I ran back the way I came, barely looking at my feet, falling down more than once, my hands and knees muddied and stinging. When I got to the Outback, I gunned the engine, backing up hard into a tree stump. I then accelerated too fast and hit another one in front of me.

I flew down the access lane and onto the main mountain road, crying as I drove. I got home in record time. It wasn't even 3:00. I ran up the stairs and stopped on the landing, taking in the chair from Michael's room, still in front of my bedroom mirror. I immediately felt the bile coming up again and ran to the toilet. I collapsed to the floor, my arms hugging the seat. Mud-caked boots, wet pants, mascara running, I threw up again and again, alternating between dry heaves and choking. This was how Michael found me.

I looked up at his perplexed face as he stood in the bathroom doorway. "Oh, you know, your mom's not feeling well, but I'll be fine," I managed to say. He asked if I needed anything, and I shook my head, staying silent until he walked away.

I wasn't fine, or maybe, finally, I was fine, because that was the end of Craig and me. I couldn't think of him or us without wanting to throw up. While he texted me one, then two question marks after our 3:00 planned rendezvous that afternoon, I simply stopped texting him back. I must admit, he didn't seem that put out. After his second, maybe third coded text on where to meet a few days later was met by no response, I never heard from him again. Our carnal knowledge was over, but the rest of the problems in Langdon were just beginning.

Chapter 7
present

One night in the loft I was having a dream, not of the building lot, but of a beefy cop named Karl, questioning me repeatedly to go over my story. He was trying to trip me up, and I think he may have been in cahoots with another cop looking smug next to him. In the dream he kept saying, "Who were you meeting? Tell us, who?" I got bold and replied back, "It's none of your fucking business." I looked pleased with myself and remembered looking in the one-way mirror those interrogation rooms on TV always have and hearing applause. I smiled and made a motion like, *'Come on, clap some more.'* Definitely hints of *Orange is the New Black,* I thought when I woke up.

It was a Saturday and the sun was streaming through the skylights of the loft. I could see dust particles settling in on the old bottles and a prism forming on the opposite wall. I watched it for a while.

When Jeffrey asked me why Bristol, I said, "Why not?'

"It makes no sense," he responded, and I knew to some degree he was right. But a lot had happened, and I needed to leave. That, we didn't disagree on. I didn't dare tell him that I had closed my eyes, standing in front of Michael's wall map of New England in his bedroom, and Bristol is where my finger landed.

Would Michael like it here? I wondered. I think he'd feel sorry for me, reduced to one big room in a seaside town, closed up tight as soon as Labor Day passed. November was around the corner and then the holidays. While I did not anticipate seeing Michael, I still held out hope that he'd want to see me. I wrestled back and forth with the idea of contacting Lexi, but I did not. I didn't want to place her in the middle of this. Jeffrey, I believed, was doing his best to get Michael to move from his position of hating me.

As Jeffrey tried to describe it: "It's not exactly disgust, and it's not really hate. It's just well, I think, um, well he's just...Yeah, okay, it's hate right now. But you know, that's awfully hard to keep up, especially when you really love the person."

Coming down the stairs from the loft, the day was chilly despite the sun. I'd decided to take a drive to a couple of the secondhand stores I had seen in the area. I needed a night stand for my bedroom. As I was pulling out of the wharf's parking lot, a big Escalade pulled in and instantly rolled down its window. Inside was a pretty woman with long red hair and freckles, and she was wearing a heavy cream-colored cable knit sweater. I could hear the chatter of children in the back.

"Hey, I don't mean to weird you out at all, but I'm Robert's—" she pointed to the Robert's Tackle and Bait sign down the wharf—"wife Shaina. You're Sara, right?"

I nodded.

"I thought so. He was supposedly going to ask you, like a hundred days ago, to come to a party at our house tonight." She smiled at me, and I instantly smiled back.

"Oh, wow, thank you. Your husband and I haven't really spoken, yet, at all."

"Well, it'd be great to get to know you, so come if you can. Google Robert and Shaina O'Brien of Bristol for our address. We aren't far. Oh, and dress warm, we'll be out in the back with a fire much of the night." And off she sped.

I watched her leave the parking lot. I had no intention of going to the party, but it was a nice gesture on her part. As I drove to the secondhand store, I wondered if the O'Brien name was common in these parts.

Bristol Antiques and Treasures was full of wonderful displays of baskets, dolls, wooden toys, antique tables, dressers, old postcards, books, frames, mirrors, and rocking chairs of all sizes and vintage. A strong scent of apple and cinnamon permeated the shop.

I liked a small maple end table and wondered if I should call out to someone. I had not seen any shop clerk yet. Suddenly, a woman in her seventies came out from a back room and looked up. "Hey, there!" she said, smiling and coming down an aisle between the displays. "Why, I haven't seen you here before."

She introduced herself as Louise Bishop, the shop owner. I told her the table I was interested in, and she smiled again. "Just like me, in great shape but an antique. Now, what's your story dear?" Her whole manner was warm and inviting.

I told her where I was renting and that I was a long-term sub at one of the elementary schools in the area. She reached out to touch my arm. "Ah, I know right where you are, in one of Peter O'Brien's designs. The second home owners love him. He can design then build those places he designs like nobody else."

"I met him briefly, he seems nice," I replied.

"And none too shabby to look at either!" Her laugh was infectious.

We loaded the stand in the back of my Subaru, and I beeped as I drove off. My hair smelled of apple and cinnamon.

Chapter 8
past

What do I remember of the time right after the 'old man and the boy' encounter? I remember thinking that any kind of sex was appalling and violent, because what I had witnessed for all of four or five seconds was so graphic and ugly. I needed some sort of processing or counseling to digest what I had witnessed, but I was also realistic. Our first and only session would go something like this: "I was planning on a good time with this guy and, to get a head start on how best to greet him in my porno spread, I arrived early and saw a disgusting sight I can't get over." End of session.

Counseling was out, talking to anyone about it was out. I went through the motions of my life and got through it, barely. But the reel was active, especially in my commute to and from school. Hammering away at me was the guilt of being at that house, wanting Craig the way I had and then seeing what I saw and feeling there could be something terribly wrong. And my abstinence started to affect Jeffrey. He couldn't put his hands on me without my recoiling from his touch.

I was reading through some essays my students had written one early evening, about a week later. Jeffrey came up from behind and lifted my hair. He tried to kiss the back of my neck. I reared up from his touch and turned around. "What the fuck are you doing?"

He looked as if I had slapped him. "Sara, what's wrong?"

I had gotten up, without saying a word, and retreated to our bedroom. I feigned sleep when he climbed into bed later that night. He knew something had happened, but, like me, he didn't know how to address it. This distance, especially at night, became our new normal.

"What is going on, Sara? Please," he asked me, trying to at least broach the subject.

He reached for me and I moved away from him. "I don't want to be touched, Jeffrey, it's that simple."

"Why, what's happened?" he whispered.

I turned away from him. "I'm tired, I need sleep." Eventually, I heard him sigh and turn, our backs to each other.

Jeannie came by another morning. We were going out walking. I was exhausted but had missed so many of our walks already, I felt obligated. Jeffrey was sweeping out the garage and had stopped to chat with her. I walked by him.

"Sara, wait." He reached up to straighten the collar of my jacket. I cringed, and he dropped his hands.

Impatiently, I said, "I'm fine, just leave me alone."

His face turned red—I had embarrassed him in front of Jeannie.

"What are you so pissed at him about?" Jeannie asked as we rounded the top of Dunsmore Street.

"It's complicated," I replied. "And sometimes people are just assholes." Normally I would have delivered an observation of this nature laughingly, and Jeannie would have landed a well-placed zinger, but she sensed I was troubled and we walked in silence.

My abhorrence gave way to depression. Spring, a time for renewal, suddenly felt overwhelming to me, and I started to worry that Michael could sense this. He and Lexi were coasting into the last weeks of their time at Langdon High. To them, everything was poignant.

One night, Michael implored me to go to the girls' softball game under the lights. They were playing a Division 2 team and our girls this year were formidable. "Come on, Mom, I know it's going to be a good game. You love the night games. I'll buy you a burger there."

Reluctantly, I went and sat in the stands. I watched Michael and his buddies, wear maroon and white war paint, along with Lexi and her besties in pigtails with maroon and white ribbons. The whole town showed up to cheer the girls on. I caught sight of Jeannie but didn't have the desire or energy to move to sit with her.

I walked home alone. The high school kids, heading out of the field's parking lot, beeped their car horns as they passed by me. Langdon had trampled the Division 2 team by a whopping 10-2.

I was not eating or sleeping well. I started to experience flashbacks of the man and the teenager, especially in the middle of the night, as Jeffrey slept beside me. In these flashbacks, sometimes I would see bits and pieces of Craig and me, or Jeffrey and me, always sexual and always with someone saying, *"Come, baby, come,"* or some similar beseeching phrase.

During this stretch of time, I decided to drive down to Harwich Port on the Cape for the weekend. I thought getting out of Langdon would be good, and I wanted the comfort of Claire, Jeffrey's youngest sister, who I was and am still very close to. I thought some distance and time away might help me reset.

When Jeffrey and I got married, we discovered Claire and I were only one day apart, she the older. Over the next eighteen years, she and I had formed a very close bond. She was a lab technician, married to a wonderful guy who painted houses. Together they had three beautiful girls, now eleven, seventeen and nineteen. Michael loved his cousins, and our early times around the girls helped shape him into the kind and gentle boy Lexi knew.

During the drive, about four hours down to the Cape, something popped up in my thoughts. My flashbacks were jumbled, but I hadn't dwelled on the actual words the old man had used. He had said, "Not yet, not yet," over and over. That was very different than Craig or Jeffrey wanting me to find sexual satisfaction with, "Come, baby, come."

I reviewed it. He was telling himself to hold off, with no regard for the boy. I had only watched seconds, but suddenly, with awful clarity, I said out loud, "Oh my God, was the kid non-complicit?" I had assumed otherwise because of his size. He was a young adult, I thought, as old as my Michael or even older.

I almost pulled the car to the shoulder of the interstate, but the Mass Pike was busy, and I kept driving. But I admonished myself, several times, for not seeing the real possibility that a teenager was being sexually abused right before my very eyes.

Along with two of her girls, Claire and I spent the day at the retail outlets and ate out at their favorite seafood restaurant. On Sunday we woke early and drank our morning coffee as we walked the beach. Paul, her husband, joined us and I noticed how sweet the two of them were, holding hands and clearly enjoying each other's company.

The contrast between our two marriages was jarringly evident to me.

The depression I was feeling and my revulsion at sexual contact gave way to self-loathing as I returned home to Vermont. I had thought, as I scampered off to meet Craig time and time again, that my life wasn't going to blow up, that I could deny this moral bankruptcy by believing that we were just two people getting our rocks off. No one would get hurt. *It's just incredible sex.* But now Jeffrey was clearly hurt and bewildered, Michael didn't have an involved mother in what should be the happiest stretch of his high school career, and I was pissed at myself for so many reasons. *How could I have been so off the mark in what I had witnessed between the old man and the teenage boy? And was I actually off the mark?* I needed to find out.

Chapter 9
present

Thanksgiving break was starting in a couple of hours. Unlike Langdon, filled with snow and skiers at this time of year, Bristol was still somewhat balmy with a bare ground. Most of the third, fourth, and fifth graders were outdoors for an extra recess with the paraeducators mulling about, anxious to be heading home.

Looking out the window, I could see Maddie and another one of my students, Sam, combing the perimeters of the soccer field, picking up various rocks. I had settled nicely into the class and this school. Erasing the whiteboard, it occurred to me that I'd spent almost as much time with this group as Kristen O'Brien had at the beginning of the year. I wondered if she was home for Thanksgiving with her baby.

I had learned more about Maddie and her circumstances. She lived with her grandmother up Route 101 in a trailer park behind the big, miniature golf park. I'd driven her home a few times, after tutoring her in reading after school. Her grandmother had a portable breathing machine, and

Maddie liked to describe all her chores, especially how she cleaned the filter and air vents on the machine.

Right now, she and Sam were making their way to the classroom window, holding up a few rocks in their hands. I cranked open the window. "What do you have there?"

Maddie was beaming. "Sam's found some precious gemstones, Mrs. Scott. We're gonna sell 'em!"

Sam held open his hands. He had shale, various sand-stone, and while I wasn't positive, I thought what I was looking at might be bits of black tourmaline and possibly quartz, both gems. "The playground is full of cool rocks and stones. You should see what I've taken home, Mrs. Scott!"

Just then the whistle blew, and I watched as Maddie and Sam ran back to get in line. One of the paras, Rosalyn Holloway, was a character and often played line games. Today I waited to see what she would do.

"All right people, we're on safari now. So, look out!" Some of the students cupped their hands over their eyes, others fashioned binoculars and pretended they were seeing exotic animals off in the distance. As they rounded the basketball court, she called out, "Now it's 'slo-mo' cause it's way too nice to go back inside!" And seamlessly the children switched to slow motion with exaggerated effort in walking the rest of the way ih.

The next day, was Thanksgiving. I had bought a Cornish hen to roast with some of my favorite fixings. It was almost noon. The Macy's Thanksgiving Day Parade was starting, and I had made myself a plate of aged cheddar cheese, sesame seed crackers, and smoked sausage. I also had a rather bold, spicy Bloody Mary to sip. Watching the parade was something we always did as a family, and I started to grow melancholy. I knew, by Jeffrey's most recent email, that Michael wasn't having Thanksgiving dinner even with him, but I still felt an ache. Lexi, Marilyn, and Michael were driving out to Marilyn's brother's house on Long Island, then going into the Big Apple for the weekend. Lexi would post on Instagram, and I looked forward to seeing her photos. I never acknowledged or made comments, unsure if Michael read her posts. His banishment of me was definitely wearing on my psyche. But risking a repeat of his fury and wrath from the summer kept me in check.

"Time and distance can work wonders," Claire had said. "Give him time, and he'll come the distance."

"But it still hurts," I said out loud to Bryant Gumbel and Alisyn Camerota as they narrated the parade.

When my cell rang, it startled me. "Hello?"

"Hey, Sara, it's Shaina, Robert's wife. Happy Thanksgiving!"

I smiled. "You too!"

"I'm inviting you over to have dessert at our house tonight. We'll have a bit of the O'Briens and the Stuarts— that's my family—and friends. Come, if you can, about six. You should know that we consider beer and wine dessert."

I chuckled at that. "I'd like that, Shaina. It's pretty quiet here."

"We're not far, about a mile out on Sandstone Road. You'll see the cars."

I hung up, not knowing how I'd feel later, but appreciating her gesture once again.

Chapter 10
past

A host of thoughts flooded me now that I thought the teenager may have been coerced into giving that old man the blow job. I thought, at the very least, I needed to report it to the Department of Children and Family Services. As a teacher, I was a mandated reporter and had made DCF calls before. But I knew this was different. First off, I had no idea who the man and the boy were. I knew the date, time, place, and the what, but I did not know their identities. Could I describe them well enough for—what was it called, an artist's rendering? Also, while I replayed the vulgar slamming of the man into the boy and his hands against the back of the boy's head, I was not one hundred percent sure the boy wasn't a willing participant. The age of consent in Vermont was sixteen. He looked even older than that to me.

A few days after my trip to the Cape, I came home from the store with groceries in the back of the car. I didn't get out. I sat at the steering wheel for many minutes. Michael came out, onto the porch, then down and around to my driver's side door. I hadn't noticed him; I was deep in thought, realizing that I was stuck. I couldn't report what I saw, I didn't have enough information, nor could I stop the images I kept seeing.

He knocked on my window, making me jump. "Mom, what's going on? You smoking a doobie in there?"

I got out and walked towards the backyard, hearing Michael call out, in a sarcastic voice, "No problema, Mama Mia, I'll unload."

We had a stonewall not far from the house. I sat down on it and thought, *I can't do nothing, but nothing is what I'm doing.* My thoughts on the boy were unclear, mixed in with how I was treating Jeffrey.

Just the day before, he had asked me, "How long is this going to go on, Sara?" He was standing on the landing as I took the vacuum into our bedroom.

"Can you lower your voice? The kids are right outside, under our window."

He came in and sat on the bed. He looked tired. "When you look at me, it's like I'm vile. I have racked my brain, trying to figure out what I've done to make you so...so, I don't even know how to describe it. It's like you loathe me, like I'm a fucking asshole to the tenth degree." His voice was cracking, on the verge of tears.

I looked up, moved by his emotions. With more attention than I'd given him in weeks, I replied, "Jeffrey, it's not you who's the asshole, okay? It's me. I'm sorry I'm acting this way, but I need some space. Will you please give that to me, please?"

He'd gotten up, still looking hurt and, I think, dismayed. Dismayed that we'd come to such a point that he no longer recognized me or our marriage.

I woke up to an empty house the Sunday of Memorial Day weekend. Jeffrey and Michael left me a note; they had gone up to Castleton to watch Luke, one of Michael's older buddies, practice pitching for a possible shot in a summer league game coming up. They were going to surprise Luke and take him out to lunch after. They had mentioned it the night before, but it garnished little interest on my part.

I decided I'd take a walk after my coffee and yogurt. I started down through Main Street. Town was busy, but nowhere to the degree of a weekend in the winter months. I smelled bacon and saw a pile of Sunday newspapers outside the Café. I stopped. A big breakfast with the paper was what I wanted more than a walk.

While the Café was busy, I found a booth open near the kitchen. I sat down, placing the Sunday paper on the opposite side of the table, then reached into its Living Arts section and started reading. A cute girl from Michael's class came over. "Hey, Bailey," I said. I ordered eggs over-easy, bacon, whole-wheat toast, and coffee.

She smiled. "Got it, Mrs. Scott."

I was turning the page to continue reading Willem Lang's column when Bailey brought me my breakfast. I salt-and-peppered my eggs and started eating. It all tasted delicious, and I was quite happy with my decision to forgo the walk in favor of food. Besides, I could walk afterwards, I rationalized. I devoured all the bacon and returned to the paper.

A man was talking, rather loudly, across from me. Something about his voice caught my attention, and I looked up. He was sitting next to another man, and a third man had his back to me. They were laughing over something the first man had said. My heart started to race, and I couldn't look away from their table. That first man, directly in my view, looked familiar. His face was puffy and pockmarked, and his hair, combed to the side, was white with flakes of dandruff evident even from where I sat. He had too much Brylcreem in his hair, giving his whole appearance an unclean look. His green polo shirt stretched over his bulging stomach.

A bus boy, walking by the table of men, knelt down on the floor, in front of me, to tie his shoe. The first man said something to the boy while he was still kneeling. The boy cocked his head up to the man, turning slightly to the right, towards me. The look emanating from the first man's face was one of utter contempt. The boy got up quickly with his bucket of dishes and went into the kitchen.

My knees began to shake, and I felt sick. The bacon and coffee I had just consumed started to make their way back up. Pulsating into every fiber of my being was the rising realization that I knew this man across from me was 'the old man' and the teenager who had just left was 'the boy.' I knew it beyond a doubt. How? Why? Because in the pool of pants and boxers at the feet of the man, there had been a belt. I had forgotten that. On that belt was a buckle, with an "R" etched in silver. This man was wearing that same belt, and because his girth was so big, the buckle was prominently displayed as he sat back and laughed. I knew I had identified the two beyond all reasonable doubt. I sat stunned and disgusted.

The three men stood up and out from the kitchen came Stu, the owner of the Café. He shook their hands; they patted his back and more laughter ensued.

I heard Bailey, sweet Bailey, say, "Thank you, Mr. Rice. You're always so generous to me."

The man with the belt buckle said, "Of course, sweetheart. Now you get that essay to us as soon as you can—I know there's a scholarship with your name on it."

Mr. Rice broke away for a brief minute, seconds really, and walked over to the counter. The bus boy, now behind it, was putting glasses up on the top shelf. I heard him say, "Come here." The boy turned and went over to Mr. Rice. The old man reached out and put something in the boy's left breast pocket. No smile, no words, just a, "Come here." The boy disappeared into the kitchen again.

I knew that it was one of the Rices, Gerald I think, who owned The Mountain. Two brothers and their families had owned it forever. I was guessing this was the older brother, a widower, about seventy years old. He left the Café with the other two men.

My mind was racing, pleading for me to do something. The boy was back in the dining room, now clearing the table they had just vacated. Whatever had been given to him was in his front shirt pocket; I had seen the old man slide it in, turn and leave. I felt an urgency to do something...I just didn't know what.

Without much of a plan, I took out my iPhone and secretly snapped some pictures of the boy's back, especially of his head. His right ear stuck our further than his left. Then, with my cell still out and in picture ready mode, I called the boy over.

"Hey, could you come here for a second, please?"

He did so, hesitantly. He was shy and very thin for his height. He carried the look of poverty: pasty coloring, in need of a haircut, dull white shirt, pants too big.

"Can you, um, change my plate?"

He looked puzzled.

"I've spilled coffee on it, and it's spoiled the eggs."

He bent over to take the plate. In a move that surprised me, I reached into his left breast pocket and pulled out what was there. It was a crisp $100 bill. I glanced up at him and then turned the bill over. In ink, below the face of Benjamin, was '9am-B9' written in black sharpie, in distinct block lettering.

I quickly took a picture of it, and then held the bill back out to the boy. He grabbed it.

"I saw you and Rice up at that building lot. Is he—" I searched his face. "Do you need help?"

The boy's face contorted in anguish as if I had hit him. He fled into the kitchen. I stood up and followed him, stopping suddenly at the kitchen's swinging door. I turned, went back to the table and grabbed my phone. I went out the door. I hadn't paid for my breakfast.

I didn't realize where I was going until I stopped at Marilyn's house. It was a small, blue, two-story home, meticulously painted and cared for. I banged on her door and went in.

"Marilyn, Marilyn, where are you?" I was yelling and noticed the basement door open, the light on. "Marilyn, are you down there?" I started to make my way down the narrow stairs.

She appeared at the bottom of the stairs. "Sara, oh my God, are the kids alright? What's wrong?"

I barreled into her. "They're fine, I'm sure, although I don't exactly know where Lexi is, she's not with Michael, or maybe she is."

Her look of relief was palpable.

I smelled strong turpentine and wood-stain. Two straight back chairs, newly caned, were in various states of refinishing. I was breathing hard and still scaring Marilyn, even though she knew this wasn't about the kids.

"Yes, Lexi did end up going with them today," Marilyn replied and continued to look at me with a degree of alarm.

I nodded in a dismissive way and sat on the bottom step of the stairs, still catching my breath. Marilyn waited patiently for me to speak.

"I need you to answer a question I'm about to ask you, okay, Marilyn? But listen, it's got to be from a place of non-judgment and without thinking of ramifications or any repercussions. Okay? I just need you to give me your gut answer without thinking."

She was wearing an old smock over leggings and her hair was pulled tight in an elastic, giving her a severe look. I knew she would answer me honestly, and this was the reason I had practically run here before knowing why.

"Alright," she responded, looking mildly amused but still concerned.

"Here I go." I looked at her directly. "Have you ever, ever, Marilyn." I paused. "In your ten years of working for Gerald Rice, gotten the feeling that he was into boys, teenagers, possibly even a pedophile?"

Marilyn's face drained of all color, and she instantly sat down on one of the caned chairs. I wanted to caution her about the stain, but I knew it didn't matter. In a whisper, looking at me intently, she replied, "Yes," and put her hands up, covering her mouth.

As soon as it was out, I could tell Marilyn wanted to take it back. I understood. All her hopes and dreams for Lexi were directly tied to her position as Rice's executive secretary. She made decent money, and The Mountain gave generous scholarships for employees' kids. Lexi was a favorite, and I knew Marilyn had counted every possible revenue stream for Lexi to make her first college choice possible, regardless of cost.

I remained looking at Marilyn and stood up. Now she stood. She didn't ask me why I wanted to know—I think it may have been because it would have opened up more feelings of betrayal, or possibly put her career into further jeopardy. I did say, "Thank you. This stays between us," and I meant it.

On the walk home, satisfaction was replacing my earlier shock. I knew now it had been Gerald Rice with the boy. I was ninety-nine point nine percent sure that the boy's right ear was in my memory bank too, now that I remembered the belt buckle. But I still didn't know the boy's name and what his level of consent was in the actual sexual act. I had ruined it by telling him, right out like that in a public setting, what I'd seen. I felt horrible and realized that even if he towered over my 5'5" frame, he was still just a kid, like Michael. I tried to think of what my next move should be.

I went into Jeffrey's office and started to write my thoughts down and what my options were. More than anything, I needed to find out who the bus boy was at the Café. I couldn't report anything without that vital information. I knew Bailey and could ask. But I had left without paying. That could be fixed too—in fact, it was my reason to see her again. I'd go back and pay and nonchalantly ask for the boy's name.

As I grabbed my keys to go out the kitchen door, I ran smack into Marilyn. It was clear she had been crying; her face was red and blotchy.

"Here." She handed me a manila envelope. "This may have what you need to know. Please, Sara, keep your promise and keep me out of it." She turned and left.

Chapter 11
present

I had a general knowledge of where Shaina lived. What I wasn't prepared for was the house as I drove up the driveway. It was beautiful in a traditional Cape way, but with a veranda that stretched the length of the front of the house. Big rocking chairs with blue paisley pillows were lined up along the way, and wrought iron lanterns added a glow, casting the outside glimmer stone of the walkway in soft ambiance. Lights were on inside, and I could see people in the windows. I heard Van Morrison coming from inside the house.

I followed a couple, a man and woman holding hands, through the garage and into the kitchen. Shaina saw me and yelled out, "Hey everybody, Sara came!" At which point everyone seemed to call out, welcoming me in with assorted greetings.

I went over to Shaina and said, "Your house is gorgeous."

She smiled, taking my bottle of wine. "Thank you! There's the builder right there."

I turned to see 'Mr. O'Brien' again, the man who had retrieved the items from the classroom.

Holding a bottle of beer, he smiled at me. "My name's Peter, and you're Mrs. Scott, right?" He was leaning against the large granite countertop. His brown eyes were cheerful, laugh lines creasing his face. He was dressed in a casual dress shirt and khaki pants and had clearly attempted to tamp down his hair. It wasn't working. I thought he was about my age, may be a little older.

"It's Sara."

"Well, hello Sara, then," he said rather charmingly. "I'm glad you came. Shaina told me she had invited you." All his awkwardness from the day in the classroom was definitely gone.

"Folks, it's help yourself—desserts on the dining room table, coffee and tea on the island, and adult beverages, well, all over." Shaina's cheeks were red. Robert, her husband, brushed by her, patting her tush. It was the kind of pat that married couples do to one another without thinking.

I met many people in the span of fifteen to twenty minutes—most were O'Briens, some Stuarts, and many of their friends. The house was warm. I had worn a sweater but now regretted it. My face felt flush. I held a glass of white wine in one hand and a piece of pumpkin pie in the other. Peter and I found ourselves once more near each other.

"I really like the loft," I said to him. "It's got a great feel to it. It's practical and pretty at the same time."

"Thank you. That pleases me."

I went into detail, like how you could hear the rain drumming on the skylights and the joy the motorized blinds brought me.

"Best thing about waking up is that remote. I love it."

He looked amused.

Peter explained that his focus, as an architect and builder, was to take existing structures and repurpose their space. I asked him what had been above Robert's Tackle and Bait Shop before.

"Lobster traps, rope, inventory and a whole lot of—" He stopped and said, "Never mind."

I laughed. "What? I want to know."

"Really, you sure?" He leaned over to me and intimately whispered, "Bat poop."

I straightened up. "Oh shit, I hate bats. But you got it all, right?"

"I did, Mrs. Scott, I did, indeed." He crossed his heart, assuring me.

"Wait, now I'm wondering, are you my actual landlord?"

Peter shook his head no. "O'Brien Designs does not own the property, my cousin does. He's O'Brien Enterprises." He pointed to Robert, who sat at the head of the table. He was balancing a little boy who bore a strong resemblance to him on his lap, feeding him a bite of pie with lots of whipped cream.

Peter cleared his throat. "Sara, can I ask, are you single?"

This caught me totally off guard and I blushed, thinking, *You're pretty sure of yourself, aren't you?* I hesitated, then answered, "I'm divorced, kind of recently. I have a son who's in college. He's a sophomore. He and I, well, we've hit a bit of a road-block in our relationship."

Peter straightened up and looked down at me, gauging, I thought, his reply back. "Oh, I've got two daughters living down in Boston with their mother. I know all about road-blocks. I'll add big pot holes, washed out bridges, broken pavement, and guard rails completely gone."

I nodded, again unsure how to respond.

"Hey, can I get you more wine?" he asked, looking maybe a tad bit uncomfortable with how much he'd just shared about his daughters, however metaphorically.

"No, I'm good, thanks. Two's my limit. I'm up early tomorrow in search of a bookshelf. A big one."

"I almost built shelves in the loft, along the wall opposite of the kitchen. I should have."

I excused myself and said good-bye to Shaina and thanked her. As I made my way back through the kitchen, I saw Peter holding the little boy. He tipped his beer to me, and I waved.

I was glad I had gone to the party. The longing I felt earlier in the day was replaced now with a kind of content-ment. I started the Outback up and pulled away. *But I don't need anyone knocking at my door*, I thought, *even if he is that hot.*

Chapter 12
past

Marilyn backed her Jetta out of the driveway, into our street, and took off. I waved to her, but she wasn't having any of our usual friendly 'we're in this together' way we'd established after that first breakfast eons ago. Her coldness towards me at my porch door had alarmed me. It was sobering, and I whispered, "Slow down," to myself. I needed to think.

I didn't open the manila envelope that day, or the rest of the week. I couldn't. I needed to reset, refocus, and reevaluate everything that had happened. A certain amount of circumspect was taking hold. What would I be opening up, literally in the envelope, but also in everything to do with Craig and me and how it pertained to Jeffrey and Michael? The big question of *'why I was where I was when I saw what I saw'* was paramount and at the center of my thoughts. I hid the envelope in my underwear drawer.

After the guys—and Lexi—got back from Castleton, Jeffrey started to pack for Washington state. He was a presenter at a big Leadership Conference and would be gone for the week. He decided, and I know my recent rejections of any sexual contact played into his decision, to drive to Hartford that afternoon to catch a 7:00 a.m. flight to Seattle the next morning.

I hugged him good-bye, my first overture in some time, and wished him safe travels. I detected him lingering a bit. Was he hoping I had come out of the funk I'd been in? Or did he, like me, feel the ground shifting, the fissures that had started to appear months ago starting to widen? I was relieved he was going. I wanted space and time, and to be able to think without seeing his sadness and feeling guilt for causing it.

That week I had several assessments to give my students, and I buckled down. Michael and Lexi were basically done with school, all their courses complete with graduation looming in nine short days. They were, along with the rest of the senior class, hanging out in the hallways, signing yearbooks outside in the sun, and skipping off to swim at Parker Pond. Part of me was sure, too, that they were upstairs with his door shut for some of that time.

• • •

"JESUS, MICHAEL, YOU CANNOT DO THAT! Do you hear me?" I asked, my face serious.

The admonishment didn't faze him. "I got you real good, didn't I, Mom? I knew if I left my light on, it would throw you off."

Michael and I, over the years when Jeffrey was gone, had fun "shenanigans"— as he called them—that kept us entertained. Michael's favorite was when we would lie in wait, ready to pounce and scare the "by golly" out of the other at the most unexpected times. This started when Michael was twelve and in middle school. I remember that because he had written about it in a descriptive writing assignment for his teacher, Miss Bentley, entitled, "The Scotts' Shenanigan Show."

The very first time it happened, I had come up to bed and called out, "Turn off your light, Michael!" Jeffrey was in Michigan, it was sleeting outside, and I was reading Alice Hoffman's novel, *Second Nature*. I climbed into bed and picked up the book. Just as I settled down, pillows puffed just right, Michael reached out from under the bench, at the foot of our bed, and grabbed my leg. I screamed, jumping up and out, banging my thigh on the corner of the night stand.

It wasn't for the faint of heart. Weeks, even months could go by before the one who had been scared would retaliate.

Our house was old, circa 1890, with a cement floor throughout the different rooms in the basement. We had a Bowflex set up, just off the area where the laundry room was. There was also a chin-up bar in the corner, at one end of the room.

I was folding a load of laundry from the dryer mid-week when I heard, then saw, Michael come down into the basement. He went over to the bar. I stopped folding, realizing he had no idea I was downstairs too. The dryer was loud with a second load in. With his back to me as he did chin-ups, I tiptoed over to him. I reached up and grabbed him by the middle, yelling, "Boo!"

Michael dropped to the floor, breathless, "Oh my God, Mom, don't do that!"

I smiled, satisfied, and returned to the clothes I was now separating. Watching him resume his chin-ups, my feeling of satisfaction was soon replaced with nostalgia. Bits and pieces of him as a little boy in this house started to play out in my mind.

Folding the warm bath towels, I recalled how Michael would run through the house after his bath, his lack of modesty endearing. Totally naked, his hair damp, he'd look at me, kneeling on the bathroom mat. "Are you ready, Mommy?"

Towel in my hand, I'd respond, "On your mark, get set, go!"

He'd tear through the den, up the stairs then back down, into the living room, around the kitchen table, and come back, breathless. Reaching up, placing his hands around my face he'd say, "I'm fast, Mommy. I'm really, really fast."

And I'd scoop him up and say, "So fast you're all dry, my silly boy!"

That memory cascaded into a second one as I glanced at the Christmas decorations stored in boxes stacked along the wall of the laundry room. I remembered giving Michael his first lecture on swearing, as he was making out his Christmas list of what to get us and Auntie Jeannie.

"Auntie Jeannie needs a new car, the one she has now is a shit box." He had mimicked Jeannie perfectly and drawn one of his first J's, and beside it, a little car with two wheels. I wanted to laugh, but I kept a straight face.

I'd told him that saying 'shit box' was a swear word. "I know we sometimes say swear words, but you shouldn't, okay? Not until you're like, um, as tall as Daddy."

He had looked up at me. "Jeannie and you aren't tall like Daddy and you say those words."

"That is true."

"So, maybe I just have to wait 'til I'm as tall as you?" His dark eyes had been thoughtful. I thought him brilliant. He towered over me now.

And that memory brought me to the first Christmas of Lexi, just two years ago. I had watched Michael write Lexi's name at the top of his list of who to shop for. 'Mom' had always been the first name he'd started his list with. It's happened, just like that, I had thought, now recalling my astonishment back then.

Michael brought me back from my reverie. "You got me good, Mom, now you better beware!" and then, as he made his way further up the cellar stairs, he called out, "Love ya!" I stood motionless, my hands resting on top of the basket of clean clothes. I couldn't believe how much I had been willing to risk for a few brief moments of pleasure.

· · ·

I opened the manila envelope after Michael's graduation while he, Lexi, and their class were on their post-graduation trip to Myrtle Beach for the next five days. They left at 4:00 a.m. the morning after graduation in a big Premier Coach bus that met at the high school parking lot. The driver was a large, personable man named Mike. He welcomed all the parents and students and had them gather around to go through his expectations in a booming voice. He was full of humor, yet no nonsense. Our Michael looked at us and smiled. He was happy and excited to go away. Lexi was standing with a couple of her girlfriends in baggie sweats, a t-shirt, a blanket wrapped around her. She was clutching her pillow and ear-buds, ready to board and get back to sleep.

Once the bus pulled out, the parents spoke a little, but mostly we all went home to see if we could go back to sleep. I saw Marilyn but never acknowledged her; I didn't even try. Once home, I figured I was up for the duration of the day. I started a pot of coffee and put in some toast. Jeffrey squeezed my hand and climbed the stairs, pretty sure he could nod off again.

Michael's graduation had been a moving event for both of us, an accumulation of all we'd done right as parents. I felt more at ease around Jeffrey, and he sensed this. We had resumed some of our old, familiar ways of relating to each other. I reached over and took his hand when Michael's name was called and he walked across the stage. After, Jeffrey guided me to the punch and cookie table to talk with other families and their seniors, his hand lightly placed on my back.

It was then, predawn, sitting at the kitchen table with the counter lights on low, that I decided to open the envelope. I crept upstairs and managed to open my top drawer, feel for it, and make my way back down to the kitchen without waking Jeffrey. I sat, sipping the strong coffee and eating my toast. I felt the envelope; it was light.

"Here I go," I said softly and opened it. Inside were two articles from *The Rutland Herald*, dated February 4, 2009, and September 15, 2009 as well as a report of some sort. I immediately recalled the topic of both articles. I had seen and read them when they first came out, almost a decade ago. A local man, Chris Larson, had died on The Mountain, grooming snow one night. Somehow the grooming machine he was operating had toppled onto him, crushing him immediately. Other night-time employees had found him. The first article was the story of the actual accident and the response of the owners of The Mountain. Gerald and his brother, Edmond, said that The Mountain would make sure Chris's widow and children were taken care of. "The Mountain takes care of its people," Gerald had been quoted saying.

The second article was a picture of a woman standing in front of a small ranch house, her arms around three boys. At first glance, the boys all looked the same—towheads, staring out blankly while the woman smiled. The heading

Chapter 12

of that front-page article read, "The Mountain Makes Good on Its Promise." I read them both slowly.

It seems Gerald Rice had bought the Larson widow a house on a small tract of land once he found out that the family's small apartment was "inadequate for three growing boys." In both articles, Gerald Rice was predominantly quoted.

I turned my attention to the third piece of paper from the envelope. It was a copy of the toxicology report of Chris Larson, dated March 21, 2009 from the night he died in February. His blood alcohol level was a staggering 1.6, twice the legal limit for driving, let alone for operating powerful machinery. I suddenly was baffled. Why would The Mountain extol their commitment to a dead employee's family when it was documented that the employee was shitfaced on the job and was totally responsible for getting crushed? As soon as I asked that, I quickly picked up the second article and held the picture up closely. Three boys, ages eight, nine and ten, their names and ages in the caption under the photograph: Jamie, Jason, and Jackson Larson. I sat back.

"Gerald Rice," I said out loud in my kitchen. Was he the 'real groomer' in this story? I sat back for some time. An emerging theory was starting to take hold. The bus boy at the Café was the same boy at the lot. Was it one of the Larson boys here in this picture? Marilyn gave me the envelope with these articles for a reason. I quickly ran into Jeffrey's office. He had a magnifying glass in the side drawer of his desk. I came back with it and held up the newspaper clipping, and focused in on the three boys. The two older boys looked alike but the third boy, the youngest, named Jamie, looked different. He appeared to be as tall as his older brothers but he was thinner. I examined the boy's features. While the photo was grainy I felt it could very well be the busboy. I wasn't positively sure, though. Could that mean—I sat up in the kitchen chair, trying to grapple with an outlandish thought making its way to the surface. Has that monster Rice been sexually abusing Jamie Larson all this time? I felt sick to my stomach.

I tried to remember what I knew of the Larsons. One of them, Jason, had been in Michael's class, but I think he had dropped out of high school a couple of years ago. Something was in the paper last year. I went to retrieve my laptop and started it up. Something about an accident and getting injured in a scrap metal yard, not far out of town.

I googled *'Langdon man injured at scrap metal.'* Up popped a WCAX report on Jason Larson stealing scrap metal but getting severely injured by a pit bull on the premises. His foot was practically torn off, and the owner had to put down the dog. There was a lot of buzz generated from this incident; animal rights activists, property owners, and small businesses all weighed in. That was in 2017, one year ago. I then googled Jackson Larson from Langdon, and instantly his name came up in the Peddan police blotter. It seems Jackson was arrested for turning in watered-down sap to a large sugar-house not far from Langdon. Charges were dropped pending completion of community service. Jackson also had charges of jacking deer; those were still pending as of this winter.

In addition to the older brothers' woes with the law, I looked up Jane Larson and found her name mentioned a couple of times. She had been arrested for buying cocaine and heroin twice, in small amounts, once in 2010 and again in 2011.

I googled Jamie to see if anything came up. Nothing. If he was eight in 2009, that made him seventeen, maybe eighteen now. I looked again at the notes I had taken on Jane. Cocaine and heroin one year after this picture. The boys would have been nine, ten, and eleven. Who was taking care of them while their mother was buying and using? Gerald Rice?

I realized I needed to verify, absolutely, that the boy was Jamie. Then, I needed to make a plan on how to find out Jamie's...I tried to find the right words to jot down on my note pad. *Jamie's level of consent?* I crossed that out and wrote, *Jamie's sexual abuse?*

I slid everything, including my notes, into the manila envelope and tiptoed up the stairs. By now it was almost 8:00 a.m. and Jeffrey was stirring. I felt drained and wanted to try to sleep. He sat up as I came in, and I quickly tucked the envelope into my top drawer.

I turned to Jeffrey and said, "I think I'm ready to try to sleep. You've got coffee in the pot."

"Thanks, baby. Hope the weather's gonna be good for the kids." He stood up and moved towards the bedroom door.

I smiled, taking off my hoop earrings and placing them on the night stand. "Oh, you know them, they'll still walk the beaches even in the rain."

Hesitating, he asked, "Are you good now? I mean, are we okay?"

In my mind I answered, *No, Jeffrey, I'm not good, and we are not okay. I've been fucking someone else and now I'm embroiled in something that could be big and even uglier.*

Instead, I looked at him with his hopeful eyes, kind face and absolute focus on what my next words were going to be.

"Yeah, we're okay." I slipped out of my jeans and took off my sweatshirt as Jeffrey stood in the doorway. He came back to our bed, leaned over, and kissed me, and I returned the kiss. Then I reached out and pulled him in. He didn't hesitate. We started making our way back; he moved down my body as if it'd been years since he'd last seen me naked.

And I no longer imagined another man. I was fully present, and it was clear to me that this was Jeffrey, the man who knew me better than anyone else. Except, I realized as he moved inside me and told me how much he loved me that he didn't really know me anymore. And despite my endearments back, I knew things would never be the same. Yes, we had crossed our chasm of no sexual contact and it felt like home, but home was different now.

I was able to fall asleep for a bit after Jeffrey left to go downstairs. It wasn't a sound sleep though. Between the coffee I'd had, my betrayal, and the fear of what Jamie Larson may be experiencing, my thoughts were restless.

Chapter 13

present

I went back to Bristol Antiques and Treasures to see if Louise had any big bookcases. I told her what I was looking for, and she said that she had nothing like that but would give my quest some serious thought. She knew the surrounding dealers and was well versed in networking. What was supposed to be a quick trip into her shop ended up much longer as we talked about everything—and really, nothing—at all. I told her a little bit about my backstory, more to her than anyone else so far. My self-exile, I described, was shaping up to be better than I had expected, especially in landing Kristen O'Brien's classroom spot. I also told her about the estrangement from my son "because of something I did."

Louise recounted to me that a customer, a gentleman named Jacob, had caught her fancy. She was a hoot in expressing her plan to get him to ask her out. When I asked why she didn't just ask him, that girls do that these days, she hugged me and exclaimed, "I'll do it! In fact, why don't you ask Peter O'Brien out, then we could double-date!"

This comment caught me totally by surprise, and I looked at her, amused. "Oh, I'm sure that man has a lot of women knocking on his door."

Louise replied thoughtfully, "Actually I've never seen him with a woman since his wife left him, some years back. His daughters were little girls then. That woman broke his heart the way she ended it with him. He was the last to know, while we all, ah, enough said."

We discovered we were Anglophiles and both binging the same Netflix series: *Last Tango in Halifax*. I was one whole season behind, but I promised I'd call her when I finished season two.

"Good, dear, then I'll stop right where I am now and wait for you. I'll have you over for a 'pint and chips' and we'll pick up from there and watch the rest together."

We hugged when I left. I realized I'd made my second friend here in Bristol. I counted Shaina as my first, and *that may be pushing it a bit,* I thought.

Back at the loft, I thought about what Louise had said regarding Peter O'Brien. Maybe I was wrong and had misread his friendliness for something other than friendliness. But why did he ask me so bluntly if I was single? I wished I could call Jeannie and talk to her, to hear her interpretation of the conversation Peter and I had on Thanksgiving and what to make of it. *Jeannie's been dating for over twenty years*, I thought. *She'd be the expert.* But I didn't call, and I knew why. I had left to make a clean break but to also leave behind everyone and everything I had hurt with my actions. I needed to pay penance. While I knew Jeannie wouldn't ever say this, I thought she might agree.

Chapter 14

past

The summer weather that June and July was beautiful. Jeannie and I were walking a challenging route every day and feeling quite accomplished. Michael was working full time at the Rec Department, and Jeffrey had some down time and decided to resurface our kitchen cabinets, a huge undertaking. Lexi was just back from spending two weeks on Long Island.

It was Michael who helped me confirm one-hundred percent that the busboy was Jamie Larson. Towards the end of June, Michael and I had run into Shaw's to get a few things, mostly lunch and snack foods for his long days at Rec. He and I were walking down an aisle and passed the boy, now evidently a grocery clerk.

Michael said, very friendly-like, "Jamie! How you doing?" The boy was taller than Michael, and his thinness, even with an apron on, was very apparent. He turned and smiled. It was the first time I'd seen his smile: lopsided, shy, and endearing.

"Hey, Michael, how are you?" The boy struggled to say this.

Michael replied, "Doing great, Jamie, I like your stacking, man!" Michael reached into the cart full of canned soups and quickly juggled three cans in front of Jamie and then bowed, handing each one to Jamie with a flourish. Jamie laughed and reached over to 'hi-five' Michael.

The boy's face froze when he saw me, and he instantly turned his back on the both of us. He had recognized me from the morning of the diner.

"See ya," Michael called out, but Jamie said nothing in response.

I wanted to start asking Michael all sorts of questions, but I had to do it without causing any alarm. The boy had a speech impediment; it had been clearly evident just in the short exchange I'd witnessed.

I waited until Michael was pulling out of the Shaw's parking lot and we were heading home.

"Hey, was that Jamie Larson?" I asked casually.

"Yeah, poor kid. He's in the Community Resource room at the high school. I helped Mr. Taylor do the Special Olympics and Jamie was on the basketball team. A really sweet kid. But, man, some scary older brothers." Michael slowed down and put the blinker on at the top of Dunsmore Street.

"Why do you say that?" I asked.

Now we were pulling into our driveway, but I needed to know more. "Michael, I forgot, I need gas, let's go to the Mobil, no, the Exxon Station out by the quarry."

Michael liked to drive and was agreeable. "Okie dokie, Momma Leonie." I never knew where he came up with all the pet names he used for me. He backed up and headed out, past the Shaw's we'd just left.

I repeated my question. "Why do you say that Jamie's brothers are scary?"

"Do you remember Jason, from my grade? I had him over a few times, even once for a sleepover, I'm pretty sure."

And then it came to me: Jason Larson had been a friend of Michael's, way back in fourth, maybe fifth grade, and there had been a sleepover.

"Yes, I do, kind of." I turned to face Michael.

Pulling down his visor as he drove west out of town, Michael went on. "First of all, just looking at these dudes can send chills down your spine. They're both tattooed all over, even up their necks, and they have that look of inmates doing hard time—you know, shaved heads, wife beater shirts." He pulled up to the self-serve pumps and put the Outback in park. I handed him a $20 bill.

Before he got out to pump the gas, I reached over, touched his arm, and asked, "Michael, has Jason ever said or done something to you that wasn't okay?" I suddenly thought, *Should I brace myself?*

"Nah, he's cool with me. I'll tell you more when I get back."

Walking in front of the Subaru, he made a funny face at me then continued on into the station. He was wearing baggy athletic shorts, a maroon Langdon soccer t-shirt, and black Nike flip flops. His hair, cropped short, looked black and his nose was starting to peel from all the hours already in the sun up at the recreation camp. *He's just a kid,* I thought, and then just as quickly, *Jamie Larson's just a kid too.*

As Michael came out and started to pump gas, a white Toyota Corolla pulled in. Two girls in the front seat jumped out. One of them was Lexi, tanned, her blond hair pulled back in a high ponytail. She was wearing a little blue skort and a bright pink polo shirt. She waved at me and went up to Michael. He gave her a big bear hug, lifting her up off the pavement. The other girl, wearing a similar outfit, ran into the gas station. Lexi picked up the window squeegee and started to wash my back window, talking to Michael as she did. I heard her mention the golf course and thought she was probably heading there to work the afternoon.

The other girl came out with drinks and called to Lexi, "Let's go, love birds!"

Lexi quickly went to put the squeegee back in the container between the row of pumps, but Michael grabbed her once more and planted a big wet kiss on her lips.

"Michael, stop that, I'm going to get all wet!"

I beeped the horn and yelled out, "Hey, enough of that!"

Lexi waved and ran to the Toyota. Michael got back in the car and took a moment to look at himself up close in the rear-view mirror. He picked at a spot on his nose. "Lexi thinks I should wear zinc oxide at Rec. Do we have any?"

I didn't want to get away from our conversation on the Larson brothers so I said, somewhat impatiently, "Yes, I'm sure. If not, we can get some. Tell me about Jamie's brothers."

Backing out of our spot at the pumps, Michael replied, "Oh, yeah, where was I? Jason Larson has a mangled foot. Did you know that? "

Now we were heading home. I needed to get as much information from Michael as possible.

"Yes, I did hear that."

"He walks with a bad limp. I heard he went up against a ferocious guard dog. Anyway, one night this winter, when I was waiting with Jamie after practice, both Jackson and Jason came into the gym. They were looking for a couple of kids they heard had been picking on Jamie. I wouldn't want to be on their bad side, ever. Jackson looks like he's in perpetual motion. Like he'd hunt you down if you looked at him cross-eyed."

We were almost home. I asked, "So Jamie has low cognitive skills, besides the speech impediment?"

"What did you just ask me?" Michael frowned, glancing at me.

"So, is Jamie Special Ed?"

"Well, Mother Einstein, he was on the Special Olympics team, so you put it together."

That night, sitting in the den alone, I reviewed the notes I had placed in the envelope Marilyn had given me. I was convinced that Jamie was being abused. The $100 bill was a bribe to keep him quiet, to buy his silence. I knew grooming involved gifts, money, and privileges to keep the victim happy and beholden to the abuser. Oprah's show on the men who visited Michael Jackson's Neverland Ranch as little boys was chock-full of grooming techniques and how insidious adults were with children and teenagers—even manipulating their parents. Rice had bought Jane Larson a house, said it was because the boys needed more space, and everybody praised him for that. But really it was a ploy, a set up to worm his way into the family.

The Larsons became my new loop, and I played what I knew over and over. I wasn't commuting to school since it was summer, but I was able to play it often, during my morning cup of coffee and especially when I mowed.

We had a riding lawn mower, and I would put on headphones and the reel would start up. I think Jeffrey thought my mowing bordered on the obsessive, until one day I abruptly quit the mower and ran through the kitchen, passing him as he methodically took down the cupboards, labeling each one. I ran up to our room where my phone was charging and scrolled through my images. I had a hunch that I wasn't as helpless as I felt.

I found the photo I had taken that day in the diner of the front of the $100 bill. '9am-B9.' I interpreted it as "9:00 at building lot B9." I'd already surmised that the notation had been a code for Jamie, because, as sickening as it was for me to remember Craig's and my texts, it was similar. But it was peculiar writing—the loops in the 9s and the two loops in the B were squarer in shape than circular. If this writing matched Rice's handwriting, this image was hard evidence that he may be pressuring Jamie, a special needs student, into sex acts. I was strangely excited and satisfied that I had something that could back up and connect both interactions I had witnessed; oral sex in the half-finished mountain house and Gerald Rice reaching over and putting the bill in Jamie's shirt. I also realized it was time to talk to the Larsons.

Chapter 15

present

I was tidying up the classroom when I heard a light knock at my door. In walked the sixth grade teacher, Ms. Sanborn. While we'd had a few pleasant exchanges, I did not know her well.

"I wanted you to be the first to hear, before David even, that there's a really good possibility—like ninety percent—that I won't be returning next year. I'm hoping to head to England to join my partner. It's early, I know, but you'd be perfect to take my spot."

I sat, digesting this news. She looked at me and said, "Would you be interested?"

I'd been living in such a "state of interim"— in all facets of my life—that this was a lot, almost too much to take in. She must have thought I was a nut as I just sat there looking at her.

I finally responded, "Interested, yes. Thank you for thinking of me. Really. It puts a whole new lens on, well, everything."

"You'd have these students again. I've heard they're a great bunch."

I asked, "What does your boyfriend do, for work?"

Ms. Sanborn stood up and said, "She's a US diplomat and has just been extended three more years. I hope to be with her by the end of June." She smiled as she left my room.

I was just about to turn off the classroom lights when I heard our custodian's voice out in the hallway. "Yep, she's still here." Peter came into the classroom and stopped. We hadn't seen each other since Shaina's. He'd gotten a haircut. I liked it longer and a bit messier.

"Hello, Sara. Sorry to barge in like this. I'm just wondering, did you find that big bookcase yet?"

He appeared serious and sincere in his question. *Why, you're a lot of things, aren't you, handsome man?* I thought. *Awkward, bold, now this.*

Giving none of my thoughts away, I replied, "No, I struck out completely."

He moved closer to me, and I stepped back instinctively. He didn't seem to notice and said, "I have an idea and want to show you what I'm thinking. Completely my responsibility for all costs, yet totally up to you, your decision. If you like it, I'd go forward; if not, nothing's lost, and you keep looking."

"Hmmm, now you've got me interested." I could feel his energy. I liked it.

"Could I swing by some time? Show you my idea, and see if I've envisioned the area right and what you want. Again, only if you want."

I thought about it for a minute. "I'm heading to the loft now. You can meet me there."

Peter stood just inside the door. I watched his eyes as he took in what I had done to decorate the place— my furniture, rugs, and art.

"Wow, this is pretty refreshing. None of that coastal crap. Do you know how many lighthouses, sand-dollar wall art, and buoys I see after I've gone out of my way to give a place its distinctness?"

"I'm still getting used to the actual coastal..." I stopped; I'd almost said "crap." He was looking at me. I was glad I'd caught myself.

I walked over to the area I thought the large bookcase should go. "Here's where I thought."

He came to where I stood, then paced off the distance from the spot to the couch, and then paced it off to the kitchen wall. He took a folded paper out of his shirt pocket and came back over to me. On it was a design of a built-in bookshelf, much larger than I had imagined. "I'm thinking nine feet high by six-to-seven feet wide. Maybe with a sliding ladder to glide, like this..." He motioned with his hands along the wall.

"I like it. I have a lot of books still in storage. I could fill those shelves, for sure."

Peter nodded and folded the paper. He moved towards the door. "Sara, I'm sorry I was so, like, well, direct in asking you if you were single at Shaina's. I'd just been to counseling the day before, and my therapist told me I needed to be more, um, assertive in what I wanted. More 'carpe diem,' or whatever that means." He looked up and smiled. "I guess you were the first thing I wanted." And then his face reddened. "Jesus, that's not what I meant to say or imply. I need to stop talking. I'll keep in touch about the bookshelves." He opened the door and started to make his way down the stairs.

I quickly went to the door and called out, "Thanks Peter. Bye." He put up his hand and waved, his back to me.

I went to the large window and watched him walking fast down the wharf. *Any faster, he'd be fleeing,* I thought.

Climbing into bed that night, I had intentions of reading my book. I was rereading John Irving's, *A Widow for One Year*. I opened the book and scanned the page to find where I had left off. But I didn't begin reading. Instead, I sat there and thought about Peter. I was totally off in my impression of him. *Today, I got the real guy,* I thought. *He's kind of vulnerable.*

I went into the kitchen to get a glass of water. I brought it back to my night stand. I found the remote for the motorized blinds, pressed and down they came.

Sitting on the side of my bed, I picked up my cell and scanned Facebook. My account had been dormant for months. But tonight, a picture of Michael and me popped up. It was one of 'my memories' from eight years ago. We were on bikes, at the end of our driveway. He looked so young. I missed him.

With urgency I thought, *Whatever I do in Bristol, Maine, I am not getting involved with a man. I cannot jeopardize Michael.* I turned off my light and went to sleep.

Chapter 16

past

The Larson family's ranch house was on Gravelin Road, west of The Mountain. Not many homes sat along its winding route, and I found it soon enough. I pulled off the side of the road and took a look. The area immediately around the house was tidy, but in various spots—on both sides of the property—there were a number of things: an abandoned truck, piles of discarded scrap metal, a fake padded deer for target practice, and miscellaneous barrels of recyclables, although I couldn't tell for sure what was in them. It was summer and the grass was high; it hadn't been mowed for a couple of weeks. A lawn-mower was out, parked just below the picture window. I wondered if it was broken.

The front door, once painted a dark red, was now faded, the siding a light gray, and along the front of the house, orange tiger lilies and black-eyed susans were in bloom.

Back home, I had taken some time to decide what to do, but it always ended up with this: driving out to the Larsons. Now, here I was. I got out of the Subaru and walked up the driveway, cutting over to the walkway. It was about 10:00 a.m. on a weekday. A dark blue Jeep was in the driveway. It had oversized tires for its frame and looked like it had recently been mudding, although most of the mud on its tires and flaps appeared dry.

I heard a dog barking from within the house. I opened the outside door and knocked on the inside screen.

"Shut the fuck up, will you?" I heard the whelp of a dog, and the barking stopped.

Jason, who I had recently looked up in Michael's older yearbooks, opened the screen and leaned out. He needed time to register who I was, but he did and said, a bit affably, "Oh, hey, Mrs. Scott."

From Jason's side, Jackson peered out at me. "What do you want?"

It was one thing to decide to do this, I realized, and quite another to be actually here. Doubt flooded through me, and I almost used my backup plan in case I needed to bail. I had practiced saying, "My car's making a funny noise, can I use your phone?" Then I'd fake dial, go back to the car, and miraculously it would start and I'd get the hell out of there.

But I didn't say any of that. Instead, I smiled, encouraged by Jason's greeting. "I'm here to talk to you both. Can I come in?"

Jason, on crutches, opened the door wider.

"Jesus, she's still a MILF, ain't she?" Jackson said as I stepped in.

"Shut up, Jackson," Jason said abruptly. He wasn't afraid of his older brother, that was clear.

I ignored the comment, knowing full well what it meant.

The inside of the house appeared to be spotless, but it held the smell of cigarettes, bacon, and something else I couldn't quite discern. Jason motioned me into the living room, and I sat on the edge of a blue floral chair, which matched a blue floral couch.

The room was dark and small, heavy drapes drawn. The biggest item was a flat screen TV adjacent to the picture window. *The Price is Right* was on, its volume high. I could see, through the opening to the kitchen, a woodstove and a couple of mismatched padded chairs around it. There was an ashtray on the floor between the two chairs, overflowing with ashes and discarded cigarette butts. Even though it was summer, no windows were open, and the air stale.

Both brothers sat down and looked at me, waiting. I thought Michael's description of inmates doing time was spot on. They looked tough, with shaven heads, scraggly beards, tattoos of intimidating images. Jackson had one on his right bicep of a revolver pointed straight out with the word BANG below it. Jason was stockier than Jackson, and had, if it could be said at all, a nicer face.

Jackson looked irritated and impatient and kept wiping his nose. Jason gave me a small smile to soften Jackson's next comment. "Well, I don't got all day, what you selling?"

"Could you turn down the TV?"

Jackson, showing even more irritation than before, picked up the remote and flicked it off.

I decided to be as honest and straightforward as I could, despite how uncomfortable this encounter was shaping up to be. I needed to tell what I'd witnessed, without hesitation or judgment. I took a deep breath, taking them both in. "I saw something you should know about up in one of the half-finished houses on The Mountain."

The brothers exchanged a nervous glance. I clapped my hands tightly in my lap. "It was Jamie, and—" I paused. "He was giving, well, Gerald Rice and Jamie were engaged in a sex act."

Jackson erupted. He stood up and came at me. I thought he might strike me in the face. I braced myself.

"Get the fuck out of our house, now. I said now, you bitch!" he screamed, bending down to within six inches of my face.

I got up quickly and gathered my purse on the floor beside me. Jason couldn't look at me. Embarrassed, ashamed? I didn't know, couldn't tell. As I moved towards the hallway near the front door I had come in, Jackson was right behind me. I smelled how much he reeked of cigarettes and BO.

"If I hear you've opened your mouth, that little shit for brains mommy's boy of yours is gonna get it."

I stopped and turned around. There, on the opposite wall, was a large framed school picture of Jackson smiling, a mouth full of front teeth, freckles splattered across his tan face. His hair was unruly, his eyes bright.

I looked back at this Jackson, but what I saw was that boy in the picture, about ten, maybe eleven, the age of my sixth graders, staring at me. His anger and aggressive, bullying stance suddenly didn't scare me anymore. I was almost certain, from Jason's agonized withdrawal a moment ago and Jackson's bravado, now in my face, that they too had been sexually abused by Rice.

I pulled myself together, and, in a steady voice, loud enough for Jason to hear around the corner, said, "Jackson Larson, you and your brothers have had…" I slowed down for emphasis…"the worst possible thing done to you. The worst. But until you tell on that fucking monster on The Mountain, he's going to keep on sexually abusing our boys."

I walked out, praying he wouldn't sic the dog on me. I started up the car and took off, eyes on the rear-view mirror, scared shitless. When I got to the end of Gravelin

Road, my shaking started to subside. I turned my blinker on and hit the steering wheel once, then again.

"That fucking, fucking monster."

Chapter 17

present

The day was clear and windy. The water, once past the inlet, had white caps. I was sitting in front of the big picture window, enjoying a plate of Christmas cookies and a cup of coffee while the movie, *The Holiday*, with Cameron Diaz, played on the flat screen TV behind me. It was one of my favorite movies this time of year. My cell started to ring, startling me. I saw that the caller was Michael. I reached for it quickly.

Somewhat belligerently, Michael greeted me with, "I don't know why I've called. I've got nothing to say."

I sat back in the chair. I remembered all the times when Michael was little, and I'd fill a sippy cup with milk. He would come lay with his head in my lap while I ran my fingers through his hair. I would regale him with all the antics of the students in my classroom, embellishing their misdeeds or exaggerating their great feats of the day. I'd talk about who had been really naughty or had run the fastest—who had the biggest brain. This entertained him. I would give nicknames to the students. Michael loved those times and always remained quiet and focused on my stories, drinking that sippy cup dry.

As he got older, he continued to enjoy my musings of the day. "How were the little critters today, m'lady?" he'd call out as I'd come up onto the porch. It became his nightly greeting as he survived middle school and moved on to high school. I began including the heartaches, like the girl I had one year who was severely burned. Her father had thrown a gas can onto the fire where she was toasting marshmallows. Or the little guy who had leukemia and wanted, more than anything, to be a catcher for the Red Sox.

I responded to his belligerence calmly, "That's okay, Michael, let me tell you about my little critters." And for a bit I talked, nonstop, about my new classroom. Maddie was 'Xenia, Brave Girl Warrior,' and Sam, 'The Rock Slayer and Keeper of Precious Gemstones.' I described Rosalyn as the 'Mad Pied Piper of Holloway Hall, detailing the strange 'shuffle and gait her creatures displayed at recess.' He listened, and when I was done, he simply said, "Merry Christmas, Mom," in a voice I'd heard thousands of times in his life, as my son. It was his gift to me, and it was a start. It was the best Christmas Eve day I'd ever had.

Chapter 18

past

The morning after I visited the Larsons, our land-line rang. Like most people, we rarely used it. My iPhone was never far from me. Hearing this ring was, at first, disconcerting. I ran in time to pick it up.

"Hello?" There was some hesitancy on the other end, and I had an inkling of who it might be.

"Hey, Mrs. Scott. It's Jason Larson."

"Oh, hey, Jason." I gave him some time, thinking to myself, *Don't blow this.*

"Um, I wanted to talk to you, 'bout yesterday. Can we talk?"

This was what I'd hoped for in going to the house. I wanted to find out the truth about the Larson boys and Rice. I wanted to help them, if I could.

"Okay, Jason. What are you thinking?"

He paused. "Well, I'm not sure. My mother is over at the Walmart in Peddan; she's got a few shifts there each week. And Jackson is working down near Brattleboro for a while, helping a guy clear his land. He's gone all day. Jamie's in town at Shaw's. Truth is, I don't have a car so can't meet you anywhere unless you come pick me up. And, if that's the case, well I don't think any place in public will work. Could we, um, are you comfortable coming back to talk here, at the house?"

I looked at the clock: it was 8:40. "Have you got coffee?"

"Sure, good stuff."

"I can be there in about twenty minutes? That sound okay?"

"Yes." He hung up.

I wanted to get there as soon as I could, because I worried he might get second thoughts and decide not to talk. His voice had sounded tentative. Jeffrey was setting up an area in the garage to spray the sanded cabinets, and he had drop cloths in place—a plastic sheet up hanging from the top of the bay doors. He had watched a *This Old House* tutorial and looked organized and determined.

"I'm heading out to get groceries," I said. "I'll be a while since I have a few other stops. Do you need anything?"

"Baby, I'm good. Though a couple of big, fat steaks for grilling tonight would be nice. Michael's heading up to see Luke; he told me he might spend the night at Luke's off-campus apartment. Have we thought about that?"

I didn't want to slow my momentum and replied, "Got it, steaks and the possibility of Michael getting shitfaced at Castleton. I'll get the steaks but the talk with Michael is your deal."

Jeffrey called out, "Thanks, I think you got the better end of the stick."

I waved and replied, "Good luck."

I knew I had a good stretch of time. I hoped Jason would feel comfortable enough to disclose to me what I suspected and confirm for me what I feared.

I parked again off the side of the road and crossed over to the walkway leading up to the front door. This time the screen was open, and Jason stood there, waiting.

"Come on in."

"Okay, thanks," I said.

"Let's sit in the kitchen; it's brighter, and I can see the dog out back."

The kitchen was bigger than the living room and had a bank of windows that overlooked the yard in back. It was neat; the ashtray near the woodstove that was overflowing the day before was now empty and clean. The sink was bare, the countertops shined, and two coffee mugs were out on the kitchen table. Jason motioned for me to sit down with my back to the window. He reached over, poured coffee from a thermos, then sat down facing the backyard.

"Oh wait, do you need cream, sugar?" he asked as he started to get back up.

"No, this is good. I drink mine black. You?"

"Same."

We sat for a little bit, and I asked if his mom was doing well. Jason told me she had been out of rehab for a long stretch of time and had a couple of jobs: Walmart and watching a lady in town.

"I think she's good, for, like forever. She seems real determined and just healthier overall." He looked up at me and shook his head. "That shit can really fuck you up."

I drank my coffee and turned in my seat to see the yard and the dog. It looked like a collie mix, with some German Shepard. It was on a dog run cable, and at this moment, hunkered down enjoying what looked like a large bone or a rawhide. "Is that your dog?"

"Oh yeah, she's mine. I named her Callie. She's about eight, nine months."

"She's still a puppy then," I said as I turned back.

Jason smiled and shook his head. "Yeah, she sure is. Her barking is 'cause she's excited, but if I give her a good amount of time out, like throwing her the tennis ball and taking her for a walk, she'll settle in pretty good."

"That's the secret, isn't it, for dogs and kids? Tire 'em out and they'll sleep."

We sat quietly for a couple more minutes. I wondered if Jason had lost his nerve, or was having regrets about me coming out. "Jason, do you still want to talk?"

"Yeah, Mrs. Scott, I wanted you to come back. It's because, well, I'm ready to talk about all the shit that Gerald Rice done to me. I've been ready for some time; I just didn't know who I was ready to tell it to."

"You didn't think you could go to the police?"

"The police have never been an option, that's the truth. Gerald Rice and his brother own this town. All the police are in their back pocket. The Mountain, is well, The Mountain. It feeds a whole lot of people."

I let that hang in the air a minute before I responded. "Okay, I understand. But if what I think happened actually has, then that man should be arrested and put away for life."

"Oh, there's no doubt 'bout that. It's just, well, who's gonna believe me?"

"If it's happened to all three of you boys, then someone will."

"Jackson will never talk. Hell, he'll off himself before he ever admits to anything." Jason mimicked a gun to the temple.

"Admits? Jason, the word 'admit' implies wrong doing. You and your brothers aren't guilty. You're victims. You all should see a counselor. They could help you with this."

Jason was expressionless as he sat staring at me.

"I could recommend someone in the area. Someone good, who I know through my teaching job at school. Want me to get a list together for you?" I looked up at him.

"Actually, you'd be good to talk to, Mrs. Scott. I trust you and well, you're here, aren't you?"

"Jason, I don't have any training in counseling, I'm not experienced in this, at all."

"I think I just want someone to listen to me, outside my family, cause we all have our shit with Rice. And you, with seeing Jamie like you did, well you already know just how bad that shit is, but more important, you know I'd be telling the truth, not lying to you."

I sat quietly, took a sip of the coffee, and realized I needed to let go of my agenda, whatever it was, and be here for Jason. I could see the pain, the hurt, and this need in his eyes.

"Okay, Jason. I can listen," I said softly. "You start when you're ready."

For the next hour or so Jason recounted, in a detached, low voice, all the things Rice had done to him, and while Jackson never admitted it to Jason, he believed Rice did all these things to him too and later to Jamie.

Jason leaned back in the chair and stretched his legs. He seemed to focus on a spot just below a collage of family pictures on the kitchen wall.

"The shit started soon after we were moved in here. I remember Rice coming by, making sure we had cable, and Mom had her hook ups for the washer and dryer. That time he brought the three of us big radio remote control Monster Trucks. Mine was blue, Jackson's red, and Jamie got the yellow one, 'cause Jackson and I didn't want that one. We spent days out back, building up a track with dirt mounds, jumps, puddles we'd fill with buckets of water. We'd been living in Langdon at the low-income buildings out on

Route 11. To have this much space all to ourselves was good, really good. Mom would sit out back and get some sun. I knew we were on food stamps, welfare and anything else she could get since Dad died. Rice was the 'big guy' to her. She'd tell us at night, across this table, how much he'd done in getting the house, the appliances, and opening a charge card in her name at Bricker's Furniture Store."

Jason got up and reached into the cupboard near the sink. "I'm getting water, you want a glass?"

"No thanks," I said.

Returning to the table, he started talking again. "The toys started to change; they got bigger and better. We got X-boxes and games. Man, Rice bought us all the latest, expensive ones. For the first time, Jackson and I felt like we weren't the poor, shitty kids living in the sticks. Rice knew what he was doing, that's for sure. First time he took me for a ride all alone, it was up near one of The Mountain sheds where the ski lift chairs are stored. Hell, he dropped his pants, full hard-on going on, and said, 'You can touch it, go on, it ain't gonna bite you.' I was nine years old. Who does that to a kid?"

I sat motionless, looking at Jason. I said nothing; he didn't expect me to.

"Rice had this thing for sucking me off while masturbating. First, he let me sit on his lap and teach me how to drive, then he'd let me actually drive. He'd chuckle, 'Feel that Jason, right up near your ass? That's me, ready to explode.' We'd park and he'd pull down my pants, and start sucking me, and move his own dick until he shot off. I'd pull my pants up and ask him if I could get ice cream down in town. And sometimes he'd drive me over to the Dairy Queen in Peddan. He couldn't be seen in Langdon so out in the open, at least that's what I think now.

"After the first time I ever ejaculated came the porn—really graphic, even violent stuff, just disgusting. Rice, laughing at my bug-eyes, told me to take my time, figure out what made me want a wad off. I think I was about eleven, maybe twelve. 'Here's a little sex-ed for ya, Jason. Stuff nobody's ever gonna show ya.'

"Basically, when my dick was little it turned him on, but when I got past puberty, he wanted nothing to do with sucking me off. Now it was all about him getting blow jobs, and teaching me how to give head to his satisfaction. Once, he struck me across the face 'cause my teeth raked him. I wasn't happy about it and told him so. 'Fore the end of the week was up, two brand new Kawasaki trailbikes arrived off a trailer he was towing. Mom's eyes were all big, me looking at Jackson, knowing, really knowing then, that he was doing the same shit to Rice as me. Up to that point, I'd seen Jackson's face after he'd take his own rides with Rice. He'd come in looking confused, guilty, disgusted, just like me. But we never once talked about it. And then, every so often, there was Rice with his hundred dollar bills shoved into our pocket, getting out of the car. 'Here Jason, a little something to get by on, just between us.' I once paid for a school dance with a hundred. Coach Mason took me aside, questioned where I got it from. I was tight-lipped, told him it was Christmas money.

"Rice used to get so pissed at me when I'd run to the sink or toilet to spit out his gunk. 'You swallow it boy!' he'd yell. Mostly he'd take me to the vacant condos he owned up on The Mountain in the off season. We'd drink beer, even play cards, or watch daytime game shows. Then he'd get this glazed look, and I'd know it was time. Nice, uh? For a kid in eighth grade to be calling in sick, then spend the day up on The Mountain with that asshole, doing that shit.

"I can't tell you how many times he and I met up but it went on for years, starting in third grade 'till middle of ninth grade. I finally told him to fuck off. He kicked me out of his car, up on The Mountain. It was like three degrees out. I froze walking back into town.

"Ms. Sanders, the counselor at the elementary school, asked me a few times how things were at home. That was during the time my mother was using, doing coke, some heroin. Sometimes, after those rides with Rice, I'd come into the house and she'd be wasted, Jackson getting something for Jamie to eat, even making sure Jamie had gotten washed up, pajamas on.

"Rice swooped in and got Mom into rehab both times she went. Even paid for a lady to come take care of us. She was an okay lady, kind of nice, young. Rice paid for it all and he let us know it. 'Nobody's gonna save your mother, 'cept me and my money.' And I believed him. Thing is, it was true. How else could she have gone to rehab, twice, and had a decent lawyer? It worked. That's all I care about. She's clean.

"I didn't know—no, that's not true. I did know Rice turned to Jamie at some point. But I didn't know until yesterday that the asshole is still getting to Jamie. That I didn't know."

We sat for a little bit of time, then Jason stood up and looked out at Callie. I had kept my face as expressionless as I could during his recounting, but it was hard, and I had begun crying. I couldn't hold it back. A few times I whispered, "Sorry," and wiped my nose with my shirt-sleeve and brushed away my tears. I stood up now and got my own glass of water. Turning around, at the sink, I asked Jason, "Have you ever told your mom any of this?"

Sitting back down, looking at me intently, Jason replied, "There was a time I thought about it, but here's the thing. I think the guilt she'd feel would eat right through her and send her back down that goddamn path, with the possibility of no return."

I thought he was probably right.

We sat some more, in silence. The windows were all open; pretty yellow curtains moved in the air. I could hear the birds outside, and a fly hitting this side of the window screen.

"You know what I remember most 'bout that sleepover I had at your house?" Jason asked.

This surprised me, that he could remember one night at least seven, maybe eight years ago—especially during all the vile shit with Rice and his mother in and out of rehab.

I smiled, recalling Michael's sleepovers. "Oh, I bet you guys ate a lot of junk food and stayed up late, playing video games."

"I remember your old man, Michael's dad, coming into his bedroom. There was a book he'd started reading and Michael said, 'Go back and start at the beginning for Jason,' and he did. I can see its cover, about a boy that had an Indian come alive."

"*The Indian in the Cupboard*, one of Michael's favorites," I interjected.

"Yeah, something like that. Your old man held a flash-light to see the pages and we listened, his voice nice and low. I remembered thinking, *Is that what some dads, some men do?* They don't all yell, guzzle beer, kick the dog, and well, you know."

Jason stood up, reached for his crutches. I stood up too.

We put the coffee cups and glasses in the sink, and I, once more in less than twenty-four hours, made my way to the Larson's front door.

"I'm still going to get you a list of counselors in the area, Jason. Maybe Jamie could go with you?"

"I don't know about that."

"There are other places to report Rice besides the Langdon Police."

I heard the dog bark out back. "Thanks, Mrs. Scott. But for right now—" he opened the screen for me—"I know you'll keep all I told you confidential, right? Jackson meant what he said if he hears you telling anybody, 'specially the authorities. I don't want to see Michael get hurt."

"But what about Jamie? You guys have to stop him from getting to Jamie."

"Jackson and me, we're on it. That boy's going nowhere besides work without one of us with him."

N ow, with all the horrible details added in, the 'Larson loop' consumed me. I didn't have to be in the car or on the lawnmower to think of Jason's description of what that monster had done to him and his brothers for the past nine years.

The Mountain and the Rice brothers were the pillars of Langdon, in every facet of the town's existence. From its thriving industry—a top-notch ski resort—to its generosity in our schools, library, Rec Center, Senior Living, hospital, and golf course. You couldn't turn anywhere without seeing their name, money, and, most importantly, influence. Just last month, at Michael and Lexi's graduation, the number of scholarships granted from The Mountain brought us all to our feet in a standing ovation as graduate after graduate received notice of their award. Michael had received $3,000. Lexi, as an employee's child with stellar grades and a pre-med track at Bucknell, received The Mountain's largest award; $10,000 with a commitment of $10,000 for every year until she graduated. I recalled how, just five weeks ago, I had watched Marilyn beaming with joy as Lexi's name was called as this year's recipient of "The

Mountain's Pride." Jeffrey and I had stood and clapped for Lexi, all her hard work and determination recognized.

At the end of the graduation ceremony, Gerald Rice and his brother, Edmond, had worked the crowd. People flocked to them, and each man appeared to be gracious and patient as parents took pictures of them with their seniors. At the time, I couldn't take my eyes off Rice. I had been a witness to his graphic sex act with Jamie, but this man didn't gel with the man I'd seen that afternoon. I watched how effortlessly he socialized with the 'common folk' like a Lord coming down to the village. At one point, as Michael, Jeffrey, and I posed for a picture, Jeannie asked, "Hey, do you want one with Mr. Rice?"

I quickly said, "No. God, no."

As the days after my morning with Jason accumulated, my eyes were wide open to the full picture of the sexual abuse. It became evident to me how accurate Jason had been when he told me he could never have gone to the Langdon police. Langdon was Gerald Rice's playground, and he was truly 'king of the mountain.'

With this realization, I wondered about other places, entities to go to for help. But would help be welcomed if none of the Larsons were ready to acknowledge the abuse? I returned to my original thought of calling DCF and reporting what I had seen, both at the building lot and in the diner. I now had all the vital information I needed, along with verbal confirmation that Rice was a pedophile.

Two things stopped me from doing this. First, Jackson's threat to do harm to Michael if I talked to anyone, and second, my promise to Jason that I would keep all that he had told me confidential. Other factors weighed in as well. The possibility of Jackson harming himself—as Jason had indicated—if any of this were to come out, and of Jane possibly relapsing from the guilt. I also thought, although I had not been to town hall yet, that the Gravelin house deed was probably in Rice's name, not in Mrs. Larson's. I added the possibility of their homelessness to the scenario.

Questions of my obligation as a mandated reporter kept me awake at night. Was I a mandated reporter even if the suspected abuse was reported to me while I was not in my teaching role? In other words, was I bound by law to report suspected abuse if it involved children who were not my students? I finally came full circle—it didn't matter what the answers to these questions were, I knew I had to do something.

Chapter 19

present

During the long holiday break, I went to a fitness gym to check it out. I hadn't been walking much, and I wanted to establish an exercise routine. I wondered who Jeannie was walking with now that I was gone. I missed her, but I still wasn't ready to reach out yet. *Did she feel the same way?* A young trainer named Zeke showed me around. He was a massive guy, with huge biceps and thighs the size of tree trunks—big tree trunks. His neck was equally as large. Zeke's soft-spoken voice did not match his physical appearance, but he was kind and patient with me as I asked way too many questions.

"Hey, you live real close. This will fit nicely into your day, Sara. And SNAP is open all hours of the day, remember that." He took my check at the counter; made out for a three-month trial membership.

Zeke was leaving just as I was. "You done for the day?" I asked.

"Oh yeah, been here since six thirty this morning." He was heading to a little yellow VW Bug. I wondered how he fit in it.

I approached the Outback and felt for my car keys in my sweatshirt, then in my purse. I did not have them. I started to turn to go back inside the gym.

Zeke stopped the Bug. "You lose something?"

"I can't find my keys—do you remember seeing me with them inside?"

"If you're anything like my mom, they're in your car. She does that two, three times a week."

I nodded and went back to the Outback. Sure enough, there they were on the passenger seat in front.

"They there?" Zeke asked.

"Yep." I stood up. "I've got a spare set at the loft. Looks like I'm gonna get a little more of a work out today than I thought."

"Hop in, I'll give you a ride to get your spare. You aren't more than a fifteen minute drive there and back."

"I don't know, Zeke, is there enough room in that beetle for both of us?" I smiled.

"This beetle happens to belong to my kickass girlfriend. She's a whopping five feet, one hundred and five pounds. My car's in the shop."

As we pulled into the parking lot in front of the loft, Peter was sitting in his truck. He got out when I got out of Zeke's Bug. I could see a look of surprise dance across his face.

I walked over to him. "Hey, what's up?"

"Hi Sara, would it be alright with you if I got some measurements and took some pictures? You know the saying, 'Measure twice, cut once.'"

I looked back at Zeke who was waiting patiently. "I locked my keys in the Outback at SNAP; Zeke was going to give me a ride back with my spare set."

Peter looked over at Zeke, then back to me. His head of messy, auburn hair lifted up as the wind kicked dust around the parking lot. He was squinting in the bright sunshine. My own hair was whipping around; it was windy down here, by the wharf. I wrapped my arms around myself, shivering.

"I can give you a ride back then measure?" Peter asked, looking cold too in his festive red Carhart jacket.

"That will work—let me run and tell Zeke."

A little while later, I was climbing the stairs to the loft with Peter behind me.

"At first seeing you with that kid," he said, "well, I thought the Marines were in Port. He's a big boy, isn't he?"

I didn't know quite what to say back. I remained quiet while he measured, marking the wall, tape measure in hand. At one point he asked if it was okay for him to use the kitchen chair.

"Of course," I said. I watched as he took off his work boots and placed them over by the door. He moved the chair to three points against the wall, marking each with a short carpenter's pencil.

It felt odd to have someone in the loft. I didn't like his 'seeing you with that kid' inference, like Zeke and I had been 'together.' When Peter was all done, he put his boots back on. I felt I needed to say something, like to set the record—my record—straight. He put his hand on the door. More than anything I wanted to let him know that while he was building the bookcase for me, it didn't mean anything else.

"Hey, Peter, can we chat for a second before you go?"

"Sure." He stayed at the door, and I didn't make any overtures to have him come back in and sit. I wanted him to stay at the door.

"I'm not sure how to say this other than—" I took a deep breath and looked at him. "I'm not interested in any sort of relationship with, like, anybody. I came to Bristol because a lot of, well, for lack of a better phrase, *bad shit* happened to me and my family in Vermont. I left to get away, and…" I moved behind the couch, placing my hands on its back. "I was responsible for a lot of that bad shit. Now, more than anything, I just need to make amends with my son. And work—I just want to teach. Okay?"

Peter's face seemed to soften, and he ran his hand through his hair. It literally stood straight up in places. His eyes narrowed as he looked at me. "Okay, Sara." He turned the knob then stopped, facing the door, and said, "I've had my share of shit, so I know how, well, *shitty* it can be."

I laughed at how that sounded. He turned back to me, smiling now. He continued, "I hope it gets better for you. Time has a way of helping. And friends too. How about you regard me as a new friend, nothing more."

He understood. I replied, "That sounds good."

"Okay then, I'll call you as I get further along into building the bookshelves." He glanced up, taking the wall area in, and looked back at me. "I think you're gonna like 'em." He went out the door, down the stairs. This time when I looked out the big picture window, I saw he was moving at a clip. It was nowhere near as fast as the time before when he apologized for asking me if I was single.

Chapter 20

past

Itried to connect with Jason again, but each time I drove by the house on Gravelin Road, either Jackson's dark blue Jeep was there or, I presumed, Jane's silver Honda. I didn't dare call the house.

Jeffrey and I were focused on getting Michael ready for college. Our spare bedroom was piled high with new bedding, toiletries, new luggage, a dorm-size refrigerator, and new clothes I'd bought for Michael to replace his blown-out sweats, tattered flannel shirts, ripped t-shirts, and the pathetic grass-stained sneakers rotting on his feet.

"Mom, these are classics, you don't understand. I've worn these sneakers into burning buildings, I've climbed mountains no human being has ever scaled—when you gave birth to me, I was wearing these!"

The girl at Olympia Sports and I laughed as Michael said this. "I'll be right back with your size in this style," she called out.

I sat down at the bench, facing the wide wall of sneakers and cleats on display. It occurred to me that for the first time in many, many years, Michael would not be playing soccer this fall.

"Hey, no new cleats this trip, you okay with that?" I asked him as he stood, still looking at sneaker options.

"Yeah, the guys at Penn State are like way out of my league. Dad played intramural soccer when he went to college; he also joined some men's summer leagues. Maybe I'll do that."

"It was a good run, wasn't it, sweetie? I sure enjoyed all those years—the rain, the cold, the heat, the…actually it was mostly beautiful."

Michael came back to the bench. "I like these too. What do you think?"

I looked at the sneakers then back up at him. "You can't go wrong having a second pair with you."

Out came the girl with a couple of boxes, and Michael thanked her. "I've got another shoe I like," he said, and he handed her the second one.

He sat down next to me on the bench and started to try the sneakers on. Leaning into me, he said, "I love you Mom, Queen of Scotts."

"Ditto," I said back and thought, *My silly boy is going to college.*

Michael was headed to Penn State; his childhood dream to attend the college had become a reality. He was thinking education would be a good fit, no surprise there. With Lexi attending Bucknell, they wouldn't be too far apart—an hour and a half by car, three hours by bus. Neither of them had a car, so Lexi's statement—"Just long enough for me to study on my way to see Michael for the weekend"—was greeted by my, "Or just long enough for Michael to study on his way to see YOU for the weekend." State College and Lewisburg were very different college towns, but I knew the kids would figure it out.

I was also busy getting my classroom organized for the start of the new school year. I loved going in and spending time deciding on group reading books, writing out purchase orders, and seeing another stray teacher or two. These times inside the quiet building were laid back and gave me plenty of time to work. I did not play the Larson reel; I kept my attention focused on the sixth graders coming in.

I had made reservations in Ogunquit at the Anchorage Hotel for a two-night, three-day getaway. It was a tradition in our family to do this—our chance to crack lobster, enjoy the beach, and eat taffy as we window-shopped.

Lexi was coming this year, and, at the last minute, Jeffrey asked me, "Should we invite Marilyn?"

I thought and replied, "No, I'm sure she has a lot to do."

My true feelings were that she and I would be pretty uncomfortable with one another, knowing what we both did. One thing I did not do, ever, in all of this: I did not judge Marilyn. I understood how complicated and scary the whole 'follow the trail' could be. I was now gingerly walking down it, after galloping somewhat blindly down it since April.

How were Jeffrey and I during this period? We appeared to be on an even keel to most people, but there was still tension between us. I couldn't quite regard him—or us—as 'back to normal.' While I no longer surprised him with my sexual appetite from the winter, nor recoiled from his sexual advances of the spring, we were 'off.' Jeffrey sensed this, in subtle ways. I'd withdraw quickly from our shared bathroom when he'd come in or decline a drive with him on more than one summer evening.

"I bet the deer are out, feeding in Haskell's orchard. Want to take a ride over?" he asked once, coming into the den. We'd been driving to Haskell's orchard since Michael was three, and kept on, long after Michael stopped riding with us.

"No, I'm okay. I've got some reading to do, you go." I had embellished my responsibility in piloting a new reading program at the middle school. I mostly sat in front of my laptop, wondering what to do. I was exhausted from sleepless nights replaying Jason's ordeal and the subterfuge of the affair and what it entailed. Our marriage had been effortless these past nineteen years. The weight now of my infidelity and what had come out of it was crushing me.

That summer, the three of us had pretty distinct and unrelated focuses: Michael enjoying his last summer home before a huge transition; Jeffrey keeping busy researching and then resurfacing the kitchen cabinets; and me, living a hellish nightmare of images. Rice, the town benefactor, Rice, The Mountain monster. Seeping into all this were my troubling thoughts on the state of my marriage.

At times I asked myself, *Is it enough to have just listened to Jason? Did I need to do more?* He told me that he and Jackson would not let Rice get to Jamie again. I believed him. They were pretty scary dudes. I couldn't imagine the old man daring to cross them.

Finally, I wrote down the names of two male counselors who I knew were very good, and then I added a woman to the list. I didn't know how much the gender of the counselor might matter. After striking out on hoping to catch Jason home alone, I put the list in an envelope and mailed it. I did not enclose a note; I thought it best not to.

Chapter 21

present

I pulled up to Louise's house on time. It was a small Cape, with gray shingles and a picket fence in front. Rose bushes, now bare, were all along the fence. A beautiful berry wreath adorned her front door.

We greeted each other like old friends. She gave me a tour; everything was lovely and pleasing to the eye, just like her shop. In the dining room, a beautiful, ornate credenza was covered in photographs in an amazing collection of assorted frames. She and I started to go through them, Louise narrating each, mostly of her children and their children. Some were of her as a young woman and then with her husband. She had been gorgeous, I knew that— even now, at seventy-two, she was still attractive.

Louise pointed to a nice-looking couple in a frame, the picture from some years back. She tapped the man in it. He was dark and handsome, his arm around a petite woman with a beautiful smile. They were standing in front of a brick building; the background was filled with a gorgeous window-box, purple petunias cascading down its sides.

"See him?"

I leaned in.

"We couldn't keep our hands or our mouths," she rolled her eyes, "off of each other. Makes me blush still, thirty years later."

I looked up at her. "Wait, you mean you had an affair?"

"I don't think there's any harm in telling you that now. He's dead, his wife is dead, and I can't imagine you're going to run off and tell my grown children, are you?" She smiled.

I smiled too and shook my head. I encouraged her to go on.

"Yes, we sure did some cavorting. It was short and intense. We had no illusions—we knew it was pure unbridled lust, nothing more."

She went on. "I don't think a woman ever comes close to her full sexual peak until her forties, usually after her childbearing is done, and well, before the drumbeat of menopause. I think there's research on that."

"Who was he? And how or why did it end?" I asked.

"Oh, I'll tell you exactly. He was an emergency room doctor at the hospital, and I was often one of the nurses on his service. The minute we met, there was something electrifying between us. I can't explain it. Why did it end? Well, my son Adam was hit pretty hard one night in a big football game. Bill, my husband, had been trying to call me. It was way back before cell phones, like nineteen-eighty-eight or eighty-nine. Henry—that was his name. He and I were thirty miles down the road at the Cruise Inn...an awful motel, not even fit for a B-rated movie!"

My eyes grew bigger, and she continued, "We knew we had two hours free, and we were making the best of it."

Picking up the picture, she dusted it with her sleeve. "After, when I drove home and entered the back door of our house, a note that my neighbor had taped above the door fell to the ground. It was telling me to go to the hospital. I never saw it. A little while later, Chrissy, our daughter, found me soaking in the tub. I told everybody I'd fallen asleep and had never heard the phone ringing or the neighbor pounding on the back door."

"And you ended it like that?"

Louise set the picture down and moved to one of a handsome boy dressed in a football uniform. "Adam had fractured his leg in two places, and Doctor Abrams said it was the worst break he'd ever seen. My Adam needed me, and I guess you could say it's what woke me from my stupor of the Henry affair."

I couldn't believe her description of how the affair ended. The words 'woke' and 'stupor' were how I would best describe my ending with Craig.

I tapped the doctor's photo as Louise had done. "Did Henry ever try to talk you out of, you know, ending it? Did he want the affair to continue?"

"Oh, I don't think that he objected strenuously to calling it quits. It was a lot of work, running here and there, clothes on, clothes off." She giggled and went on. "But it's true—it was a time of no constraints and when we were alone, no restraints. It's hard to describe."

"No, no, I think I understand." Being with Louise, here and listening to her talk, I felt like I was starting to be able to identify some of the big feelings I hadn't resolved.

"Now, let's pour us a couple of pints and get ready for our show."

I had caught up to the same *Last Tango in Halifax* episode Louise was on.

"Can I ask you one more thing, Louise, about the affair? I don't mean to pry, but I'm just curious." My voice was breaking, and Louise turned back to me, searching my face.

"Oh Sara, that's what your exile is all about, isn't it? I shouldn't have prattled on and on like this."

Tears came to me unexpectedly, and I shook my head. "No, really, it's okay."

She came over and put her arms around me. I felt my mother's arms, and I surrendered to being held. When we straightened up, I blew my nose on the tissue she had given me.

"Do you still want to ask that question?"

I nodded. "What happened after the affair? I mean, in your life, like how did it change it?"

She thought for a moment, then replied, "I can't say it did much of anything, really. We each resumed our married lives, and, well, I can only speak for myself, but I never strayed again. One thing I didn't do Sara, is beat myself up over it."

She turned and went into the kitchen. I stood in front of the credenza, surrounded by her photographs of family, friends, and associates. I blew my nose again. The guilt I was carrying around was still there, but now I hoped that time and maybe hearing Louise's story would help to start to unpack it. *Michael will always be my son, no matter what,* I thought. And then I got a flash of Peter's face, smiling at my door and telling me friends can help too.

I called out to Louise, "I love your place, it's just like your shop." The scent of apple and cinnamon wafted from the swinging doors to her kitchen.

Chapter 22

past

Our seven hour drive to take Michael to State College was full of good conversation. We discussed the idea of a school merger that Langdon had recently entered into with some of the other districts in the area. I was surprised by how vehemently Michael objected to the idea of a regional high school.

"Can you imagine having to drive thirty minutes down into Colton or Peddan. It'd be horrible. Not to mention how much longer bus rides would be. As it is, some kids at Langdon are on the bus an hour to get to school. Even longer."

"I know, Michael, but school funding in Vermont is taking a hit. Our taxes are high," Jeffrey replied.

"Think about the sports programs too, everybody trying out for limited spots. Now, Coach Mason practically begs anyone with two legs to join soccer, but I like that. It makes our teams, well, pathetic, but cohesive." Michael imitated his coach with a few, "We are a cohesive unit out there. Co-hes-ive."

I chuckled at that. We entered Massachusetts and made our way south. I noticed the medians in Mass were mowed, and the signage for gas, food, and lodging were in better shape. *They've got more money in their coffers*, I thought. If Langdon's high school closed, it'd be a big, gaping hole in the town. My thoughts started to turn to Rice and The Mountain. *Nope, not going there.* I had the next forty-eight hours with Michael—the last time before his Thanksgiving break. I was going to enjoy it.

We all grew quiet. At one point I glanced back at Michael. His eyes were closed, his ear-buds in.

Jeffrey asked, "Is he asleep?"

"Hard to tell; he might just be listening to music."

"I can hear you, people," Michael sang out and shifted in his seat. I smiled at Jeffrey, and he shook his head.

When we entered Connecticut, Michael perked up. "Lexi's already in Lewisburg, she just texted me." He leaned into the center console.

"Wow, she and her mom must have left well before the crack of dawn," I replied.

"This drive isn't going to be too bad, Michael, once you do it a few times," Jeffrey said, glancing at him.

I had made a list of things I wanted to buy: Penn State sweatshirts, sweatpants, banners, and water bottles for all of us and Jeannie too. Just yesterday, as we did our loop, she and I reminisced. We remembered the times we had gone walking while little Michael rode his bike ahead of us. When he was just starting out, we were frantic, taking turns yelling, "Michael! Be careful!" Or, "Stop Michael! Up ahead. Stop!"

It was neither invigorating nor relaxing, but it was a way for us to get at least some exercise, especially when Jeffrey was out of town. When we'd get back to the house, I'd hug Jeannie before she'd get in her car and apologize, "Well, that was stressful, sorry." And she'd say something funny and dramatic back like, "We kept him alive, that's all that matters." Or, "I've aged ten years in the last hour."

Further into our walk Jeannie had said, "How about the whole TV dinner thing you two had going on?" We were passing the Café and turning onto Whitcomb Street.

"Oh my gosh, I've forgotten that." Again, when Jeffrey was traveling and in the years pre-Lexi, Michael and I tended to eat dinner early, often in front of the T.V. I knew it was a bad habit, but one I totally enjoyed with him. We'd make our decision about a movie or show and then set up our dinners side-by-side on the coffee table in the den. We never did this while Jeffrey was home; it was our little secret.

"What should we watch for dinner?" Michael would ask, instead of, "What's for dinner?" I'd say back, "Why don't you choose." He chose most of the nights: *Paw Patrol* grew into *The Lord of the Rings* trilogy into past seasons of *Survivor*. Jeannie came over sometimes and got us hooked on the early episodes of *Friends*. Michael had been flabbergasted when he discovered there were real things called "TV dinners," and we had to try them. "This is horrible, Mom, but let's buy trays like this, okay?" And we had, parceling out our meals on trays like it was hot lunch at school.

I had not gone to Penn State in the spring of Michael's junior year when he and Jeffrey first checked it out. I had a lot going on at school and had, at that point, already done a couple of college visits.

While they both had told me to prepare for a huge campus, University Park took my breath away. It was its own city within a city. The College of Education was one of fourteen colleges located on its 7,500 acres. Michael was bringing a brand-new bike with him, and I now understood why. The campus buildings were grand, the student population reaching 45,000. Its size was overwhelming to me, but Michael and Jeffrey basked in it. I understood why Lexi had chosen Bucknell, with its small campus of 3,600 students, its reputation of strong advisory groups, and its close work with medical professionals from its alumni. Here at Penn State, Michael would be in an environment completely the opposite of his first eighteen years of life; I hoped he knew what he was in for. I hoped he would adjust.

We stayed two nights and finally left Michael in the evening of the third day, standing outside his dorm, waving us off, eager to start college life. We had met his roommate, Jayden, and his parents. They seemed like very nice people, coming from a little place called Illion in upstate New York. At one point, Becky, Jayden's mom, leaned into me and whispered, "I don't know about you, but I feel like I'm going to have a nose bleed, this place is so huge."

I agreed and added, "Hope they adjust and become best friends. That would help." We exchanged cell numbers and email addresses, promising to keep in touch.

On our way home, traveling north on I-80 West, Jeffrey mentioned that he hoped—with Michael's agreement—that we'd be able to come down for at least one, possibly two Penn State football games. He added, "Maybe swing by and pick up Lexi at Bucknell."

I responded by asking, "Do you think they'll stay together? I hope they do, but I'm not so sure."

Jeffrey's confidence surprised me. "Oh, I think that boy isn't ever going to look for any other girl."

I glanced at him, and he reached over and took my hand. "Lexi is the real deal, and Michael knows it. He's got a good head on his shoulders, Sara, and he's in love, with a level of commitment that I feel is pretty mature."

I hoped he was right, but matters of the heart—or loin—weren't always so simple or clear cut, I thought.

"Penn State football games, in person, not on TV. You and Michael are in the big league now."

Jeffrey replied, "You know there was a time in two-thousand-eleven that Penn State football was in real jeopardy because of the whole Sandusky, Joe Paterno sexual abuse thing."

I sat up and said, "Tell me about it." Somehow, I knew, right then, that I was about to glean something useful from what Jeffrey was going to tell me. In hindsight, those hours in the car en route home to Langdon, listening to Jeffrey's description of Penn State's past, gave me time to formulate my next moves. Inaction was no longer a choice. We had just dropped Michael off, 450 plus miles away. Jackson's threats to hurt him were no longer valid.

Jeffrey was a voracious reader and knew a lot about the scandal and Penn State's possible cover up. He told me Sandusky had been sexually abusing middle school boys for years but had still been given 'emeritus' status in the Penn State football program and had access to their facilities. He went on to describe how Sandusky had a charity for boys plucked from poverty—again, like with Rice, the underprivileged tended to be easier targets—and that some assistant coach had seen him in the shower sexually abusing a boy. That assistant had reported it—not to the police, but to his next chain of command in the organization. "I think that was even Paterno, but I'm not positive."

Over several days, possibly weeks, other men in the football program—which was and still is a big franchise—did little with the information. Penn State was later accused of a cover up, and the state's attorney opened up an investigation.

"Sandusky went to jail, didn't he?" I asked.

"Yeah, he never admitted it, but like twenty-five victims went on record as having been sexually abused by him over many years, even his own adopted son. Civil lawsuits were settled, and Penn State agreed to shell out millions in payments to these men. Heads rolled, people were fired, including the President of the College. Actually, he may have resigned."

"If he never admitted the abuse, it must have been a jury trial, right?"

"A grand jury was convened first and looked at all the state's evidence and then it was moved to the trial courts. That's what they do when the state's evidence in cases is iffy; they get a grand jury to decide if charges are merited. In Sandusky's case, the grand jury took two years."

"Wait, two years to just investigate to determine if they had a case?"

"Yes, crazy isn't it?"

"So, in general, if a state attorney has a solid case, no grand jury is necessary?" I asked Jeffrey.

"Yes, I think that's it. The state attorney's office is full of very capable staff. It's usually the district attorney, or the state's assistant attorney and their staff who do all the leg-work and gather evidence through questioning witnesses, taking depositions, even setting up wire taps to see if charges are warranted. Then if they are, the state attorney brings a case forward. The ultimate decision rests with the state attorney on whether to go right into pressing charges or convening a grand jury."

I wished, as he was talking, that I could take notes. A plan was starting to percolate, and by the time we got home late Sunday night, I had jotted down thoughts on the back of the paper with Jayden's mother's contact information. I put those notes in the manila envelope still hidden in my top dresser drawer.

How did I feel about the momentous milestone of dropping my only child off at college? I was so focused on what I had heard in the car from Jeffrey that I didn't get a chance to reflect until later in the week. The house was quiet, there was no TV too loud, no dirty dishes left out on the counter or on the floor of his bedroom, no Lexi calling out to Michael to "Stop tickling, stop slurping, stop talking, stop making me laugh so hard," and there was no "Night, Mom" as big feet stopped on the landing outside my bedroom door.

"This sucks," I said to Jeffrey one night as we were going to bed.

"I know, but we'll adjust."

We then made love, but it was sad, like we were trying to find comfort in each other, but really, there was none left.

September came, and the weather continued to be beautiful. We did settle in some with Michael gone. Our trip to a Penn State game was set for October 12. Jeffrey made reservations at the same place we'd stayed when we dropped Michael off. It was all set, too, that we would pick up Lexi and check out Lewisburg. I thought a lot about Marilyn during this time, knowing I still had Jeffrey in the house and she now had no one. At times, I thought it'd be easier on me if I was alone. Every interaction with Jeffrey was fraught with worry that I'd give something away or show him how much turmoil I was in. I finally couldn't hold it in any longer.

On the eve of Jeffrey leaving once more for the University of Washington's Center for Educational Conference, of which he had a prominent speaking engagement, I lost it. It was a combination of missing Michael and the pressure I was under to do something about the Larsons. I had done some more reading on the Penn State pedophile scandal and started to worry, really worry that my inaction could be criminal.

Jeffrey had been recording bits and pieces of his presentation. From his office, I could hear him speaking on scaffolding lessons and strengthening critical thinking skills. On and on he went, while I sat at the kitchen table practically pulling my hair out.

I'd lost more weight and felt like I was unraveling. I couldn't take another word and marched into his office. "My God, don't you ever get tired of all this bullshit? You're all fucking theory. You never spew anything remotely needed in the classroom. You spout this and that from the lectern and all of us little minions are the ones who deal with all the shit. You don't care that teachers are having to break up fights, buy their students food, clothes, and—" I paused, raising my voice—"and call DCF because sick fucks force twelve-year-olds to give them blow jobs. Go to Washington you arrogant, educational asshole." And I stormed out.

Jeffrey tried to follow me, but I shouted, "Stay the fuck away from me." I went up into Michael's room and cried. I fell asleep for a while. Later, as dusk fell, I tiptoed out and down to the kitchen. Jeffrey was sitting in the living room, the TV on low.

"Hey, you want to talk?" he called out, in a tone of concern.

"No, not now. I'm sorry, but no, not now."

"How about when I get back at the end of the week?" he asked, again his voice low and measured.

"Yeah, sure." I added, "I'm just having a hard time."

"I miss him too."

The next morning when Jeffrey left, I gave him a hug and wished him safe travels. He looked as if he hadn't slept.

As he was backing out of the driveway, he rolled down the passenger-side window and called out, "I love you, Sara."

I nodded at him. I stood on the porch, still in my pajamas, drinking coffee. "My marriage is going south," I said out loud as he drove down the street.

Jeffrey's absence was exactly what I needed in order to get my thoughts centered on the Larson boys. *There's a way forward for this family, there has to be,* I thought.

Chapter 23
present

January rolled into Bristol, wet and chilly. I returned to school, coming off of a relaxing, recharging ten days. Michael's words—"Merry Christmas, Mom"—had restored something in me that was the core of who I was: his mother.

Passing the sixth grade teacher in the hallway, she whispered, "It's one-hundred percent, for sure that I'm going to England. Just want you to know."

"Good for you."

By 5:15, I was turning into the Wine and Cheese Shop, feeling beat after just one day back. I recognized Peter's truck in the parking lot. I quickly brushed my hair and put on a little Chapstick. Then I pinched my cheeks.

He was paying for a case of Frye's Leap from a local brewery. I had tried the local IPA at Louise's and liked it. The middle-aged woman behind the counter was vivacious and laughing loudly. She reached over the counter and patted Peter's chest, exclaiming, "Oh, I bet you're a good dancer. Really, come join us, I'll teach you a lot."

Peter was smiling and taking this all in. As he went by me to leave, I leaned back and whispered, "Didn't know you liked them so lively."

"Sara! Hey now, you be quiet." He looked pleased to see me. And I realized that my comment to him was border-line flirtatious. *Where did that come from?* I thought.

I looked down at the case and back up at him. "Been a tough day?"

He ran his fingers through his hair—now it stood out wildly—and he looked tired. "My seventeen-year-old daughter is back. Enrolled at Bristol Regional. I can't even begin to tell you what it's been like."

"Really?" I thought that may explain his more than usual disheveled look.

"I'll have to lock this in my truck." He hefted the case up by two hands. "But believe me, I'll be making lots of trips out to that truck this week, that's for sure."

"When did she decide to come back and live with you?"

"Right after spending Christmas here. But the rationale that 'she missed her dad' didn't hold up too well when Ryan Seaton came by, minutes after her decision. He's a nice kid, but I'm on high alert."

"How's her mom taking it?" I asked.

"Honestly, I think she may be relieved. It's a whole new, well, completely different level of parenting since the last time I did it."

"I wish you luck, and patience, Peter. Lots of patience."

He smiled back. "I may come by, you know, to work on the framing for the shelves. It's getting to that point. And it'll be a respite."

"I'll give you my cell number so you don't have to find me at school." I had my purse and a pad of sticky notes in it. I wrote my number out and handed it to him. "Come by anytime. I remember those teen years; I'm kind of missing them these days."

He took the sticky note and left. I looked out the window and noticed a girl in the passenger seat of his truck, boots up on the dashboard, long blond hair pulled up in a hair tie. She was looking down, I assumed at her phone. I had missed seeing her there.

She said something to her dad as he got in. Peter looked at her and laughed. *Can't be all that bad,* I thought. I wondered what Michael was doing at Penn State this chilly January evening. I decided, on the spot, to make a batch of his favorite cookies and mail them to him.

Less than a week later, while I was sleeping soundly sometime around midnight, someone called my cell. I always panic at a late night call, instantly going to the worst-case scenario: car accident, heart attack, the police. It was Peter, his voice low and apologetic. "Hey Sara, so sorry to wake you, but I've got a situation that I think I need you for."

It's his daughter, I thought and sat up. "Hey, what's up?"

"I'm at Portsmouth General, and Eula, Maddie's grandmother, has been admitted. I think she had a stroke about two hours ago. The thing is, Maddie is here, and well, I'm not sure what I should do."

I immediately got out of bed and said, "I'm coming. I'll bring her back to my place. I've got clean clothes for her, and she'll be fine. I'll be there in twenty."

"That's good, thank you."

When I arrived at the hospital, it was very quiet. I saw Peter's back—he was sitting up in a straight-back chair, in the waiting room outside the emergency room doors. As I came in further, I saw Maddie asleep with her head in Peter's lap. His eyes were also closed. I was touched by the gentleness they both emitted. I sat down in the chair beside them.

Touching his arm hesitantly, I said, "Hey Peter, I'm here."

"Oh, hey," he said, rubbing his eyes and scratching his forehead. He looked down at Maddie. "She hasn't been asleep long. She was awake when I called you. We both must have dozed off."

Peter explained that Maddie had dialed 911 and told the dispatcher that her gram was on the floor in her bedroom: "Not looking good, but still breathing." They sent out an ambulance and brought them both here. "Shaina's cousin was on the call. He phoned me, knowing Maddie needed someone, and I came."

"How's her gram?"

"I think she suffered a stroke, but I don't know any more than that. With the way privacy rules are now, it's hard to get information. But I am related somehow, like Eula is my grandmother Bertha's niece from her first marriage."

"Ah, the O'Brien clan strikes again."

"That it does. Hell, you and I are probably related."

"No, I'm pretty sure we're not." I laughed.

"Okay, well, let's save that for another day. How about I carry her to your car and follow you home? I'll get her up your stairs."

"That's a plan."

I called in sick the next morning—for the first time—and told Tami where my sub plans were.

She laughed. "Sub plans for the sub." She already knew Maddie was home with me—word travels fast. I let the child sleep as long as she could, curled up on my sleeper sofa.

When Peter had first placed her down on it the night before, I woke her up softly and suggested she go to the bathroom. She was a little trooper and did, coming right back and climbing in. "Hi, Mrs. Scott," she whispered as I tucked her in. "You smell good." Tide Fresh Scent was my detergent of choice now.

Peter and I had talked quietly in my kitchen. I was voicing my concern that her gram may not be well enough to take care of Maddie for some time.

"That was how some people felt even before this stroke. There's an aunt up in Lincoln who tried to get Maddie just last year—Eula's youngest daughter, I can't think of her name. But Eula convinced her she could still manage. I think Maddie was on the fence about going."

"Is Lincoln a nice area, a good school?"

"I think so. Aunt Kelly, that's her name. She's Maddie's mother's sister. Nice girl, done okay for herself, married, a couple of kids, husband works for the highway department. I'll give her a call in the morning."

Peter left at about 1:30 a.m. I sat for a few minutes and reviewed our night. *He's a pretty decent guy,* I thought.

Chapter 24
past

O n Wednesday of the week Jeffrey had left, I came home from school and sat in my driveway for a minute before backing out and driving straight to Shaw's. I was craving one of their rosemary and garlic whole-roasted chickens. I also grabbed a premade salad and a pint bottle of Harpoon.

I was coming out, anticipating the mouth-savoring chicken, when I heard a raspy, deep voice call out to me. "Hey, Mrs. Scott, over here."

I looked over and saw the dark blue Jeep and Jackson Larson smoking a cigarette, its smoke curling out the window. I thought, but couldn't tell for sure, that Jason was in the passenger side. I came over, my plastic bag hanging in my hand, banging at my side.

"Hi Jackson, what's up?"

He flung the cigarette out of the car in a perfect arc. I watched it land two parking spots over. It was still lit, its embers glowing.

"We're ready to do it."

"I beg your pardon?" I asked, now confirming it was Jason across from him, and Jamie in the backseat.

"We're ready to report that fucker, that monster, and we need your help. The son of a bitch tried to get Jamie again, then kicked him out of his car, somewhere up there." He pointed to The Mountain. "Some asshole picked him up and got him home to us."

I placed my free hand on Jackson's door and looked at him, sitting behind the wheel. "Well, then Jackson, that someone wasn't an asshole, was he? He got Jamie home safe." In that one statement, the dynamics between Jackson and me changed.

"Follow me to my house," I told him and turned to head home to eat.

The three boys stood in my kitchen while I cut the chicken and scooped a serving of the potato salad onto a plate. I poured a glass of Harpoon. I couldn't remember eating any lunch at school, and I was too hungry not to eat. I had made chocolate chip cookies the night before and put the tin out, motioning for them to help themselves. They stood awkwardly; no one reached for a cookie. I stayed standing too, eating and looking at the three of them.

Jamie was the tallest and by far the thinnest. His shoulders were concave, his clothes too big. He wouldn't look at me.

I wiped my mouth with the back of my hand and said, "Jamie, what I said to you in the diner was not okay. I was wrong to have said that. I want you to know this."

He neither looked at me or said anything in acknowledgment.

"He's a retard, he don't talk much. Thought you knew that," Jackson said.

"Don't call him that, it's not okay. And he will talk, he'll have to." I gave Jackson a look I reserved for the toughest kids I'd had in my years of teaching. It was a 'not up for discussion' look.

"Jason, what about your mother? What's going to happen to her when you report this?"

Looking at me seriously and thoughtfully, Jason replied, "She knows now, Mrs. Scott. I told her. She said maybe that's why she's gotten so strong these last few years. The Good Lord was bracing her."

I turned to Jackson. "Are you ready, Jackson, to talk about what Rice did to you?"

He looked at me intently and said, "If I don't talk, I'll kill the bastard. But here's the thing, I don't want to rot in jail. So, yeah, I'm ready to talk."

I'd had enough to eat, and I stood, taking them all in. I put my plate in the sink. My kitchen clock was ticking. It was 5:30, on September 19.

"You boys have to listen to me carefully." I made sure I had everyone's attention. "You're not only going to bring that monster down and send him to jail for life; you're going to sue the hell out of him and The Mountain for all this..." I searched for the right words. "This terrible wrong."

"And you—" I pointed to Jackson. "You're going to quit that tough guy act and do exactly as I, as they, tell you. Do you understand?"

Jackson nodded yes.

"Good, because I won't go forward unless you can take directions."

"Who's they, Mrs. Scott?" Jason asked.

"I'm working on that, Jason." I didn't smile. "We're staying clear of Langdon Police. You called that right. We need to get Rice to confess. Can you do that, Jackson, without putting your hands on him?"

Jackson raised his eyebrows, and a smile, one that wasn't at all friendly, appeared. "I can do that, Mrs. Scott."

"Good. Now, no talking to anybody and wait until I get back to you." I handed Jamie the cookie tin and told him to take it home to his mother.

Just like that, my inaction became action. We had a plan.

Chapter 25

present

I ended up having Maddie at my place, with Aunt Kelly's permission, for eleven days. Eula had suffered a massive stroke and would not be returning to the trailer. Maddie and I had gone out and gathered up her clothes, stuffed animals, and toys, and brought them back to the loft. We also went to the hospital, a trip that had not been pleasant for Maddie. She was distressed to see her gram was so out of it, with all those tubes connected to her.

We went together every day to school and left together every afternoon. Sometimes, as she lay in the sofa bed at night, I would pat her back. She said her gram would do that when sleep didn't come easily. A couple of those times, I wondered what it would have been like to be the mother to a daughter. It would have been different but I think I would have liked it.

Aunt Kelly came to pick up Maddie. Peter was over to break the ice since I didn't know her or her husband. I was glad Maddie was excited to go. She kept telling me about all the animals on their farm. She'd spent a month with them the summer before.

Kelly was soft spoken and sweet, early thirties, chubby with red, curly hair. Her husband had run to fill up the car, and now, I could hear him coming up the stairs. Peter opened the door.

Something about him immediately repulsed me, sending shock waves through my body. He was short and rather heavy. His hair was slicked to the side, and I could see dandruff. He bore a strong resemblance to Gerald Rice, or what I imagined Rice would have looked like as a forty-year-old. Uncle Don and Peter were chatting back and forth. I couldn't take my eyes off of him. Maddie quickly came to me and took my hand. It struck me as an odd reaction. She was staring at Uncle Don, too, and seemed wary.

Aunt Kelly was gathering up all of Maddie things, while I stood watching Don. I called Peter over and motioned for him to follow me. I walked into the bathroom and closed the door and turned on the fan and the water faucet. Peter wasn't amused; he could see my face, and I looked as sick as I felt.

"Peter, that man, Don...we shouldn't let Maddie go."

"What do you mean?"

"I think he's—there's something about him that is giving me bad...I mean *really* bad vibes."

Peter ran his fingers through his hair, a habit I now recognized he did when he was stressed.

"Okay, Sara." He stood still, thinking. "Why don't we keep Maddie here a little bit longer, and let me vet Don. You know, check him out with Lincoln's police and the school, if they'll talk to me. And then—only then—if things are cool, we'll drive Maddie up there ourselves. Okay?"

I nodded, but then suddenly let go. I slipped to the floor and began sobbing. Peter bent down and touched my shoulder.

"I'm going to get them to go, Sara, and then I'll get Maddie settled in."

I didn't hear what Peter said to them or Maddie. I kept the fan and water running as I lay on the bathroom floor. After a bit, I washed my face and came out. Peter and Maddie were cuddled up on the couch, spoons in their hands, a pint of ice cream between them. Peter leaned his head back and said, "QVC Shopping Channel." He held up the Breyers. "Hope this is okay to take from your freezer."

I walked up behind him on the couch, leaned down close to his ear and whispered, "Thank you for having my back." Peter nodded to me as the woman on the shopping channel announced the evening's special offering.

Chapter 26
past

I called in sick the next morning and drove down to
Peddan, straight to the lawyer's house who had settled
my mother's estate. His name was Freddy and he was a
brother to a very dear coworker, Sal. I'd met him socially a
number of times, and liked him a lot. Kind of a hippie still,
he wore his hair long and shaggy. He was cute, in a teddy
bear sort of way.

When I knocked, just after 7:30 a.m., he shuffled to the
door and was clearly surprised to see my face. I didn't care.
I told him I needed to see him as soon as possible. "In fact,
it's a matter of life and possible death," I pleaded, believing
that Jackson might actually kill Rice if we didn't report the
sexual abuse.

Freddy looked like he didn't know whether to be amused
or frightened by my statement. He told me to meet him at
his office in an hour. I went and got coffee, parked, and added a few more thoughts to the notes I'd written up after the
boys left my house the night before. I had Marilyn's manila
envelope on the seat next to me.

After Freddy's execution of my mother's estate, Jeffrey told me that it was pretty evident Freddy had a crush on me. "He couldn't stop looking at you, Sara. I was embarrassed for him."

That part was not what I had remembered—nor what I now needed—from my dealings with Freddy. What I recalled most about Freddy happened when Jeffrey and I were in his office one afternoon.

Jeffrey had said, "Must be nice hanging with the big boys." He was pointing to a picture behind Freddy's desk.

Freddy had swiveled around and looked up at the picture of himself with two other men, holding some decent-sized fish. "Lake Ontario, in Pulaski, New York. Great salmon fishing. Have you ever been?"

Jeffrey had replied, "No, but it looks like you guys caught some big ones."

Freddy had responded by pointing to one of the men. "Only in Vermont does the State's Attorney coach Little League for his son's team." And he pointed to the second man. "And the Assistant State's Attorney asks me, an old hippie friend, to be his daughter's godfather."

Now, Freddy came out to the waiting room of his office and smiled. "You look good, Sara."

I followed into his office and sat down across from him. "Thanks for seeing me, Freddy. I'll get right to it. If I talk too fast, slow me down, and, well, you'll need to take out a legal pad, because I think you're going to want to take some notes. I've got a lot to say."

I began with the moment in the building lot B10 on April 24 and what I witnessed. I ended with the Larson boys standing in my kitchen, a little over fourteen hours ago. I left nothing out. I took my phone and showed him the photo of the front of the $100 bill, with its strange block printing of '9am-B9', along with the pictures I had taken of

Jamie in the diner. I reached in and took out *The Rutland Herald* articles and the toxicology report. Freddy took extensive notes, needing to turn the legal pad over once, twice before I stopped talking.

"Sara, I'm just an estate planning lawyer. Why come to me with all this?"

I stood and walked around his desk. I touched the picture. "You've got fishing buddies in high places, Freddy—where this needs to go. Get me to them, and I'll bring the boys. Jackson, the oldest one, says he'll talk and swears he can get Rice to confess." I returned to the chair.

Freddy sat, tapping his pen against the legal pad and looking at me. He glanced down at his notes and asked, "How'd you get the toxicology report?"

"Doesn't matter—you can verify its accuracy."

"Okay." He paused, then looked up at me. "Sara, why were you there at that building lot in the first place?"

And just like that, all the moral wrestling about what to do was over for me. I had decided that I would pay the personal price, the high cost, to make sure Rice was punished for all the horrors of his actions. It was payment time. In order to seal the deal, I had to be completely honest.

"I was having an affair with a guy who worked on The Mountain. I got to our meeting place early that afternoon. Rice was already there with Jamie." I felt a strange sense of relief saying the words aloud.

I watched Freddy closely. My eyes never wavered; I was daring him to say something. I could have lied, said I was out walking, but that wouldn't have been credible. I needed to give the Larsons' story the credibility it deserved—*they* deserved. I needed to tell my truth, just as the boys had.

Freddy sat for a few minutes, then stood up from his desk and said, "The shit's going to hit the fan, Sara. You ready for that?"

"No, but what's the alternative, Freddy? Rice may have his eyes, and maybe a whole lot more, on a new boy, about nine. Check out the Langdon Shopper, the 'Pinewood Derby Winner' picture on page six. It's of Rice and the boy. This kid lives with his grandmother, no father in his life, on the edge of poverty. That's been his M.O."

"Jesus, I will." He walked me to his office door. "Keep your cell close by, and tell those boys of yours...well, just make sure they're ready too."

"I will, and Freddy, remember that the youngest boy, Jamie, has cognitive disabilities along with a speech impediment. Please make sure they plan for that, like you would with a young child."

"Anything else, Sara?"

"Yes, the boys are going to sue the hell out of Rice and The Mountain for what he's done to them. Read up on civil law, Freddy, 'cause you're our guy."

I opened his office door. A woman was now behind the receptionist's desk. A very elderly man sat in the chair I had just vacated an hour earlier.

I turned back to Freddy. "Oh, and the name of the guy I was meeting is immaterial. He never saw anything."

Chapter 27

present

A week later, I was talking with Uncle Don and Kelly in the driveway of their farm. My initial strong reaction to Uncle Don seemed strange to me now. He and Kelly had greeted Maddie warmly, with Maddie hugging them without reservation. Their two children—a boy and a girl, a little bit younger than Maddie—had run to her, the three of them toppling like puppies onto the hard ground outside Peter's truck.

My impression was that this family, this farm, was exactly what Maddie needed. While Eula had done her best, it was time for Maddie to be surrounded by siblings, animals, and young parents.

Peter had vetted Don and, by everyone's account, he was a hardworking family man. He worked for the Lincoln Highway department while the farm was Kelly's deal. Goats, pigs, and two miniature horses were milling in a nearby pasture—we could see them from where we stood in the driveway. While the old clapboard house needed paint, the bright red rockers told me that Kelly had flair. The barn had a colorful green and yellow hex sign above its doors.

These colorful bits gave me joy as Maddie came running across the yard, barreling into me. I had never seen her eyes so lively, even out at recess. "Sorry, Mrs. Scott." And off she ran, the two little ones chasing after her.

We didn't stay long. I looked at Maddie's small belongings and said, "Wait, I've got to get the Fresh Scent."

Kelly smiled. "Sara, don't bother. I know all 'bout that. I've got some."

We said our goodbyes. I called out, "I love you, Maddie girl."

"Love you too," she said, as she skipped onto the porch and went inside.

We were about twenty minutes into our return trip back to Bristol when I said, "Thanks for this, Peter. I don't know why I was so suspicious of Don. I was ridiculous."

"There was a time I had some pretty irrational thoughts. It was Eula who got me some help."

I turned to face Peter. "Eula, really?"

"After my ex-wife left and took the girls, I did some, well, unhealthy things, including a lot of nights of dark thoughts. Eula came by and said something like, 'If I can bury a daughter who overdosed and take in her fourteen-month-old, at sixty-seven and on disability, you can survive this.'"

He paused. "I still see a therapist once a month. His name is Wiles; he and his wife are in practice together. I hear she's great—I think her name is Katherine. I've got their card."

This was Peter's way of saying *you need help,* without actually saying it aloud.

While my insomnia at night had subsided some, I still thought a lot about what I'd done in Langdon, especially with Rice and the Larsons. Chance and fate were still in question, but now I had new thoughts on the concept of free will. I had made my own choices all along the way; I had exercised free will in choosing my course of action. Did I ever think the consequence of those choices, my actions, would play out to the degree that they had? That I'd be living alone, isolated from Michael, the one person I had built and centered my life around? Yet, to have chosen differently would have meant not to have acted at all.

When I was at Keene State, I had taken a course on the Holocaust. I recalled the topic of one of the papers I had written during a particularly hard night where sleep and my thoughts were in conflict. I'd gotten up, turned on the light, and sat for what seemed like hours. The paper was about people who had been members of the Resistance and hidden Jews during WWII. Why had only a minority of people back then acted, while a majority had not, despite the horror of the time? A book I'd read, *The Hand of Compassion,* examined the attributes of those who stood up, did something. Those rescuers were shaped by strong identities and the ability to see other perspectives, along with the aptitude to value others' needs as much as their own. I remembered the term 'moral salience.' It was like Atticus Finch telling Jem and Scout that you have to walk in other people's shoes before judging them. None of the people had second thoughts or misgivings in helping. They did not question their role in rescuing—in fact, they said they had no choice.

I knew my situation didn't compare, in the least, to the danger and personal sacrifices that those brave rescuers experienced back then. But it did give me something to think on. Even in my loneliness, and with the issues that my reaction to Don had illustrated, I couldn't see another way around what had happened, what I'd chosen to do. I felt bad that I hadn't done more.

In the truck, as Peter drove, I thought how I had witnessed the sexual abuse firsthand. That had such an indelible effect on me. All the other times I had called DCF in my years of teaching, none of those reports had touched me in the visceral way that Jamie's experience had.

If I felt I had no choice, then I didn't exercise free will, did I? But I *had* exercised free will, because no one forced me to do anything. Along with fate and chance, I now added free will to my mumbled, jumbled ponderings in the middle of the night. Could someone listen and help me sort through all this?

Peter and I drove a bit in silence, but it was comfortable. I jotted a few things down about calling Maddie's new school in Lincoln, especially to include her most recent reading scores. While the scores had shown growth, she would still benefit from reading intervention. Also, I'd suggest an eye exam. Her squinting was still noticeable.

I finally broke the silence by asking about Peter's daughter, and he described how both of them had settled into a routine of cohabitating in his small place, which was attached to his large shop and office. Katie was her name. "She's pretty heavy into Ryan, but we're making headway."

"I'm glad things are better for you both."

As we drove into Bristol, I asked Peter what I had been meaning to but kept forgetting. "Hey, what did you say to Kelly and Don last week when I lost it in the bathroom? About not letting Maddie go with them?"

He raised his eyebrows, and said, "You sure you want to know?"

"Yes, well, I think so." I turned in the passenger seat to face him. "Now, you have to tell me, for sure."

"I told them you were in the bathroom throwing up. That a stomach bug was going through your classroom, and you had just gotten it. Maddie was bound to get it too. It was debilitating. I went into great detail, saying it started out as throwing up, but then well, it took other routes. They couldn't get down the stairs fast enough."

I sat, marveling at this. He'd been brilliant. He looked at me quickly, and his eyes, a dark brown, were filled with mirth. "I can think fast on my feet, Mrs. Scott, as well as hammer a nail."

"Yes, you can."

When we got to the wharf, I thanked him again, and as I started to leave the truck, I came back to his driver's side door. He unrolled the window.

"You have that card for your therapist on you?"

"That I do, Mrs. Scott." He reached into his back pocket and took out his wallet. In a moment, he handed me a business card.

I took it and glanced at the name. "Peter, call me Sara, 'kay? I'm not married anymore."

He nodded slowly, then smiled. "Take care, Sara."

It had been a good day and only got better when I checked Lexi's Instagram posts. The kids were skiing on The Mountain, with a whole bunch of Langdon classmates. Her caption read, "Class Reunion." Michael was beaming, looking so much older. I hesitated, and then liked all the pictures. Maybe next time I'd even comment.

Chapter 28
past

J effrey was gone until Friday night. I knew, after telling
Freddy, that I needed to tell Jeffrey everything now. I
dreaded this, but I also knew the weight of lying had
taken its toll on me.

On the way home from Freddy's, I swung by the Larsons. Only the silver Honda was there. I had not planned on
stopping, but while I had spoken to all the boys (if you
counted my apology to Jamie), I had not spoken to Jane. I
owed her that much before we were all thrust into revealing
the chaotic nightmare of the monster's abuse.

Jane invited me in. She looked good, as Jason had said to
me. She was younger than I was, maybe by about five years.
She was a tall, thin woman, and I could see that Jamie
looked a lot like her. She had light reddish brown hair that
was cut short and a pale complexion. The other two boys
must favor their father, I thought.

We sat in the kitchen, and Jane offered me coffee. I took
it despite thinking I'd already had my caffeine quota of the
morning. It wasn't 11:00 yet, but the fall day was bright and
warm.

Two to three sets of white sheets were hanging out on the clothes-line. I wondered if Callie was out on her dog run, blocked from my view, maybe enjoying a rawhide.

"I miss the smell of sheets hung to dry." I smiled. "My mother never put them in the dryer. She would die—well she already did, but you know what I mean—if she knew I never hung mine out."

Jane replied, "Well, I have no idea how to make cookies from scratch like my mother did." She pushed forward the familiar tin I had sent Jamie home with. "I buy the frozen dough, cut it, slap it on the cookie sheet and there, I think I've made homemade cookies."

We laughed, and I sensed the tension leaving us.

"Jane, the boys talked to you?"

"Yes, Sara—can I call you Sara?"

"Of course. Please, tell me what you're thinking?"

"Ooh." She sighed deeply. "What I'm thinking...that's hard. But I'll try."

She went to the sink and turned off the faucet. Had it been dripping? I never noticed.

"I've known something wasn't right with the boys for a long time, especially Jason. I thought Jackson's anger was about his father's death and, well, Chris wasn't a very nice man. Jackson has a lot of his father in him. Jamie is slow... that's from his difficult birth. He was without oxygen for some time—really only seconds—but that's why he has a low IQ and difficulties in speech. Then there's Jason. Jason is the son that everybody deserves. But things aren't right with him either."

"He finally told you why?"

"Yes." Jane started to cry. She got up and went to the counter and tore off some paper towels.

"You must think I'm a terrible mother." She blew her nose.

"Jane, pedophiles like Rice groom the parents of their victims, just as much or even more than the victims. They've got to fool you into believing that they're wonderful people who think you and your children are special and that they want nothing more than to bestow their good fortune on your family."

Jane had returned, and I reached across the table and put my hand over hers. "They want you to trust them so you'll let them take your child. They lull you into this state of being where you believe that they love your child just as much as you do."

She was watching me intently. "I think you just described how I viewed Rice for the last decade."

"He bought you this house, and the toys, and then the bigger toys for the boys. He sent you to rehab, got you a lawyer, and made you believe that he wanted nothing from you in return. But Jane, he orchestrated every move to win you and those boys over. It would have been hard for anyone—" I held her hand tighter—"anyone, me included, to see the truth of how insidious he was."

"But, Sara, I never even questioned his attention. Not once. And I never asked the boys if everything was okay, not once."

I paused and then replied, "Jason and Jackson grew up sleeping in the very same room, think of that. They never once spoke to each other about the abuse. If they weren't opening up to each other, why do you think they'd open up to you?"

We sat some more. I told her about my trip to Freddy's office that morning. "We're in a holding pattern until Freddy can get what I told him to the State's Attorney's office. Tell the boys to stick around. When I get the call, we may need to go meet with them.

Jane walked me out to my car; this time I had parked in their driveway. We hugged each other. At the end of Gravelin Road, my cell started ringing. It was Freddy. I had left his office at 9:45. It was now 11:30.

"Hey, what's up?"

"I got you in, Sara. The Assistant State's Attorney's criminal division is on board. They're going to be the main guys here in charge of everything. They'll be involved in all aspects of the case from this point on and will work in conjunction with the local police in interviewing witnesses and gathering and reviewing evidence. They'll be deciding the charges, making the actual arrest, trying the case in court, and ultimately, if it gets that far, they're involved in sentencing and appeals hearings. Mark Flanders is the Assistant State Attorney whom I spoke with. One of the men in the fishing picture. He's going to devote serious man-power to this Sara. He's a good guy."

"No, no, Freddy." My voice carried panic—I tried to keep calm, but I was failing. "Do you know—does he know—not to use any Langdon law enforcement? Please, this is really important. Rice owns those guys. Evidence will be ruined or fabricated, the boys will get hurt. Please get to him to make sure."

"I'll call you right back," Freddy replied, hanging up fast.

I turned towards home but pulled off to the shoulder about a mile out to take Freddy's call back.

"Sara, I just got off the phone with him. He's using law enforcement from outside the county. He assured me that no one employed by The Mountain or residing in Langdon will be on this case in any way. Wow, you had me freaking out too."

"Good, that's good, Freddy."

"Sara, even if those boys wanted to pull out now, this train, this freight train has just left the station."

Chapter 29
present

S ara, are you interested in the sixth grade spot?" I wasn't prepared for this question so soon and in such a direct manner. I imagined I would have had time to think, to get my resume, references, and transcripts in order if I did decide to apply.

David Parks looked at me across the row of desks. "Your level of engagement with your students and your strong classroom management skills are stand-outs. I would be thrilled to have you on our faculty full-time."

"Thank you, I appreciate that."

Just then, the walkie-talkie on David's belt started to crackle, and he reached down and turned it off. He looked back up at me. My students were in Music, and we had a few minutes left.

"I think I need some time, David. I'm not sure what I want, you know...as in long-term. I originally came to Bristol on a temporary basis—" I hesitated then moved closer, leaning on a student's desk near where he stood. "Without going into details, I was involved in a mess last year. Not professionally." I quickly looked up to make sure he understood this.

He smiled. "No, I didn't think that at all." He had a kind, fatherly way about him. I wondered if he was nearing retirement.

"It's all personal stuff, and I'm not sure where things will stand for me. The lease for the place I'm renting is up at the end of August."

"Which, Sara, would correspond nicely with the start of next year's school year." He raised his eyebrows and waited.

"When would I have to make my decision by—that is, if you did offer me a contract?"

"Off the record, I can tell you that the job is yours, if you want it. The middle school teaching team sent me to you. They're chomping at the bit, hoping you're interested. As far as an actual date, I'd like to know and have a signed contract back by May first, no later."

The PA system came on; the secretary was paging his name. I smiled at him as he started to leave. He turned back. "I have a daughter about your age. She lives down in Eustis, Florida—that's horse country. Has two great kids. But, unfortunately, she and her husband are getting a divorce. Too bad, I really like him."

My entire ride home, every store I passed that I frequented—SNAP, Hannaford's, the Mobil, and now the Wine and Cheese shop—took on new significance. I asked each one, "Are you gonna be my place forever?"

By the time I walked down the wharf, I felt stressed. David Parks had thrown a curve ball into my timeline. I had been honest with him, giving him no indication of my choice—because I didn't know what I was going to do.

Chapter 30

past

We gave our depositions the next day. I had to take a second sick day from school. Freddy's office was in Peddan, in an unassuming building at the end of the town sprawl. Mark Flanders' staff, who was working on our case, had moved into two unoccupied office spaces next to Freddy's. There was no furniture, but folding chairs with card tables had been set up in each office, still with their bright orange price stickers on them.

I waved to Jason and Jackson and smiled at Jane as we were directed into our respective interrogation rooms. It was just past 8:00 a.m. I was nervous about being seen in Peddan after calling in sick, so I made sure to park behind the building. I came in the back door, surprising two investigators smoking cigarettes.

Staff from the Assistant State's Attorney's office explained to me that these sworn oral testimonies, given while out of court, would be transcribed and could be used in court or for discovery. I asked one of the two investigators across from me what discovery meant, and she explained that what we swore to now in our statements would most likely be read by Rice's defense lawyers in preparation for trial—if charges were filed, and he was arrested.

I told her to make sure Jackson and Jason understood how important it was to be thorough and honest in their depositions. She smiled at me, clearly having no intention of interrupting their depositions to tell them what I'd said. I worried about Jackson and hoped he wasn't trying to keep the most painful parts of the sexual abuse he suffered private in order to save face. He needs some of Jason's detachment, I thought, instead of all that fury in his gut. This investigator's name was Sarah, she had said, but, "With an h."

"You're doing really great, Sara. We want to go back now through all your testimony, but this time we'll ask you, at different points, to give us more detail if you're able to. Okay?"

The investigator took a sip of water from a red Solo cup and adjusted her cream-colored shirt. She was dressed in a blue pant suit and wore black flats. Her brown hair was pulled back and she wore no makeup. I thought she was about my age. I responded to her kindness by smiling back. She was definitely the lead between the two of them.

"Okay, that sounds good." I looked at the man, trying to remember his name.

Our introductions seemed hours ago, although I knew we'd only been at it for a couple of hours tops. He nodded, pushing 'play' on the small, black recorder placed near me on the card table.

Hearing my voice startled me.

"Sorry. I meant to hit record," he said, quickly doing so.

In what little I heard of the recording, I sounded confident—a lot different from the nervousness I really felt. I wiped my sweaty palms on my pants and sat up.

My back was to the large glass window at the entrance of the office. Someone had hung sheets of butcher paper to cover every inch of the glass. I couldn't see out into the corridor or hear anyone moving about.

I focused in on what Sarah was asking. "Describe to us once more what Jamie was wearing in the unfinished house, but in more detail if you can. You said—" she looked down at her notes—"blue sweatshirt and jeans."

I placed my elbows on the card table and brought both hands up to my face, fingers pressed together like the 'steeple of the church' from the hand game I used to play with Michael.

I stared at the recorder, remembering the moment, and then answered, "It was a royal blue, faded sweatshirt. The hood was frayed. It drooped down from his neck. I could see two of his vertebrae, like knobs, sticking out as he moved. If you don't know Jamie...well, he's very thin."

"Was anything written on the back of the sweatshirt? Any logo, picture? Please, try to remember." Again, Sarah's kind eyes met mine.

I looked down at the carpet and followed the weave of blue-green-gold to the baseboard below the window. "No, I don't think so. Jamie's sweatshirt was all stretched out around his neck, like I just said, but it was too small. The sleeves were short on his arms. I saw that when both his hands were on Rice's legs as Rice was, well as Jamie's head was moving."

I looked at them both and took a sip from the water. I was getting hungry; I wondered what time it was.

I continued, "He was wearing Levi jeans. I could see the little red logo tag. There was a rip in the right pocket like it was worn out from carrying a wallet." My stomach growled. "Jeffrey, my husband, wears Levi's, and he gets that same 'wearing thin thing.'" I grew quiet and then added, "That's what I remember about what Jamie was wearing."

Both investigators exchanged slight nods, and the man stopped the recorder. I asked, "Is everything okay?"

Sarah replied, "Yes, but let's take a break. We'll get you a little something to eat. I think there's muffins and juice."

The man got up and started for the door, then turned to me and said, "You're actually doing very well here. It's clear you have a memory for detail."

"Thanks." I turned to Sarah and asked if Jamie had special accommodations, because I had not seen him earlier with the rest of the Larson family members.

She assured me that that was the case. "The people doing the interviews with the sexual abuse victims are highly trained. They're extremely sensitive and skillful in bringing out information, no matter the age of the victim."

I mulled this over, and then hesitantly said, "At first I thought what Rice was doing with Jamie was consensual. Did you know that?"

Sarah looked down at her notes, scanning what was written, then looked back at me. "Jamie's over six feet, and seventeen years old. I can understand why you may have thought that. There are a lot of teenagers in this country who slip through the cracks especially those teens living out on the streets. They'll sell sex for money to buy food to eat, endure all sorts of humiliation in order to get a roof over their heads. It's just as horrible when teenagers are still forced into sexual acts with their abusers too."

I stood up to stretch, and the door opened. It was the second investigator back with a plate of muffins and a pitcher of orange juice. He smiled and placed them down on the card table.

"I, for one, am snagging the banana nut," He reached out and took it, smiling at us both. All the muffins appeared to be banana nut.

I had done some recent reading on child sexual exploitation cases, and thought that Jamie's cognitive age, much younger than his chronological age, definitely played a factor in Rice's continued 'exploitation.' I wanted that bastard nailed, humiliated, reduced to nothing.

As soon as my muffin was gone, Sarah nodded at the other investigator, and we positioned ourselves around the recorder again.

"Now, let's return to the house and try to get as much detail around what Rice was wearing, including what he wasn't wearing but what was still visible at the bottom of his feet. Take your time."

Sarah's acknowledgment—that she understood how I could have assumed it was consensual—gave me a brief sense of validation. I thought, *Maybe I wasn't such an idiot at first.*

When I was done at 1:00, I noticed the dark blue Jeep still parked out front when I drove by. I only had one afternoon and one breakfast to describe in detail to the state's investigators. The Larsons had almost ten years. I later found out that the Larson boys' depositions took two and a half days.

Chapter 31
present

I came clamoring down the wharf from the parking lot—
school bag, lunch bag, gym bag, and purse all wrapped
around me as I walked. When I got to the overhang and
stairs, I set down what I could. I needed to reach into my
purse for the loft's keys. I was a little off-kilter; I usually
only went to the gym in the afternoons, but today, for the
first time, I had gone before school. As I reached up to
bring my purse forward, my hair got tangled in one of my
hoop earrings. I impatiently pulled at it, and I heard the
earring drop onto the wharf.

The earrings were not especially expensive, but they
were from Michael. I had worn the hoops for the past four
or so years, and now, with so little of Michael in my life, the
earrings had taken on 'monumental, sentimental, out of
proportion' status. When I heard the earring fall, I immediately took everything off from around my neck and hunkered down, intent on finding the missing hoop. I concentrated on the area under the overhang in front of the stairs
to the loft. When that didn't net the earring, I branched out
onto the wharf, passing the door to the tackle and bait shop,

now on my knees combing the wooden planks. This was absurd: I knew I had the earrings on when I passed the shop, but I was growing desperate.

The wharf was empty, and I grew more frantic. I pounded on the closed shop door, but it did no good. At one point I started to cry, and I had become inconsolable. When Peter knelt down next to me, just feet from the shop's entrance, he had to ask several times what was wrong. My crying was messy, my words garbled; I was incoherent. Finally, he understood.

"Sara, let's get up and go upstairs, okay? We'll look for the earring again tomorrow. I promise." Poor Peter. He had a hysterical woman on his hands again—literally on her hands, looking for a silver hoop that was long gone. I imagined it through the slats of the wooden wharf, falling in several inches of swirling water, and settling slowly into thick, black muck.

Up in the loft, Peter made a salad and then began rinsing the cheese ravioli he had found in my freezer. He was heating up half a jar of pasta sauce on top of the stove. I had recovered from my full-blown hysteria but felt depleted. I didn't know what to say to him. He seemed intent on feeding me. Getting up from the couch, I walked into the galley kitchen and stood with my back to the table, looking at him. "Peter, you must think I am a total disaster. First Maddie and now this, with the earring."

He looked up from the sink. "If this is your worst stretch, I'm fine with it. Mine was trying to figure out all the ways to..." but he didn't finish.

He turned with a plate of ravioli and handed it to me, smiling. "You don't have any dangerous items in the loft, do you?"

I held up what he had used for the salad. "Only a paring knife." I couldn't help but smile back.

"Okay, let's sit down and make a safety plan for that paring knife."

I ate a little bit but felt I needed sleep more than food. I didn't know how to send Peter on his way. He seemed committed to staying, making sure I was okay.

"Hey Peter, I'm good, really. Thank you for—"Looking at him, now standing at my refrigerator with the jar of sauce in his hands, made me feel suddenly bereft of all hope. Like he was the only person on earth who knew I existed, and here he was, practically a stranger. I couldn't finish the sentence.

I started to cry again. Peter got me to the alcove. I took off my shoes, and he helped pull the afghan at the foot of my bed up and over me.

"Sara, I'll let myself out. You go to sleep."

When I woke before dawn, too early to get up, I heard the TV on. Some infomercial was selling gourmet frying pans at a huge discount. Peter was asleep, sideways on the couch. I turned the TV off and crept back to my bed.

The next time I woke, he was gone. There was a note on the table. *"Coffee ready to hit, shelves done."* I realized that's why he had been coming down to the wharf, to make a time to work inside my place.

I reviewed what had happened as I sipped my black coffee. The French term 'raison d'etre' came to me. I thought, *Was Michael my 'reason for being?'* He had been once, but now he no longer needed me—that was evident.

I put the motorized blinds up. The gray sky matched the water, and it looked like rain was imminent. *I need to get a life, apart from Michael.* I knew I'd be at this same point even if Jeffrey and I were still together.

Peter was the only person who knew how much I was struggling, and he had stayed. But all my thoughts and actions were to push him away like he was a threat. *Why am*

I tying whatever feelings I have for that man to Michael? I thought. *They aren't connected—one doesn't preclude the other.* It was clear to me that I had put Peter on the same level as Craig; that because he wasn't Jeffrey, I was betraying Michael. But this made no sense at all.

I added 'raison d'etre' now to the free will, chance, and fate debate in my lonely musings of the loft. I felt that any more of what I dubbed 'my night time philosophical battles' would send me over the edge, even more so than I apparently already was. I moved the Wiles counseling card from my dresser drawer into my school bag. I needed to make that call.

Chapter 32

past

On the drive home from school, the day after our depositions and two days after my trip to Freddy's, I braced myself. It was time to tell Jeffrey everything.

I met him on the porch. He looked tired but happy to see me. We hugged, and I helped carry in his luggage. I'd made a big antipasto salad with crusty Italian bread. Glancing at Jeffrey, I saw that he looked older, thinner. *I look older, thinner too,* I thought.

Putting the plates down on each of our placemats, I looked over at him. He'd been watching me, sipping from his glass of red wine. I smiled. "Want to sit?"

He came to the table. "Sara, I called your school, what's going on there?" He was scooping up bits of the antipasto salad onto his plate, but when he spoke he stopped and looked at me.

My faced turned red. I replied defensively, "What are you talking about?"

"I called your school on Wednesday and then Thursday, and they said you had called in sick both days. Yet, you didn't mention that when we talked later in the day."

I took a sip of my wine and tore off a piece of bread. I didn't know what to say.

He went on, "You've lost weight, at least ten pounds, probably more." He moved his plate to the side and brought his elbows onto the table. Leaning toward me with concern, he asked, "Are you sick?"

I looked at him. I did feel sick, but not in the way he imagined. My face must have carried the weight of what I was about to do, because he took my hand and said softly, "Baby, whatever it is, we'll face it together. Please know that."

I pulled my hand back. He looked up, surprised.

"I'm not sick, at least not physically, Jeffrey. I'm fine. But I have been—" I stopped; I didn't know how to go on, but I knew I had to. "You'll wish I was sick rather than this." I paused, but just for a moment before I looked directly at him. "I've been unfaithful to you."

His face looked puzzled, but then my words registered.

I hurriedly said, "It's not still going on, it's been over with for months. It meant absolutely nothing, and it sickens me when I think of it and what I did. But Jeffrey..." I stopped and watched him get up and walk around the table to the kitchen counter. His back was to me.

In a louder voice than I intended, I continued, "I've become involved in a situation stemming from this..." I faltered. "This affair."

There, I've said it, I thought. *Now and forever that word, that thing that will measure our marriage in the time before, and in the time after.*

He turned and faced me. "Do you want me to go on?" I asked.

He nodded.

The only time I stopped was when I needed a glass of water. Jeffrey moved further down the counter when I approached the sink. His growing repulsion of me was obvious. I returned to the kitchen table.

To Freddy, my timeline began on the day at the building lot. Now, with Jeffrey, I started on the December morning of the accident in the Gulf. As I made my way through it all—the affair, the construction site, the moment in the diner, Jason's reported sexual abuse, and my trip to Freddy's office—I tried to gauge Jeffrey's reaction. He remained undemonstrative, looking down at the kitchen floor. The only flicker of a reaction I saw was when he flinched at the details about Craig and my first sexual encounter outside the Rec Center. I left out all the specifics, but I did not downplay how consumed I had been. I think he was already connecting the dots to the times I had been different with him. I was rushing, talking fast. A dam had broken.

I stopped speaking when I reached the events of yesterday and how I gave my deposition.

I sat quietly. Jeffrey remained standing. The kitchen clock ticked on, despite our world having just blown up.

Jeffrey's voice broke the silence, vicious and cold. "Who the fuck is he, Sara? Tell me." What I had thought was an undemonstrative reaction a minute ago had actually been quiet seething. Now it was deepening into a red fury. I had never seen Jeffrey this angry; his jaw was set, his eyes glaring. "Is it someone we know? I know?" He moved closer to the table.

I pushed back in my chair. "Jeffrey, stop! He was just a guy I met—no one you or I knew before."

His expression was incredulous. "So you were willing to throw us away for some guy you just met? I don't get it, Sara. Just tell me his name."

"No, I'm not going to give you a name, Jeffrey. His name doesn't matter, okay?" My own voice was rising to match his.

"Tell me his name," he commanded.

Again, I held my ground. "No, I'm not going to. His life doesn't have to be ruined."

Shaking his head in disbelief, Jeffrey replied in a heavily sarcastic tone, "Wait, let me get this straight. He can ruin our lives, but you're worried you might ruin his? You have got to be shitting me. This guy can waltz into the Scotts, do a number, then waltz right out? Who the hell is he?"

I got up from the table, feeling as if I might explode. "He didn't waltz into my life, Jeffrey. He looked at me and smiled—that's all it took. I'm the one who decided I'd fuck him. This wasn't something done to me. I was more than a willing participant. Are you happy now?"

I started to leave the kitchen, but then I turned back. Jeffrey was crying.

"Look at me," I pleaded. He didn't. "I've been lost since Michael has grown up. Haven't you noticed that Jeffrey?" My voice was breaking. "I don't know who I am. And us—you and me? We're lovely to each other, but we don't connect anymore. It's like we're friends with benefits who get along really, really, well. We never fight, we never yell and," I paused, "we never ever feel."

I left the kitchen and went into the downstairs bathroom. I sat down on the floor, my back up against the vanity. *All he wants is to know who fucked me.* I felt I was going to be sick to my stomach and scooted closer to the toilet.

What is it I want? I asked myself. Mindlessly, I reached up and grabbed the aloe cream, squeezing some from the pump. As I rubbed it into my hands, I thought, *The affair is too big for us.* We were at a precipitous point.

I stood up and looked out the bathroom window. I could see the light in the First United Church's steeple, and a sliver of The Mountain. I put my forehead against the window pane, feeling overwhelmed with all the awfulness of the Larson's ordeal, the ugliness of my affair, and the fury I'd just witnessed from both me and Jeffrey. *My marriage has been my home as much as this house has,* I thought. But what if this 'home' was too damaged now? I turned to the door and whispered, "I destroyed it months ago." The full weight of my actions hit me.

When I re-entered the kitchen, Jeffrey said, "You need a lawyer."

"Okay," I said softly, sitting back down at the table. He remained at the counter. His eyes were red, but he was no longer crying.

Spreading my hands out on the table, I cleared my throat and looked at him. "I'm so sorry, Jeffrey. I know all of this is shocking and awful and hard, but this guy meant nothing to me. Absolutely nothing. My actions are inexcusable. I don't even re—"

He cut me off. "I don't mean a lawyer about our marriage. I'm not sure what route that's going to take. I mean about your involvement in this sexual abuse case, with Rice and the whole Mountain. Freddy's ill-equipped and not able to represent you in anyway. You need a lawyer to navigate this all with just your best interest in mind. Do you understand?"

"Are you saying I did something wrong? That I could be in trouble?"

Jeffrey sat down, looking exhausted and disturbed. "I am saying that we need someone who's well versed in criminal law who can represent you—as in making sure you're not in trouble."

I sat, digesting this. I looked out the window. The backyard was covered in darkness; it was nearing midnight.

Jeffrey left the room. I stayed at the kitchen table but shimmied over to Michael's spot on the bench seat. I couldn't remember the last time I had sat and looked out at the kitchen from this angle. The white resurfaced cabinets Jeffrey worked so hard on looked good but under the recessed lighting the colorful pottery above the cabinets needed a good washing. It seemed like a huge undertaking I wasn't up for.

I filled my glass with more red wine and took a long drink. I picked out the olives and the provolone cheese from the antipasto salad and made little sandwiches, tearing off chunks of the Italian bread. At one point I reached over and drank all of the wine that Jeffrey had left in his glass. I then finished the bottle.

I laid my head down, one arm draped across the table. I closed my eyes. I started to spin. Images flooded me: of Jeffrey crying, his shoulders shaking; Jackson flicking his cigarette; Sarah with an 'h' leaning in, wanting more; Freddy turning the pages as he wrote; and Jason staring at me, asking, "Who does that to a child?"

The toilet flushed upstairs, and I heard Jeffrey directly above me in Michael's room. *I'm drunk*, I thought and lay like that a bit longer before finally getting up.

Minutes later, Jeffrey passed by our bedroom and whispered, "Did you lock up?"

"No, I forgot," I replied, bone weary.

"Sara, I'm glad you're not sick."

It was 9:30 when I woke up the next morning. I hadn't slept that late on a Saturday morning in years. My head was groggy, and I felt awful.

I came downstairs and went into the kitchen. Jeffrey was measuring a spot above our coat hooks where he wanted to hang a shelf. He turned when I came in and went to the coffee pot. He reached up into the cupboard and brought down the mug I drank my coffee in every morning. There had been a fundraiser in Michael's classroom years ago. The coffee cup's design was Michael's own rudimentary drawing of a red tug boat, a fish dangling from a hook on its rigging. Jeffrey gingerly handed me the cup of coffee.

"Thanks," I replied. I wasn't sure how things were going to go between us this morning, but I felt Jeffrey knew. He seemed purposeful. I moved over to the kitchen table and sat down. I was still in my pajamas and hadn't brushed my hair or washed my face. The dinner dishes from the night before were gone; the dishwasher was humming. I felt a sticky spot near where I placed my hand and moved it. I looked up at Jeffrey and took a sip of the strong coffee.

"I'd be a hypocrite, Sara, if I didn't confess to you my own indiscretion in our marriage."

"Holy shit," I whispered. I sat up and faced him, shocked.

Jeffrey didn't acknowledge my comment, but he stared at me, watching for my reaction.

"I guess it's your turn for show-and-tell today, huh?" My sarcasm was not flattering; I disliked the snide tone I had just used.

He asked, "Do you want me to go on?"

"Gee, Jeffrey, I don't know. I'm feeling a wee bit ambushed right now. Will you give me a minute?"

He got himself a glass of water and drank it all down. I watched him as he turned back around.

"I should have told you a long time ago. On one of my trips to Austin, I drank too much at the hotel bar. I met a woman there, a complete stranger. I can't even recall her face. I went back to her room." He walked over to the kitchen window and stood, facing out, his back to me.

"That had never happened before and hasn't happened since." He turned and faced me.

This seemed more surreal to me than the night before.

Jeffrey continued, "I came home and almost changed direction in my career. Remember? I applied to those super-intendent openings? You couldn't understand why I was even interested. Well, that was why."

"Wait, was this the trip with the French, like ten years ago?" I asked him, incredulously.

"Yes," he whispered. His eyes full of sorrow.

"Oh my God." I moved my hands to my face, holding back my hair.

He started to say more, but I held up one of my hands and stopped him.

My head was pounding from the wine the night before and, now, from everything I was hearing.

I leaned my chair against the kitchen wall and closed my eyes. I remembered that trip and the night he came home. We had been standing here, in this kitchen. I was pissed at Jeffrey when he got back. It sometimes took me the first hour or two after he returned to stop resenting his absences, especially after those particularly long, whole week trips.

This trip had been an even longer one: two weeks in Austin. He had taken forever tucking Michael in that night, and when he finally came down, I was ready to pepper him with guilt. "Thank God Jeannie was able to pick Michael up on Wednesday; our staff meeting went way over." And I had looked at him reproachfully. "The sink upstairs is backed up again. It's impossible to wash our faces and then brush our teeth."

But Jeffrey had taken these hits happily and had asked me lots of questions about everything he had missed: Michael's games, his parent-teacher conference, and my work news. When I felt I had punished him enough, my tone had changed, and we sat down for dinner.

Opening a bottle of wine, he had looked over at me, twisting the cork out of the corkscrew. "My video presentation was in French for about the first minute or two."

"You're kidding, really?" I had lit a candle on this very table.

Pouring our wine, Jeffrey had explained, "I stood there and the tech guy came out on stage and scrolled through my settings. Then I remembered Michael and me fooling around with that translation app."

"What did you say to the audience?"

"I said, 'Sorry folks, Quebec is next week.' I got a big laugh," Jeffrey had replied, pleased with himself.

I had giggled at that and admired his quick wit. And he and I had used that phrase with each other—"Sorry folks, Quebec is next week"—from then on, whenever either one of us royally screwed up.

I remembered something else about that trip back from Austin. I had gotten up and moved to Jeffrey's lap. He had lifted my hair and kissed the nape of my neck and whispered, "I want to stay home. I want you more, Sara. I need you more." And he had carried me to this very counter and undressed me. Then, lifting me up, he cupped his hands beneath and entered me, and we rocked, slowly at first and then faster. I had held on to him, thinking then how much I wanted and needed him too.

Now, Jeffrey was still talking. "But I couldn't change careers. We didn't want to relocate, uproot Michael, have you lose seniority."

"Or you didn't want to stop those temptations," I said, my snide tone returning, my face feeling warm.

He didn't respond.

I looked up at him and tried to make sense of what this all meant. We stayed motionless for minutes. How many times did I use "Sorry folks, Quebec is next week" in his presence? But saying it had been a reference to that trip and his deceit. I thought, *Fuck you, you've probably been screwing around for years. Now we're even.*

Abruptly, I stood up from the table and left the kitchen. I said nothing more.

How did I feel about his own confession? I wish I could say I was devastated and hurt. But I wasn't. I was furious, growing more pissed by the minute. This reaction of mine, this affront to my social standing in his life as Mrs. Scott was the root of my anger—not the breaking of my heart, not the fact that he had been unfaithful. This was the second bomb dropped onto our marriage in less than twenty-four hours. *No, actually,* I thought, *we've been taking hits for years. We just didn't know it.* We didn't speak for hours that day; we both avoided the other.

Toward evening, Jeffrey found me on the porch. He had located a potential law firm in Albany after researching on the internet. "Sara, do you agree that you need legal representation?"

It was growing cooler, and the trees in our yard were letting go of their leaves. I said, "Yes, I think so. Should I call?"

"I'll leave a message with them tomorrow and hopefully set up a conference call when you're done teaching."

I worried about the cost. I'm sure Jeffrey did too.

Jeffrey remained in Michael's room, and I slept soundly in our bed. I was physically better the next morning, but I still felt numb. I was glad to be leaving the house early that Monday morning for school.

As it turned out, we never got a call back from Reed and Associates, or an opportunity to ask questions. Things moved rather quickly that week, and the week after that.

Chapter 33
present

Iliked Katherine Wiles, the therapist Peter recommend-
ed. She was open, kind, and soft-spoken. While my
strong, irrational reactions to Uncle Don and the lost
earring were the impetus that brought me to her office, I
had so much unresolved shit to work through.

At our first session, she asked me to give her my background. "Tell me how you came to be in Bristol, Maine,
teaching at Morris Elementary. And what brought you to
see me."

I smiled and replied, "Oh boy, I'll give you the short
version, as best as I can." I looked around her office, taking
in the bookshelf, the plants, her desk, the diplomas on the
wall, and the oriental rug.

"I had an affair, got involved in a big, sexual abuse case,
quit my job, and left town when my husband and I divorced. My son hasn't spoken to me in months—well, that's
not exactly accurate. He did wish me a Merry Christmas. I
picked Bristol out of the blue and got a long-term sub
position, as you know, at Morris. Then, well, I've had a

couple of weird episodes—crying a lot, scared, irrational thoughts. Peter O'Brien—" I paused, looking out the window behind her desk, remembering his kindness—"happened to be with me both times when I lost it. He gave me your card, and, voila, here I am."

She had written something down as I spoke, and I wondered if it was, *"This is one fucked up lady."*

"That's a lot, Sara, even for the short version." She then asked, "Where did you live before here?"

"Langdon, Vermont." I watched her face and thought she recognized it.

"Is there a connection to the affair you had and the sexual abuse case?"

"Yes." I replied, trying to figure how best to explain it.

Katherine was patient, and encouraging.

"Well, I was having this affair and literally saw Rice, the owner of the ski resort in Langdon, sexually abusing a seventeen-year-old special ed kid. I saw this going on when I happened to be at the same isolated place waiting to meet—well, I think you get the picture."

I watched as Katherine sat back, and exhaled. "Wow."

She suggested we meet each Wednesday for a while, and then we could decide what I needed. I wholeheartedly agreed.

It was during my third meeting with Katherine that she asked me to specifically focus on my marriage. "Let's talk about you and Jeffrey. What your marriage looked like before all this, then, well, what changed and what led you to decide to divorce?"

I corrected her, "We both decided to divorce, it wasn't just me."

"Okay, Sara." She smiled. "I want to know what led you both to decide to divorce." We had developed a comfortable rapport, and I liked the way she rephrased my correction. The only thing was, I wasn't exactly sure it happened that way.

"Actually, I think Jeffrey accepted it. Accepted our getting a divorce."

"Okay, got it." She waited for me to start.

I talked about our many years of raising Michael, how we'd loved Langdon and had gotten involved in the community.

"What did your marriage look like during this? Not in relation to Michael, or the community, but in relation to each other?"

I quietly sat and took some time to reflect. "We were good. He traveled a lot, but then he'd come home for stretches at a time. I think people saw us as a happy couple. Our sex life was good. I got pregnant at twenty-two. I'd never had a serious relationship before that and hadn't been sexually active with anyone else before Jeffrey. Not really." I hesitated, then added, "But you should know, after I told Jeffrey about my affair, he confessed that he'd slept with a woman on one of his trips."

I watched Katherine digest this. "How did that make you feel, Sara?"

I remembered that morning after, in the kitchen. "Pissed, really pissed."

After a few weeks of seeing Katherine, I met Peter coming out of the office next door by chance. We smiled and went outside together. It was raining. "Where's all the snow?" I asked, putting up the hood on my slicker.

"Ah, that's right, you must miss the snow in Vermont."

I smiled up at him.

"Do you like her?" he asked.

I knew he meant Katherine. "Absolutely, I can't thank you enough."

We stopped at the bottom of the ramp. His truck was parked beside my car. "Take care, Peter," I said and started to walk toward mine.

He cleared his throat. "Hey, Sara, want to get a beer?"

I turned back to him.

"You know, you paying me back for Katherine with your company?"

"You buying?" I asked, smiling.

He smiled back. "Absolutely! Let's drop your car at the wharf, and I'll drive us to McKinley's."

Once there, we settled into a booth near the jukebox with a couple of pints. I quickly got up and brought our coats over to one of the hooks on the wall.

"Thanks," he said when I returned. Looking out the window, we could see the rain was coming down harder now and the wind was picking up.

It was a lively place, with a cross section of people. I watched Rosalyn, from school, seductively dancing with a man who wore his hair in a long, white ponytail. They were swaying to Tracy Chapman's "Fast Car." Peter was watching too. We sipped our beers.

Looking at him, I realized I liked everything about him: his calmness, the way he sat with one hand resting on his thigh, the other flat on the table. I also liked his face, lined from time spent outdoors, open and honest. His thick, red-brown hair was messy and curling at the ends, and it had bits of gray just above his ears. *He's got eyes as dark as mine,* I realized.

He may have felt uncomfortable under my scrutiny, because he leaned forward, drummed both hands on the table and asked, "You been okay?"

I knew he was referring to the two crying episodes I'd had in his presence. Without thinking, I reached over and placed both my hands on top of his. "Yes, I've been okay."

He didn't pull back. Instead he turned his hands over and held both of mine. He squeezed them and smiled. "Good."

I felt something spark between us before he leaned back and drank his beer. "You hungry?"

"I could eat something, for sure."

He seemed at ease with me, and this made me feel good, especially since he had seen me at my lowest points in the last month. He wasn't running from me, and I had definitely dropped the random equation I had made in my mind: *If I date Peter, then there's no chance of a Michael patch up.* In fact, I was hard-pressed to remember what my rationale for that line of thinking had been. Now, sitting across from him, I was feeling good, hopeful even for something I had no name for.

A waitress came over, and Peter chided her about the dent he noticed in her black Nissan when we drove into the parking lot.

"I don't know, Suzie, looks to me like you had a few too many."

She was young and had very short, spiky hair. She hit Peter's arm and told him to shut up. "Someone backed into me, so there."

Peter ordered first after I asked for a little more time to read the menu. Suzie then turned her attention to me, and I ordered a burger and fries, same as Peter.

As we waited, another song came on the jukebox: Springsteen's "I'm On Fire." Again, Rosalyn and her partner got up. I glanced at Peter. I was attracted to him. It was the first stirrings I'd felt in many months.

He looked at me thoughtfully and said, "Rosalyn and Curt, they've been together since high school. I don't think too many people are that lucky."

"Lucky? What do you mean?" I asked.

"Oh, you know, finding the love-of-your-life kind of lucky," Peter replied.

I asked him, my tone growing serious, "Was your wife, your ex-wife I mean, was she the love of yours?"

He was contemplative. "I used to think so, but now I kind of think it's got to be reciprocated. Otherwise, the timing's all off. Like, two people have to feel the same way, to the same degree, and for some time to meet the 'love of my life criteria.'" Sitting back, he added, "At least that's what I think."

I thought of Jeffrey and me. I was starting some serious processing with Katherine, but now here with Peter, it wasn't the time, nor the place, nor the who, I wanted to be thinking about.

I changed the subject. "Hey, how's Katie?"

Peter replied, "Oh, Jesus, let me order two more beers before I tell you the latest." He waved to one of the bartenders by holding up his beer, then signaling with two fingers.

"Gotcha, Pete," the bartender called out.

He stood up. "Drink up. I'll be right back."

I was amused and watched him walk up to the bar. I bit my lip and thought, *My, oh my, that man has a nice backside too.*

Upon his return, I smiled. "Oh, come now, it can't be all that bad."

He told me that he had found Katie and her boyfriend Ryan practically 'doing it' on the couch of his apartment. He described how he had yelled at his daughter and kicked Ryan out, clothes and all. As he talked, I watched his expressive face and tried not to laugh.

When he was done, I leaned in and said, "Peter, you've got to get her to a doctor for birth control options—that is if she's hasn't been already. You tell her it's what big girls do. And make a rule: her bedroom door has to stay open when Ryan's there, period."

He looked at me and raised his beer. "This is great advice, thank you."

While Peter paid for the bill, I walked over to retrieve our raincoats. Something fell out of his coat pocket. It was the little yellow sticky-note I'd given him in the Wine and Cheese Shop with my number on it. I was just about to put it back when I saw something drawn on the other side. It was a small stick figure with long hair, holding onto a tiny, hollow heart. The initials 'S.S.' were written below it.

I glanced up at him as he was putting his wallet away. When he turned to me, I smiled. *This is okay,* I thought. *'It's okay for me to be happy.'*

When we reached the wharf, Peter put the truck in park and looked at me. I didn't move. He leaned over to kiss me. I pulled back, just out of his reach.

Puzzled, he said, "Sara, I'm sorry."

"It's not. It's just that I don't want to…not in the truck, but—" I pointed out the front window to the street light, illuminating my car in the rain—"I do like street lights."

Under that street lamp, he pulled me close. He gathered his dark green slicker up over his head like an umbrella and shielded me from the rain. We kissed and kissed and kissed some more. He was delicious and warm and salty. Finally, we stopped, and he walked me down the wharf to my door. In the covered overhang of the stairs, he kissed me again. I returned the kiss, now pressing my body against his. I wanted him and teetered on inviting him up. He pulled back and looked at me. "Hey, let's plan to go out on a proper date. This weekend. I'll make dinner reservations some place nice, okay?"

I smiled and said, "Yes." I turned to go up the stairs.

"Sara?" he called out.

I turned around.

"Are we in a hurry?"

"No, not at all. This—" I pointed to him and then back to myself—"is a nice feeling, and we should savor it."

When I climbed the stairs to the loft, I felt my hair and clothes. They were soaking wet.

Chapter 34
past

As planned that Tuesday, Jackson wore a wire. The set up was that he'd park outside the Café for the next three mornings. Rice ate there a minimum of four mornings a week, always sometime between 7:15 and 8:30. The prosecutors believed that this was the best chance at catching Rice in a relaxed, unguarded state. "Most natural" was the phrase they used.

While I was nowhere near the Café during this time, Freddy called me at school after Jackson successfully had a 'chat' with the monster on the second morning of the stakeout.

Freddy let me read the transcript.

Jackson, upon seeing Rice come out of the Café, called out, "Hey, Mr. Rice, could I speak to you for a second?"

Rice had replied, "Sure, Jackson, come on over, sit a minute."

Jackson climbed into Rice's big black Suburban. Freddy said the reception had been exceptional; the police van was disguised as a Plumbing and Heating outfit parked in the same lot.

J: "Hey I'm here to ask you to lay off
       Jamie."

GR: "What'd he do? Spit out to you what
       happened between us? (pause). I'll
       always take care of you boys and your
       mother, you know that."

J: "The thing is, you don't have to
       anymore. We're all working. Doing good.
       We want you out of our lives. Ain't
       exactly fond memories, you know?"

GR: "You boys learned how to cream your
       pants with me. Nothing wrong with
       that."

       (pause)

J: "You done with Jamie?"

GR: "Where you working these days? And
       what's Jason doing?"

J: "I got some work helping a guy clear
       about twenty acres down off Route 30 in
       Dummerston. I'll be there for a while.
       He's paying me good. Jason's in a little
       bit of a lull right now. He just
       finished mending a lady's fencing, you
       know the farm further up on Gravelin?
       He'll get something soon, always does.
       And Jamie, well … he's moved on over to
       Shaw's. I don't think he liked seeing
       you just about every day here at the
       Café. You know why."

       (pause)

GR: "Waved to your mom last week, coming
       out of Mrs. Johnson's house. She looks
       good, staying healthy."

J: "Why do you think that, Mr. Rice? That Jamie went to the grocery store instead of seeing you so much?"

GR: "Listen Jackson, you came to me this morning in a respectful manner. I appreciate that. What do you want me to say? He's a tough kid to deal with. Okay, I'll stop."

J: "I appreciate that, Mr. Rice. Really. You spent time with all three of us at some point, right? One on one, up there on that mountain of yours?"

(pause)

GR: "Damn, that boy can't give head worth shit. You now, you could."

J: "Well, you taught me, didn't you? How old was I when we first started?"

GR: "What, you mean when I sucked you off? Or you did me?"

J: "In general, I guess."

GR: "Hell, it's got to be almost nine, ten years."

J: "Jason, too?"

GR: "Yeah, Jason too."

J: "Okay, well, now you're done with the Larson boys. Time to move on."

GR: "I can do that."

I was dumbfounded at Jackson's composure when I read the transcript of the exchange. "Cool as a cucumber," Freddy had said. There would be no need for a grand jury—Rice admitted the abuse in graphic terms. I had become immune to the graphic terms.

Assistant Attorney Mark Flanders reported it was one of the most successful wires ever executed by his office. Gerald Rice was arrested the following morning, again coming out of the Café. His Suburban was loaded onto a wrecker before he'd even ducked his head to get into the police cruiser. I imagined his usual sunny disposition changed pretty quickly.

Accounts of his arrest vary, but most concur that Rice was shouting, "Don't you know who I am? I'm the fucking Mountain." And, "I'll sue the State's Attorney's office, do you hear me? This is slander!"

Some eye witnesses worried Rice might suffer a heart attack. He tried to resist the handcuffs and turned beet red, spitting out his tooth-pick—and bits of his breakfast—onto the County Sheriff reading him his Miranda rights. He refused to hand over the keys to the Suburban. When one officer finally reached into Rice's pocket to retrieve them, the old man attempted to kick him, almost landing flat on the pavement of the parking lot. Breathing hard, he continued to sputter, "This is bullshit. Just you wait until my lawyers…"

Stu, the owner of the Café, stood outside, hands on his hips, along with Rice's breakfast cronies. A few of them were on their cell phones, faces incredulous, pointing to Rice as the County Sheriff climbed in and drove him away. Powerless to stop the events of the morning, they gave up and put their phones away. Two hours later, people were still outside the Café, hovering in small groups, unsure of exactly what had happened. In the bright sunshine of the fall day, the traffic through Langdon remained heavy, as leaf peepers from out-of-state, were oblivious to the town's unfolding drama.

Two dozen staffers, working out of Flanders' office at the temporary location in Peddan, swooped in and gathered financial records, clothing—including the belt I had seen—a cache of pornographic materials, and a whole lot more I had no idea about or ever would. The Larsons provided photo albums (Jane loved taking pictures of her boys, holding up all those new toys and gaming systems), bank statements from all of them, the deed to the house, and specific clothing worn by Jamie.

Here's the real kicker: Jamie's sworn testimony led to the most concrete evidence in the State's Attorney's case against Gerald Rice. This evidence was in the form of a Fanny Farmer box of candy and a perfectly lifted fingerprint. The wire Jackson had worn was the nail in the proverbial coffin.

During his deposition, Jamie revealed that he had six crisp $100 bills stashed in a Fanny Farmer two-tiered candy box right out on his dresser—including the one I had the photo of with the block lettering. Also, Jamie's fingerprints were lifted off the back door of Rice's Suburban. It turns out there was more to the story of the night Rice kicked Jamie out of the car up on The Mountain. Jamie had opened the door and jumped. I was beginning to question Jamie's cognitive abilities—were they as low as everyone thought? Or was it the speech impediment coupled with the sexual abuse trauma that made him appear much less aware than he actually was?

Bail was set at $250,000. Rice had to surrender his passport. The Mountain and Langdon were ablaze with the news. By noon the following day, several news vans and reporters were broadcasting live, positioned all up and down Main Street. It was a maelstrom of shit. By 4:00 p.m. Rice had posted bail and was out, after being arraigned on fourteen counts of sex crimes against young boys, three counts of corruption of minors, five counts of endangering the welfare of a child, and eleven counts of indecent assault and other offenses. Apparently, the Assistant State's Attorney's office works around the clock when it's warranted.

Even Michael called home that night, instead of his usual texting. "What the hell is going on in Langdon, Mom? Facebook is lit up."

I'd been watching WCAX and replied, "Gerald Rice has been sexually abusing boys for a while. Someone finally told."

"Huge, Mom, really huge. Got to go, love you."

I thought how simple the call had been. Would it stay this simple, I wondered, knowing that he might possibly find out, one day, that I was that 'someone?'

The Mountain house, as well as the other ones in the development, had finally gotten all the permits it needed. B-10 was much further along than that April day when I'd seen Rice and Jamie. I tried to get my bearings. The investigators were thorough; we walked the path to and from the house, over the roots and fallen trees. I knelt at the window, now glass, and pointed to where the wall had been. I watched them measure out twelve feet, and then measure the distance and angle from where my eyes were—my line of vision. They had a cut out of a man the same size as Rice.

I was called into Mark Flander's makeshift office early the next day. I'd lost track of the number of days I'd already missed at school. I wondered about taking a short leave of absence, just to make things in my classroom run smoother. My principal knew my level of involvement in the Rice case.

While she did not know any of the specifics, she did tell me to do what I needed to do. She was confident that I wouldn't be negligent in my sub plans or take advantage of the situation.

I sat across from Flanders, a big, red-haired Irishman around my age, who—I imagined—did not mince words or make small talk.

I was correct. He got right to it. "The two older boys and their mother insist that you sit in with them to hear the state's case, how we're planning to proceed, and, in general, what to expect. While you're our only eye-witness to one of the actual sex acts, I would normally not allow this. But I sense, you're their—for lack of a better word—rock in this whole thing. So, I'm granting you this status, okay?"

"Okay," I replied.

"Generational poverty sucks, doesn't it?" he asked.

I knew exactly where he was coming from. "Yes, but that's going to change for this family."

His next words were measured as he continued to look at me. "Make sure they get reputable financial representation and services. Help them not to be victims again in another domain."

I hadn't thought that far ahead. I made a mental note to get on it, like right away. "I will. Thanks. Is that all?" I asked.

"Yes," he said, hesitantly.

I stood to leave.

"Mrs. Scott?" Flanders seemed unsure whether to continue.

I gave him a smile and said, "Go ahead."

"I was the one Freddy called right after you told him about Rice's abuse. You were so sure that Jackson would wear a wire. And that it'd work. How did you know?"

I thought for a minute. "I've taught for a lot of years. Playground bullies love to boast about their conquests. And in their minds, their actions don't seem so outside, well, society's norms. I've also seen Rice work a crowd; he wants to be liked. Jackson is bright but flies off the handle. Once I thought he had a degree of trust in me, I figured he'd be loyal and follow directions. I believed we'd get what we got."

He smiled. "You ever think of a career in criminal law?"

I ignored his comment. "And I also didn't want them going through the nightmare of something like the two-year grand jury thing with the Sandusky case. We needed a confession, proof from Rice himself that he was a monster. You know their house deed wasn't in Jane's name? I worried about where they'd live, if it dragged on. What if people in Langdon, including the Langdon police figured out it was them? Their safety could have been in question."

Flanders looked pensive, then reached over and extended his hand to me. I took it and shook it firmly.

Unbeknownst to either of us, during our brief meeting, Gerald Rice had walked out onto the massive deck of his multi-million dollar home and put a bullet in his head. The shot reverberated around The Mountain.

Chapter 35

present

A few days after my first date with Peter, I received an interesting email from Diana Church, a friend of mine from Langdon. We had met at one of Langdon's many art shows over the years and hit it off. We occasionally had dinners out, mostly when Jeffrey was on one of his many trips and Michael was happy to be home with pizza and a video game.

Diana was fun to be with. She'd been a counselor in her own practice for years. Then in her mid-forties, she'd decided she wanted to paint full time. That had been almost ten years ago. She was an attractive blond with a fantastic figure. She had never married. She dated prominent men in and around Langdon and always kept me entertained with antics from her love life, usually on the latest one she was seeing. Diana was classy and sweet, definitely with a healthy dose of self-confidence.

Once she was able to give her art the time it deserved, Diana came to be known as an excellent painter in the area. Her preferred medium was watercolors. I had bought one of her paintings—a barn I loved to pass in the countryside outside of Langdon. It was beautiful, capturing the colors of sunrise on a winter morning, with its pinks, purples, and yellows against the stark gray of an old barn. It was not unusual to see Diana set up her easel and paints around town or on the rolling hills. The State Building in Montpelier displayed many of her Vermont scenes along its corridor, and the logo for The Mountain had been taken from one of her earlier sketches, many years ago.

I had also commissioned Diana to paint Michael from a photograph I had taken of him sitting in a window of our den. It was when he was about twelve. It did not show his face, only his profile. You could already see how handsome Michael would someday be. Much to my surprise and pleasure, Diana had chosen to sketch it in black and shades of gray. The end result was a beautiful custom-framed portrait hanging in our home.

Diana had walked through our downstairs, wine glass in hand, helping me decide where it should go. It ended up in the den, close to the window where the original picture had been taken.

In the email, Diana asked if I would be okay if she started a relationship with Jeffrey. She wrote that they had run into one another out and about and had started a friendly acquaintance. Now the two of them had progressed to the point that they felt they wanted to be more of a couple. I wasn't quite sure from the email if this meant that they were ready to have sexual relations or go so far as to share a residence.

I responded, *"Dear Diana, clarification needed: do you want to sleep with Jeffrey or move in with him? And are you asking me for permission OR what I think?"* I hit send.

Within twenty minutes Diana responded, *"My dear, I was being too oblique, wasn't I? I will clarify. Are you okay if I move into the house on Dunsmore? Does that idea upset you, devastate you, or?"*

I smiled and wrote, *"The house on Dunsmore is no longer mine, nor is the man who owns it. But the boy who comes home and calls out 'Dad' is. Please be the woman I know you to be and give that boy your kindness and love. He is deserving. P.S. the man is deserving too. P.P.S. I did not take my two paintings. I think it only fair that I get the two paintings. P.P.P.S. Can we meet halfway with the two paintings? P.P.P.P.S. I am kind of happy for you and him."*

Diana responded promptly, *"You may be a better housekeeper than me, but I'm the better gardener. And where is halfway?"*

My last email back: *"Agreed. XOX."*

As the weeks went by, I thought a lot about Jeffrey and Diana living in the house. I wasn't jealous, but then that wasn't totally true. I was envious that they were willing to try to make something work between them. That despite the same old formula, they saw their relationship capable of maybe making it. And what did 'making it' mean, anyway? Going the distance? Lasting into old age? I didn't know.

I never answered her back on where the halfway mark was. I wasn't going to push it.

With this knowledge now of Jeffrey and Diana, there were times when I was just about to fall asleep that I played a new reel. It was a scene, cast in slow motion, of Michael coming up onto the porch and into the kitchen. I watch him putting down his duffle bag, full of dirty clothes, kicking off his sneakers and going immediately to the refrigerator. He grabs a honeycrisp apple and a block of cheddar cheese. With the apple in his mouth, he cuts a chunk of cheese, grabs a long sleeve of Ritz crackers from the cupboard, and continues moving further into the house to the den. He flips on the TV and plops heavily onto the couch—cheese, crackers, and apple placed on the coffee table. No napkin, no plate, the sound of basketball, maybe soccer blaring. I then add Diana and see her come into the den. The imaginary scene plays out and she smiles and says something nice to Michael as she hands him a plate for his food. He says 'thanks' automatically, smiles and gathers up his food onto the plate, never taking his eyes off the action of the game. I think I've gotten it right, and I'm okay with it.

I continued to miss Michael terribly, but there was movement on that front. After the third tin of cookies, he texted me, *"Keep them coming, thanks."*

Chapter 36
past

The Mountain, along with Langdon, was turned upside down. First, Gerald Rice's arraignment had sent shockwaves through the community, and now, coupled with his suicide in a matter of days, we were experiencing a tsunami. The events even made national news. You couldn't go anywhere within a fifty mile radius without it being the talk of the restaurants, convenience stores, gift shops, bars, teachers' rooms, country clubs, waiting rooms, and, of course, the actual employees as they gathered in small groups, whispering, "What does this mean for The Mountain?" Which, when translated, really meant, "What does this mean for me, my family, our mortgage?"

Every facet of Rice's life was discussed and dissected. Many people felt the pedophile scandal would be a blight on Langdon for years, possibly leading to its demise. I thought of Penn State and the Sandusky case. While its reputation suffered and people were fired or forced to resign, Penn State had recovered. Its freshman enrollment was the largest ever; the Paterno Library was one of its most impressive buildings on campus. I had read all this and wanted to appease people of their fears, but I kept quiet, as did Jeffrey. We were hunkering down, not sure where this left me, as a key witness, in a criminal case now with no defendant.

As of yet there had still been no return call from the law firm in Albany where Jeffrey had left a message. I asked him if we should call again, but now, with the suicide, he wasn't sure.

We were cautious with one another, but also, in our nineteenth year of marriage, comfortable with our uncomfortableness, I guess. If that made any sense. I felt that if the shockwaves followed by the tsunami of our own infidelities had not decimated us, we could coast for some time before we would have to confront 'us' and the future of our marriage.

Even though it was fall and snow would not be coming for weeks, our area was a major attraction for tourists coming up to experience the proverbial Vermont fall. Inns and motels, including The Mountain Hotel, were booked. Restaurants and pubs were fully stocked in anticipation. The weather was beautiful, the foliage striking as the poplars turned yellow, the sumacs orange, and the maples a fiery red.

We walked up to the chili cook-off in the town square, within walking distance of our house on Dunsmore Street. In the past it was always a favorite of ours, but now we were subdued and watched the tourists drinking and excitedly tasting the entries. We walked back home, and I noticed one of our front shutters was broken and hanging off its hinges. Jeffrey saw it too. He was usually good at keeping up with the old house. We didn't say a word to each other about what we saw. We were both distracted—our marriage and the unknown legal ramifications weighing heavily on us.

We had changed places. I was now sleeping in Michael's bedroom, and Jeffrey was back in our bed. It had happened a week or so before. He'd come in as I was getting ready for bed.

"Sara, we should talk," he'd said, after silently sitting through many of our previous dinners.

"I think what you're really here for is to get laid, right, Jeffrey? Been awhile, eh?" I was sarcastic and had gotten up, walked past him and crawled into Michael's bed. "I'm in here now, until I ...." I had left it at that. We went through the motions of our days, just void of any of 'us.' Riding waves of anger, I'd start to say something to him, but his look of bafflement silenced me. He, who knew so much, knew nothing now.

The town's select board dismissed each of its next two meetings early amid concern that it had no answers and did not want to appear as powerless as it felt. I had heard, and I imagined Marilyn had also heard with relief, that all college awards were covered, including those for each succeeding year, for its most recent graduating class. But nothing for the future, pertaining to The Mountain, was guaranteed. I wondered about Marilyn's position as Executive Assistant to Gerald Rice.

I knew she had been to Peddan, in the very same office, next to Freddy's, facing a table of strange investigators, like all of us, to give her deposition. Freddy had mentioned that Rice's secretary had provided a wealth of information, including the location of a private, handwritten ledger that the monster had kept. In this ledger, Rice had written in distinct block lettering every dollar he had spent on 'gifts' and each $100 bill he'd stuffed into the pockets of his victims. "This secretary," Freddy had added, "shed light on possible identities from the initials Rice marked in the ledger."

Freddy had said, "There may have been more victims than the Larson boys."

I had driven home, wondering how far back the sick bastard's perversion had gone.

I experienced a poignant, passing moment with Jane Larson in Shaw's during this heightened state of Langdon. I was getting some groceries—now that Michael was gone, I only bought a couple of days' worth at a time. I came around the aisle of cereals and coffee to find Jane, reading glasses on, examining a box of granola.

"I like granola" I said. She straightened up, appearing guarded, but when she saw me she smiled.

"You sure you want to associate with me? We'll soon be banished to the leper colony, I fear."

I looked at her and whispered, "It's against the law for anyone to release the names of sexual abuse victims."

"Well, someone forgot to tell that to the couple of pickup trucks that have been gunning their engines up and down Gravelin Road, all hours of the night."

"Really? Are you guys okay?"

"Oh, you know, Jackson is in his 'hyped up, high alert mode.' Jason is trying to make sure all of us are okay, and Jamie—well, Jamie is…I'm not sure. He doesn't talk much."

I recalled a school training we had, not long ago, on adverse childhood experiences. It detailed the ways in which children respond to trauma in their lives. Disassociation was when a child withdraws or detaches from the experience, escapes to a different place in their mind while the actual event is happening, as well as after, when they're recalling the event and trying to make sense of what happened. It's our 'freeze' response. I thought that best described Jason and possibly Jamie's way of coping with Rice's molestation. A second way was one of hyperarousal, where the senses and mind are—as Jane described Jackson—on high alert. It was the 'fight or flight' response, and Jackson was the living, breathing example of a person in a constant state of hypervigilance. All three boys would need years of counseling. The chances of the brothers becoming abusers themselves was possibly there too, but intervention and support could make a huge difference. "Abuse is a life sentence," our presenter had said, stressing the need for treatment throughout a person's life. I hoped Jane would consider counseling too, sometime down the line.

"Jane, if something isn't right, call me, please. I don't know what happens to the case now with the suicide, but I do know that Mark Flanders wants you and your boys to be safe. And to report anything suspicious."

"Thank you. I know we're not alone; his office made that very clear to us." Jane looked at me, weighing, I think, what she could safely tell me in the grocery store, on aisle seven, next to the healthier cereal choices and across from all the coffee blends and flavors.

"I did have to call the County Sheriff two nights ago. Seems those trucks were getting bolder every time they drove up, then came back down Gravelin Road. Finally, Jackson went out and basically stood in front of the road when he heard them start down again. Their usual deal was to drive by, stop, then rev their engines and squeal out, causing all sorts of skid marks in front of the house."

"Did something happen, Jane? Did Jackson threaten them?" I pushed my cart to the side and let an elderly woman pass by us both. Jane waited until she moved further on, out of hearing distance.

"Yes, he did. Shot out of the house..." Jane watched my eyes grow big and quickly corrected herself. "No, no, I don't mean shot, as in shot a gun, but, well, he hightailed it outside the minute he heard them this past Tuesday night, about seven. 'No way are they gonna do this to us every night,' he yelled and grabbed his hunting rifle to take with him. Jason was right behind, telling Jackson to calm down. Didn't do any good, though. The pickup trucks came barreling back down the road and there's Jackson standing in the middle of it. He wasn't like aiming at them. Just standing there holding his rifle. Then Jason stood there with him too, and before you know it, there's Jamie going out the door. So I went out. I was already in my bathrobe, but I didn't care. I needed to be there."

"Who were they, do you know?" I asked in a hushed voice as I scanned the end of the aisle. A young mother and two children were just starting to make their way down, stopping at the rows of breakfast bars and fruit snacks.

Jane took note of them too and whispered, "I recognized just one of the boys, but my boys definitely knew them all. Jamie maybe not so much, but the two older boys did. Most of them work The Mountain seasonally, and actually, one is the son of their dad's best friend, at least he was years ago. Will Sherwood.

"I know a Sherwood boy, Kevin, in Michael's class. Not a bad kid, at least I didn't think so."

"Now all three of my boys are standing there blocking the road. It's just about dusk and the guys in the two pickups get out. I've got my cell ready to call, thinking there's about to be some physical stuff and my boys are gonna get the raw end of the deal, being so outnumbered. Jackson's got enough piss and vinegar for two, maybe three men, but still."

"Oh Jane, how scary it must have been for you." I searched her face and thought she looked tired, definitely paler since the first time I saw her back at their house in September.

"Basically, I yelled, 'I'll call the County Sheriff if there's any fighting on anybody's part!' But none of them seemed at all interested in what I was saying or took my threat seriously, Jackson least of all."

Hesitantly, and afraid of the answer, I asked, "Did they fight?"

"Almost, but no. Just a lot of blow-hard testosterone on show, thank God. The Mountain boys yelled that my boys were 'pussies,' and that they must of 'liked it with Rice,' 'cause 'Rice sure as hell wasn't forcing them to do any of it.' One of them was really agitated, puffing out his chest something fierce."

I interrupted her and said, "Your boys don't need to hear any of that kind of shit, Jane."

Jane leaned on her cart. "Jason started to yell, 'You shut up, you have no idea what you're talking about.' And then Jackson, if I remember right, started to shift around his rifle some, daring any one of them to say it again, you know, that 'they liked it.'"

"But here's the thing, it was Jamie who left his brothers and walked right up to the four, maybe five guys standing outside their trucks, and said, clear as Jamie is ever capable of saying anything, 'It wasn't right what he done.' And he repeated it, with even more conviction the second time."

"His words and him trying so hard to say what he did, well, it took all the steam out of the crazy confrontation, and they all stopped. The boys got in their trucks and started to drive off. When the Sherwood boy went by, driving the bigger rig, he slowed down and said to Jason, loud enough for all of us to hear, 'We're done, man. We won't be back.' So I think we're okay for now, Sara. But I did take a picture of their license plates when they left and called their numbers in to the County Sheriff's office. I don't think they'll be back, but just in case."

"I'm so glad no one got hurt, that would have been awful." I thought, *And so much worse if it had gotten out, verifying that it was the Larson boys.* I knew some people had put it together, but that was still just speculation and nothing had been confirmed. I thought about Jackson and his temper, how wound up tight he must be. I hoped their connection to all this would remain out of the public eye, and he could hang on. All of them just needed to hang on.

Jane reached up and took a second box of granola and dropped it into her cart. "How about that Jamie? Never talks 'cept when it's absolutely necessary and then he nails it."

I knew she was referring to his deposition and how his testimony helped solidify the case against Rice, as well as defusing the standoff on Gravelin Road.

I reached out, patted Jane's arm and started to leave, moving down the aisle. She called out to me, as I was about halfway down, "Sara, we've got to stay brave, don't we?"

And just like that, I replied, "Yes, Jane. Those boys need us."

Chapter 37

present

One school night, while watching the Celtics, eating popcorn and drinking beers, Peter and I took our relationship to the next level.

It had been almost two years since that afternoon when I met Craig at Dickerson and Whitcomb Street, and well over a year since Jeffrey and I had been intimate. I'd had my moments on my own, for sure. Once Jeannie had said to me, as we walked, "All a woman really needs are Egyptian sheets, a silk nightie, Netflix, and a glass of wine." We giggled as we rounded the indoor track. Along the way, in my self-imposed exile, I had bought the Egyptian cotton sheets. I had everything else.

I definitely thought, for some time, that I was going to need more processing with Katherine before anyone joined me in that new bed of mine. But, well, things happened.

Peter and I were sitting on the couch, my feet in his lap. I noticed his hand was getting more familiar with my upper leg. I looked at him and pulled my feet away. "I think I need a little more time, Peter, you know, before we're over there." I nodded to the alcove.

"Is that like time measured in nanoseconds?" he asked, reaching for my feet again.

I giggled. "No it's, um, never mind." He leaned over and pulled me to him, kissing me, his hands on my collarbone and then slowly moving down to my chest. I reached up and took off my sweater. His hands traveled over my breasts, my stomach, and then his fingers were on my zipper. I stood up and stepped out of my jeans, now in a camisole and undies.

"God, you're beautiful," he whispered. I pulled him close to me, thinking how wonderful it was to feel a man and want a man like I did, at this moment. Soon we *were* over there.

He stayed the night. In the early morning hour, way before dawn, he had gotten up and accidentally knocked a little basket from the maple night-stand. I turned on the bedside lamp and watched him scoop up the sand dollars I had collected recently on a cold, sunny beach outing with Louise.

As he stood, with all of them once again in the basket, he exclaimed, "Sand dollars, in the loft! Please don't tell me you've succumbed!"

I lay there, looking at him. It'd been a long time since I thoroughly appreciated the beauty of a naked man.

But more processing did happen, not long after Peter spent the night. This was what I was coming to understand. All the times Craig and I were together, I always relived it in my mind through our physical interactions and the sexual sensations. Never were there any big feelings or emotions connected to our relationship—not ever. We never made 'love,' we coupled in pretty base ways: mostly in his truck, a few times in the woods, standing behind trees or woodpiles on deserted Mountain properties.

Katherine said my processing was spot on and to go one step further, now imagining that description for Peter and me. I laughed. I had only to recall that recent afternoon, night, and the following morning to see the stark difference. My feelings for Peter were wrapped in friendship, romance, and hope, in that order. It was far more than sensations, although that recent morning when we were showering, I had said as I passed the soap, "I'm teaching adverbs today. So, let's start: loudly, wet, often, deep, happily, and—"

Peter sang out, "Hugely!" The shower had almost run out of hot water. I blushed in front of Katherine, keeping the memory deliciously to myself.

I asked Katherine, "But what about my guilt? The guilt of losing Michael and Jeffrey?"

She looked at me and said, "Sara, from the first time we discussed Jeffrey you related him to others: Michael, the different people he worked with on community projects, his speaking engagements. Rarely did you discuss him in terms of you."

I turned, looking out her window and frowning, trying to make sense of that. "What does that mean? I don't get it."

"Just sit a minute and think about this," she had encouraged.

And I sat for a bit, and then replied, "I saw Jeffrey in the way I perceived others saw him, especially as Michael's father. But." I shook my head. "This is hard, Katherine."

"You're doing great," she replied.

"I think we both lacked the insight to see each other as individuals in our marriage. I think we lacked that ability to be 'just us.'"

But Katherine wasn't done. She pointedly asked, "And as far as Michael and the guilt you feel, who called you Christmas Eve day? And who wants more cookies?"

Chapter 38
past

About five weeks after Rice's suicide, the prosecutors filed a request to dismiss the charges and a Vermont judge approved. The defendant had died while the case was pending and so, before a final judgment was issued, they stated: 'The Indictment must be dismissed under rule of abatement.' The indictment was wiped clean. But future legal matters involving Rice's estate or his associates were very possible.

As I had mentioned to Freddy that first morning, the Larsons were planning on filing a major civil lawsuit against Rice and The Mountain. Freddy had done his homework and the wheels were in motion. A firm from Burlington—well-versed in civil lawsuits—was handling the case. The lead attorney had told Freddy that Rice's suicide would likely accelerate the battle over his estate. Their position was that his entire estate should be given to the victims. I had been shocked to hear this, but I now better understood Flanders' initial warning to make sure the Larsons had credible representation and financial services.

"They could be granted millions of dollars?" I had asked Freddy.

He clarified, "Each boy could be granted millions of dollars, Sara."

Langdon was soon bracing itself for the winter ski season. Unsure how much the scandal would affect the season, the people who made all their livelihood from the tourist industry held their breath. The weather was cooperating and, by Thanksgiving, The Mountain was covered in white powder. Early indications were that the Rice sexual abuse/suicide scandal had not dented the numbers one bit. People exhaled, and businesses and the hospitality trade kicked into high gear as they always did. Langdon, fully decorated in holiday cheer, welcomed the skiers in their Range Rovers with their Italian leather wallets stuffed with credit cards.

Michael and Lexi came home for winter break. It was wonderful to hear their sing-song voices throughout the house. I kept the refrigerator stocked full of Michael's favorite foods and noticed that while neither one had put on the proverbial freshman fifteen, they had both put on some. Lexi had excelled at Bucknell her first semester; the faculty and her advisor had already taken notice. I imagined they'd immediately seen that she was determined, extremely bright, and had a natural empathy for a field in medicine. Michael had done 'fair,' according to his own characterization of receiving a 2.6 grade point average.

I had looked at Jeffrey and nodded when he said, "I'll talk to him once the holidays are over." Jeffrey was always good at these 'talks' in our parenting journey, much better than I. Sometimes this surprised me because of my fairly successful practice at tackling some tough issues with my sixth graders in Peddan. Michael tended to melt my heart and left me woefully inadequate when the 'going got tough.'

Maybe that's why I moved back into our bedroom before Michael came home. I had passed Jeffrey going through our recycling and garbage bins in the garage and told him I was moving back into our bedroom. "Michael needs a relaxing break home. I don't want him to sense any tension between us."

"Okay, Sara, anything else you want to inform me of?"

I detected his resentment. I wondered if he felt like I was calling all the shots.

"No, nothing else. I just don't want you to get the wrong idea."

Marilyn and I found ourselves sitting across from each other at our favorite Italian restaurant as we blended families for an early Christmas Eve dinner out. It was our first time together since she had handed me the manila envelope on the porch that May morning. At one point, while the kids and Jeffrey were chatting at a nearby table filled with other returning college students and their parents, Marilyn had grabbed my hand.

"Sara, what a mess, with all that's come out!"

I looked at her and asked, "Work-wise, where does this leave you, Marilyn? Are you worried?"

"I'll be just fine. I've got feelers out, and—truth be told—coming down off that mountain wouldn't upset me in the least. I'd welcome it."

"Thank you, for, well...I heard you were helpful to the State's Assistant Attorney's office."

Just then the kids and Jeffrey returned to the table. We had a wonderful dinner with our children and topped it off with tiramisu for dessert. I looked at everyone and proposed what was possibly our third toast of the evening: "To our children." Michael and Lexi kissed—Michael a little too robustly, and Marilyn raised her eyebrows at me. I burst out laughing; I knew she and I were remembering our summer breakfast of long ago.

As Jeffrey and I followed the kids and Marilyn out of the restaurant, Jeannie caught my attention. She was at the bar with a man who looked better than her usual sort.

"Hey, good to see you, Sara. You look really happy," she said. We hugged and when we pulled back, Jeannie said, "Really happy — like the old times."

"Michael and Lexi are home, and it's Christmas Eve in Langdon, Jeannie!" I then whispered, motioning to the man beside her, "He looks decent."

Shifting her body totally away from him, she leaned into me, "We're just having a drink. It's the first Christmas without his little girl—the ex has her. He's kind of being morbid about it. But, hey, if I ply him with enough drinks, maybe I'll get lucky and he'll forget about the kid."

I left, laughing, and took Jeffrey's hand without thinking as we crossed the street to our car.

That night, Jeffrey and I put out all the gifts for the following morning and filled the stockings. There were definitely less boxes, ribbons, and bows than in the past—our shopping for each other was clearly strained this year. But what we lacked in buying for one another we made up for in Michael's gifts. Even Lexi had a surprising number of wrapped items.

I made us our traditional Kahlúa and cream on the rocks as we speculated about which gifts he'd like the most—reminiscent of the years when Michael still believed in Santa. This year we agreed that it'd probably be the brand-new MacBook Air to take back to school. Jeffrey spent hours deciding which computer and software would best fit his needs.

Heading up to bed, I noticed Michael's light was still on. I could hear him on his phone, speaking low to Lexi. When I climbed into our bed, Jeffrey turned to me and said, "He seems great, doesn't he?"

I whispered, "At least that's something we've done right."

Without any preamble, Jeffrey moved to me. I didn't withdraw. I responded to his touch, to our shared history and we quietly made love, as if all the shit that had happened in the last year was a blur and this was our only focus.

In the morning, our tension with one another returned, and we resumed our distance, but never to the point that Michael caught on. *Betrayal is a gut punch*, I thought as I watched Michael and Jeffrey open their gifts.

The afternoon of New Year's Day, I was at the same Italian restaurant where we'd had our Christmas Eve dinner, only this time I was sitting at the bar and waiting for Jeannie to arrive. She had just texted me that she was running a little late. On the flat-screen TV above the rows of wine glasses, a football game was turned on low. The servers were setting up the dining room. I could hear the kitchen staff bantering back and forth, and someone was answering the telephone, taking reservations. I ordered an Irish coffee and hoped Jeannie would want to split a dessert with me. I was the only one at the bar. I imagined the skiers were on their last runs of the day on The Mountain.

"The pot won't take long at all," the bartender said as she measured out a jigger of Irish whiskey. Waiting for the fresh brew to finish, I thought about how Michael had always been what gave Jeffrey and me the equilibrium in our marriage. We'd gotten pregnant soon after we'd met and never really had a chance to develop as a couple before parenthood was upon us. That wasn't necessarily a bad thing. Maybe most couples with children would define themselves first as parents, then as spouses. I just think the gap between the parent part and the spouse part with Jeffrey and me was wider than with most couples. And now it was damaged. For the umpteenth time, I wondered if it was irreparable.

I loved the five weeks that our big boy was home, and I loved every second I had with Lexi. When Marilyn drove them back to Pennsylvania, I cried, looking out the window as she backed up and left our driveway. Lexi knew to text me when they were safely to Lewisburg. Michael was staying with her for two days before taking the bus back to Penn State.

Michael surprised me on Christmas day by coming up behind me and placing his hands on my shoulder as I sat at the kitchen table, checking my phone. "I love, love the black-and-white photograph of Lexi that you enlarged and framed for me, Mom. It's my favorite gift."

I had looked up at him, surprised. "She's a beautiful girl, Michael, and you're a lucky boy."

His grown up, reflective response had equally taken me aback. "I hope I'm worthy of her."

I had turned around and looked at him. "That look of wonderment I captured in her eyes? She was looking at you, right out there on the stone wall. You were pretending you were some tightrope walker, about to fall. I grabbed my phone and took it. I captured her love for you, Michael. That picture is her love."

He had nodded and stood, looking out at the stone wall, now covered in snow and barely discernible.

I thought Jeffrey may have been right. Michael's regard for Lexi seemed to be the most mature thing about him.

After their departure, the words 'just getting by' once again characterized our marriage. Jeffrey had a busy travel schedule for his consulting practice, and I returned to school, hitting the academic gut of the school year and focusing on the growth and progress of my students. SBACs, the regional standardized testing, was slated for March, and I had some areas to cover in preparation.

When Jeffrey finally left town, I was already en route to school. Our distance from each other was amplified by our actual distance.

Chapter 39
present

I told Louise about Peter. I was bursting with feelings for him and it showed, especially when I was in her company. She was happy for me and felt that Peter had taken a great leap forward as well. "People need relationships, need connection. Believe me, I'm all for 'finding one's self,' but it's so much fun to travel this earth with someone who you're compatible with." We toasted to this new development of mine with a glass of sherry, poured into two beautiful 'Dublin crystal' cordial glasses. I wasn't sure I liked the nutty, caramel taste, but I wanted to please Louise and drank it slowly, sharing a small plate of shortbread cookies.

One Friday mid-morning, Peter texted me at school: *"Come to my place, tonight? Katie is going to Boston to see her mother and sister."*

"Really?" I texted back.

"Yes, I've been cleaning a lot! I'll make my bisque." Peter had told me he wasn't much of a cook, but his lobster bisque was excellent. *"Bring your toothbrush."*

I sent him an *"OK"* emoji then texted back, *"What time?"*

"Five, Six, no Five."

I had a wonderful day with my class. They were focused and collaborative in almost everything that we covered. But I still couldn't wait to shoo them out the door, to the buses, their parents' waiting cars, and onto the neighborhood sidewalks. My usual planning time after school, alone in my classroom, was cut short.

As I walked down the hallway, our custodian called out, "Leaving early, Sara? You got a hot date?"

I replied back, "Yes, I do!"

Peter's actual residence was small, a two-bedroom apartment attached to a much bigger—almost three times the size of the apartment—workshop and office. It had been a roller-skating rink from years ago: built in 1938, to be exact.

"Roller skating was big back then," Peter told me. "We even had the famous Gloria Nord come here."

I looked at him and smiled, "I'm sorry, but I don't know who that is."

In a humorous and rather boastful manner, Peter replied, "Why, she was a pinup girl on skates—fully clothed, mind you—for the boys and men fighting in WWII."

Skylights, rafters, and the original narrow, hardwood flooring all blended to make a huge area for storing various planks and types of wood, windows, doors, electric saws, ladders, and random buckets of things. His office off the shop was enclosed in glass, and it was neat and small, with a drafting table, a large desk-top computer, and a bookshelf full of architecture reference and specification books. I walked up to the framed black-and-white pictures of the building as a rink in the 1940s. One showed Gloria Nord standing just inside the entrance.

"Wow, she was beautiful, wasn't she?"

In one corner of the work-room was a ladder made of red cedar, like the beams in the loft. It looked finished, leaning against the wall. "Hey, do me a favor," Peter said when he saw me looking at it. "Climb up the ladder, please. I want to make sure I've done the dimensions right, and that the distance between the rungs is good for you."

"Okay." I put down the glass of wine he'd given me and climbed. Peter watched from the floor.

"That right there—that would be the best angle if ever I wanted to sell the shelves with a custom-built ladder."

Looking back at him, I said, "What are you talking about?"

"You, in those jeans with your hair down your back makes a grown man, well..."

I climbed back down and went into his arms. We barely made it to the couch in his living room. We didn't hold back. It had been a long week.

I can't exactly say where we were in our 'not holding back,' but suddenly the outside door to the apartment opened up and in burst Katie. She was alone. She froze—as did we—trying to take in what she was seeing. "For fuck's sake, Dad, use your room!" We immediately put our clothes on, and Katie came back out to the living room. "Have you seen my charger? I know it's here somewhere. But you've moved all my shit around."

Peter stood up and said, "Hey, Katie, I'd like you to meet Sara Scott. We're, um..." His voice trailed off.

Katie was tall with blond hair, a long neck, sharp eyes, and she seemed to be in constant motion. "Hey, there, Sara." She stopped just long enough to extend her hand to me. I was surprised at her strong grip. Her smile was fleeting.

"Where is that goddamn charger?" And off she went again, around the apartment. "Got it!" she exclaimed, and was zooming to the entrance again, her hand on the door-knob, ready to go.

She paused and turned back to us. She looked directly at me, "Hey, you're still young. Be a big girl now. You know what that means!" She zipped out the door, slamming it just as hard as Michael would have.

Peter looked at me then at the door and said, "So that's Katie."

I burst out laughing. He immediately started the thing with his hair, running his fingers through it until it stood straight up. He seemed frazzled, unable to say anything else.

I came up and took his hands away from his head and put them around my waist. I held him there, smiling. "Well, she's got a point. And condoms aren't much fun, are they?"

"When I laid down the rule—you know, about her bedroom door being open, and that she should be going to the doctor to take care of business or something like that—she asked who I'd been talking to. She said it sounded like someone with half a brain. So I think, in some way, she just paid you a compliment."

We ate Peter's excellent lobster bisque with a loaf of crusty artisan bread and then settled back on the same couch to watch a scary movie: *A Quiet Place*. Peter jumped even more than I did, commenting, "And this is supposed to be entertaining?"

When we made our way to his bedroom, he said, "I'll be right back. I've got to hit the lights and lock up the shop."

I went in to the small bathroom off his bedroom and washed my face then brushed my teeth. With my night bag on the toilet seat, I hesitated. I wasn't sure what to do: wear the pajamas I had brought, crawl into his bed naked, or sit on the bed fully clothed and wait for him. This was a new situation for me. I didn't want to appear too prim, but I also didn't want to appear too eager, either. I smiled at my reflection, wishing I could call Jeannie. I imagined our conversation and her advice, delivered with such expert knowledge.

Vacillating between the three choices, I put on the t-shirt and cotton shorts and climbed into his bed. As I waited for him, looking around his bedroom, I realized this was my first time in a man's bed other than Jeffrey's since I was twenty-two. Craig and I had never gotten that far. I quickly squashed any further thought of the both of them.

Peter came back and said, "Sorry 'bout that." After using the bathroom, he took off all his clothes and climbed in. Reaching for me, he felt my tee then my shorts and whispered, "Hey, I thought I told you just your toothbrush." And off they came. *Duly noted,* I thought. *No clothes next time.*

We were so new in our closeness that at times things felt awkward. Yet at other moments, it was unbelievably natural. Lying in his bed after our love making, I teetered on whether to ask him about his own low points after his wife took the girls and left Bristol. But I didn't. We'd had a great evening once the Katie debacle had receded. Soon, Peter fell asleep with his arms wrapped tightly around me. I nestled in, feeling perfectly content.

Chapter 40
past

Freddy and I communicated less and less. I figured I would hear from him or Jane or Jason if the need arose. I knew civil lawsuits were complex, and, unlike the criminal charges, I held no role in these. As for referring the Larsons to legitimate and reputable financial services, Freddy had asked the law firm in Burlington to give him a head's up when the lawsuits started to take definite shape and if and when any noteworthy progress was made.

Toward the end of February, The Mountain made a surprise announcement through a press release that it was filing for Chapter 11 protection. I knew this wasn't bankruptcy, but it was the first step to avoiding bankruptcy. The Mountain needed to reorganize its business affairs, debts, and assets. Most importantly, the filing would protect the company's assets while they negotiated new terms with their creditors.

I called Freddy and asked him to explain what this meant. "In layman's terms, because the lawsuit was in progress when The Mountain filed, the Larson's case will come to a stop. This is an automatic stay, a court order, or injunction that prohibits—and this is either the key or the tricky part—a creditor from collecting a debt."

I had been fussing with my indoor plants, clipping and turning the geraniums to the sun. I stopped, perplexed. "But the Larsons aren't really a debt of The Mountain's, are they?"

"That's the debate, Sara. But now a bankruptcy judge will have to approve before the Larsons can continue any action against The Mountain. What I can only surmise, and believe me I am not an expert, is that the income The Mountain is raking in may be lower than what they fear the payout could be to the Larsons."

I sat down in the old rocker near the kitchen window, "Holy shit, Freddy."

"Yeah, Sara, this thing is big."

"But now they're screwed because it's on hold?" I rocked in the chair, trying to understand.

I heard Freddy speaking to someone on the side. "Sorry, I had to sign something. My understanding is that a company can be sued after it files Chapter 11, but only if it meets certain conditions."

I now moved into the den, carrying the watering can. Freddy continued, "While the case is pending, the Larsons' lawyers must file a motion to lift the automatic stay. Continuing the litigation without the bankruptcy court's permission could sink us and negate our chances of ever suing The Mountain. But here's a key element: the Chapter Eleven filing adds a layer of court supervision."

I needed to stop and digest this. Moving to the den's window, I looked out and saw the sliver of The Mountain that was visible on this side of our house. On this cold morning, it looked regal. "Freddy, in your opinion—and you've made it very clear that you're not an expert—are the

Larsons' civil lawsuits against The Mountain good enough reason for a bankruptcy court to lift the stay? And I'm not talking about Rice's estate, but the lawsuits against The Mountain."

"Yes, I think they are. And I'll tell you why. This whole time you've thought the Larson house was in Rice's name. I didn't correct you, Sara, but now I will. The house was bought and paid for by The Mountain. The Mountain placed those little boys in that house, so one of its owners could set them up to be sexually abused for a decade. The Mountain had a part in grooming that family, Sara. They have their own responsibility in this nightmare."

When I hung up with Freddy, I started to cry, thinking, *How does a thing like this happen?* With The Mountain looming and my energy sapped, I didn't finish the plants.

L angdon and The Mountain were soon hit a third time. This time it was cataclysmic. Filing Chapter 11 was a chance for The Mountain to reorganize, to prevent total liquidation and to avoid a Chapter 7 bankruptcy and no chance to stay afloat. The difference between filing Chapter 11 and Chapter 7 was lost on a lot of people.

"The Mountain is folding." "Our property values just dropped ninety-percent." And worst yet, "Who the hell is behind this?" The initial shock at what Rice had done was now replaced by anger, resentment, and an even greater fear.

It didn't take long for the Larsons to be identified, and they were given protection. A couple of state troopers were assigned to watch the house 24/7 in unmarked cars. Jane stopped working; the boys had stopped a while before. They became prisoners in their own home—the home provided to them by a monster and a mountain.

I called a couple of times a week to see how they were. Sometimes it was a short exchange, letting me know everything was fine. But sometimes Jane would talk, taking the phone out on the back steps to her kitchen. We'd go over what had happened, and how each of the boys were doing. One night, Jason surprised me and stayed on the phone. He told me they'd all been talking. "It'd be good to get gone. We're thinking Orlando—we always wanted to go to Disney World. Why not live there?"

I thought, but didn't say, *You may be able to buy Disney World after all this, if you stay safe and out of sight.*

Instead, we chatted, and I told him, I'd never been there either. "Maybe I'd come down and visit."

And that boy, the same age as my own, had said, "Mrs. Scott, wherever we go, I hope you come visit." I thought how much I would have liked to have been his teacher.

One night, in the middle of March, as I was coming back from Jeannie's, I could see a Langdon Police cruiser coming up fast behind me in my rear-view mirror. It got really close but didn't turn on its lights. I saw two officers in the front seat—a chubby cop behind the wheel, laughing. It hit me that they were doing this to scare me and had no intentions of actually stopping me. I was sure it was because of my involvement with the Larson case. I realized my role in all this would eventually be leaked.

We were on a secondary road, and I slowed down then slammed on my brakes. It was almost dark. I grabbed my car keys from the ignition. I had one of those tiny but powerful flashlights hooked on the key chain. The cop car had braked quickly too, coming within inches of my rear-end bumper. I got out, walked up to the driver's side of their car, and shone the light in on them. We must have been near a swamp because the spring peepers were loud, almost deafening.

"What, you boys trying to scare me? Scare me? You think you can scare me, uh? I brought that goddamn monster down."

The other officer—just a kid, really—said urgently, "Get out of here, Karl, now." And they backed up, turned, and left.

Their attempt to intimidate me had failed. Standing in the near darkness, I felt invincible.

Chapter 41

present

I took the paper and looked down at it. "Thank you, David. I feel good about my decision." It was a one-page contract for the following school year. The school secretary looked up from her desk at us. "Sara, this is such great news. We'll all love having you here permanently."

Smiling, I replied, "I'm excited too. Thanks."

"Just get it in soon. It's budget time."

I wanted to tell Peter about the contract so I called him when I was in my Subaru on the way out of the school's parking lot. He didn't pick up. I decided to go to his shop.

Driving over, I replayed our most recent dinner out. We'd gone up the coast to a fine dining restaurant, Emmanuel's, right on the water. I had gone out of my way to look nice: a little more makeup, a refresh of Donna's lowlights, and a new black dress. Peter had whistled when I came out of the alcove, and the rest of the night felt magical. The bartender had teased us while we waited for our table. "Only couple here who doesn't mind the wait; must be nice to be in love." I had turned red, but Peter didn't. "Yes, it is," he'd replied, reaching for my hand without an ounce of awkwardness. That had solidified my decision; I was going to stay put and follow this thing with Peter. I was taking the position at Morris Elementary. I was going to make Bristol my permanent spot.

As I came down the side street of the entrance to Peter's apartment and workshop, I slowed down and then stopped. Peter was in front of me, just outside the apartment door, hugging a woman who looked an awful lot like Katie—tall, blond, and, well, beautiful. She had her hair pulled back, and it was striking against the black coat she wore. I knew who she was immediately. The black BMW parked on the street ahead confirmed it. Massachusetts plates.

I watched Peter say something to her, and this time he reached down and touched her face—a very intimate act between lovers. "The love of his life," I said out loud and slowly backed up the Subaru. I turned around and left. Looking in the rear-view mirror, I saw them continue to embrace.

I started to cry as I got out at the wharf and made my way down to my place. Once inside the loft, I went to the couch and sat with my coat still on. I replayed what I had just seen. "What a fool I am," I said out loud. "Fool, fool, fool." All of the elation I felt when I reached over and took the contract from David's extended hand was directly tied to a future here in Bristol with Peter.

I quickly changed into my sweatpants and sweatshirt and picked up my hand weights. I thought, *I'm either going to power walk or drink. And if I drink, it won't be pretty.*

As I was walking across the parking lot again, I realized that I could easily hand the unsigned contract back to David with a *"Something's come up, I can't commit."* But the disappointment I felt seemed insurmountable, and, once more, I felt bereft of hope. 'Peter and I' had been my vision for any kind of life moving forward here. *I let you in,* I thought. *And now this.* Despite the cold, I walked for miles, and at some point, I started to cry again. But I didn't let myself cry for long. Instead I steeled myself, thinking, *Sara, get your act together.*

Again, I wished for Jeannie or Claire to talk to. While Louise had become a dear friend, I did not want to burden her with anything so negative. I would not have done that with my own mother, either. *No, this development with Peter is mine and mine alone,* I thought. I turned around and came back home to the loft.

Later that night, as I was surfing Netflix, I heard the ding of a text. It was Peter. *"What's up? I've been calling, you okay?"* I wanted to text back, *"Fuck you."* Instead, I went to bed. But it was a restless night.

Chapter 42

past

The Larsons quietly settled their civil lawsuit against Gerald Rice's estate. His brother, Edmund Rice, the co-owner of The Mountain, agreed that his brother's whole estate should go to the victims of the sexual abuse.

Freddy confirmed that two other boys—now men—were also in lawsuits against the estate. As best he could figure, Gerald Rice started abusing sometime shortly after his wife of thirty-seven years died, about fourteen years ago.

"Maybe she kept his monstrous thoughts at bay."

I countered Freddy's comment with, "We really have no idea, do we? There could be victims all across his past." I quickly added, "Thank God they had no children of their own."

This March morning, Jane had asked me to accompany her and the boys to Freddy's office, feeling she needed my support. I watched her as she listened to Freddy.

Edmund's letter to Jane Larson was incredibly heartfelt and moving. He referenced his own fears that his brother might have preyed on his own sons and ended by saying, "Your boys are all our children."

Enclosed was a cashier's check, made out to Jane Larson for the sum of $1,000,000. "To be used to get by while the lawyers take care of everything." It was beyond generous, and Jane cried when they got it, the boys sitting uncomfortably in Freddy's office, now crowded with three of the Burlington lawyers they hired for their civil suits.

The lawyers approximated—and they were being conservative—that each boy should expect about $2.1 million from Gerald Rice's estate, even with the two lawsuits of the other victims in the mix.

"That's besides this check, Freddy?" Jane asked.

"Yes, Jane, that's besides this check. This is not figured into any of this." He held up Edmund's cashier's check.

One of the Burlington lawyers, who looked slicker than any lawyer I'd ever seen practicing in Vermont, said, "Mrs. Larson, the boys will get even more from their suits against The Mountain, now that the bankruptcy judge has granted the lawsuits to go forward."

Another one of the Burlington lawyers chimed in, "We plan to bring The Mountain to its knees. Conservative estimates could be as much as another eleven million each."

Jane looked aghast. It was a strange reaction to hearing that her boys—and by extension her—could possibly rake in thirty-three million more dollars, on top of the 6.3 million they were getting from the estate and the one million they could start using tomorrow.

She stood up and her boys immediately followed her. Something was wrong. Jane's eyes swept over all of us in Freddy's office. Her voice started out tentatively then grew stronger. "What Rice did to these boys was obscene. We all agree on that. But the amount of money you just said we could get from The Mountain, well, that's a different kind of obscene."

She paused. "This all has to stop, right here. I—we—don't want, don't need that additional amount to get out of town, start fresh. That check, and what's got to be settled from his estate, is plenty. I didn't quite understand the second suit, that it was all separate or could end up closing down The Mountain…" her voice trailed off, and she looked at her three sons.

Lawyer Slick said, "But Mrs. Larson, you and your boys will never have to work another day in your lives with that kind of money coming from The Mountain."

It was Jackson who piped up. "But we want to work, don't we?" He looked at his mother.

Jane's reply was strong. "Yes, Jackson, there's not a lazy bone in any of my sons. A strong work ethic is all I've been able to give you. Not working is never gonna be what any of us wants."

Jason, ever thoughtful, said, "Our beef has never been with The Mountain. We have friends who work The Mountain. Our dad died on that mountain. Last thing we want is for it to be closed down on account of us. We'll take Rice's money and move on, right Mom, right Sara?"

Jane and everybody looked at me. I cleared my throat. "I think that the four of you need to take a few minutes and talk without us here. I propose that we go into the waiting room and give the Larson family some privacy. Take as long as you need." I pointed to Freddy, the three lawyers, and Freddy's secretary.

"Yes, that would be good. Thank you, Sara." Jane looked determined.

We took seats in the waiting room, but then two of the three Burlington lawyers motioned to go out into the hallway. Their cells were already up to their ears. I thought, *They're shitting bricks. All those millions gone.*

It wasn't long before Jackson opened the door and said, "You guys can come back."

Freddy opened his outside office door and I heard him say to the two lawyers in the corridor, "They want us back."

Jane sat up straight and Jamie sat on the floor before her, his legs pulled up underneath him, his long skinny arms draped over his knees. Jason sat next to his mom, crutches off to the side, leaning against the wall. Jackson stood behind his mother, eyes bright. They looked like they'd been arranged for a family portrait.

I waited for Jane to talk, but it was Jackson who addressed us all. "We haven't been working for a while, 'cause of all this. We didn't dare go to town, not sure what would happen as people started to figure out it was us. But we still got a lot of goodness—and concern, I guess you'd call it—from people for what that monster did to us."

I watched as Jane placed her hand on Jamie's shoulder and straightened the collar of his shirt.

Jackson continued, "We've used up all of our savings to make ends meet. The check helps us right away. Here's our plan. We're heading to Orlando, Florida. We're hoping to buy a house, a couple of cars. My Jeep is unreliable and Mom's Honda is going on eight years. We all want work— who knows, maybe even at Disney World."

At that, Jamie looked back at Jackson and smiled.

Then Jane took over. "Withdraw the lawsuits against The Mountain, and settle up our bill once we get what we're gonna get from Rice's estate. If those other two victims want to sue The Mountain, well, that's their business. And thank you to everybody here, thank you."

I came over to Jane, leaned down, and whispered, "There's that fearless Momma I know."

She took my hand and squeezed it.

Chapter 43

present

Louise was standing outside her home. I pulled into the driveway, right up behind her Saab. She called across the street to a man standing outside a house similar to her own, "Yes, Anthony, that would be lovely, thank you!"

"Your neighbor?" I asked, walking up to her.

"Poor fella. His wife died this time last spring, and he's lost without her. He just told me my roses need pruning and that he'd do it for me. I usually pay to have my yard work done."

She had just returned from Boston. Jacob needed to go back to his oncologist every six months to determine if his cancer was still in remission. Louise had volunteered to ride with him. It was still good news.

I walked along Louise's side yard with her as she took note of all the perennial shoots coming up. She stopped suddenly and looked at me. "What has Peter told you about Stacey's husband? I saw her this morning. Seems her husband goes to the same doctor as Jacob. What are the odds of that?"

"Wait, what?"

Louise took hold of my arm. "Peter hasn't told you? Stacey's husband—the lawyer she ran off with—he's got pancreatic cancer. Stage four. It's advanced. The girls are devastated. Of course it goes without saying, so is she."

I looked at Louise, trying to understand what she was telling me.

She continued, "I don't wish that on anyone, even if he did wine and dine another man's wife."

I gave Louise back two books, both mysteries that I had borrowed, the first and second in a series about a small Canadian town called Three Pines. I needed to think about what she had just told me, so I cut my visit short. "I loved the books, Louise, but I've got to go."

"Wait, don't you want a cup of tea, a glass of wine?"

"I'll call you a little later. I have to get going." I couldn't wait to get home and dissect this new information. While it was awful news, there was a trace of joy spreading through me. *This explains the embrace*, I thought. *He'd been wiping her tears away, not stroking her cheek.*

By midnight, I was still up, walking the wide plank floors, growing more anxious by the minute. Peter did not know that I'd had an affair, that I'd cheated on my husband. I didn't run off like Stacey had, but I had been unfaithful. "How much should I tell him?" I worried. "Would he see me in a whole different light? Would he even want to have a relationship with me?"

We had just started to open up about our failed marriages and what we'd learned from them. Yet, I had remained guarded for good reason. I had alluded to the shit my family had experienced in Vermont because of me, way back when he first came to the loft. But now I hoped he didn't remember that comment.

Just then a text came in. I went to the kitchen counter and looked at my cell. *"You awake?"* It was Peter. I didn't answer it. I had to think.

Chapter 44
past

S o," Jeffrey said. "I've had some time to think, and I know you have too." He looked at me with thoughtful eyes and a tentative smile. He nervously brushed his hands over the cushion of the couch and then crossed his legs.

"Yes, I have," I responded.

He had traveled to three different districts in the last month, spending only short periods of time at the house. I had stayed busy at school and done very little outside of work and coming home. Most of the nights when I was in the house alone, I jotted down my thoughts and feelings. The clipboard where Michael had once placed all of his and Lexi's possibilities for college now held my own possibilities for moving forward.

"Do you want to start and tell me what you're thinking, how you're feeling about us?" he asked quietly.

It was mid-morning, and the weather outside carried the first, full promise of a spring day.

"I can." I came and sat down in the Windsor chair next to the couch. The house was quiet, and the morning light streamed in. I looked at Jeffrey and braced myself. I began, "I think it's time for us to end this slow death of our marriage."

He leaned forward, his face suddenly looking unsure. "What do you mean?"

I shifted my feet and looked directly at him. "I feel that we've both done things that have undermined the foundation—at least what I thought was the foundation—of what we had. Our trust is shot."

Jeffrey ran his hand across his face, the strain of our relationship clearly showing. He asked, "Do you think we can get back to that place of trust?"

I said nothing. Only stared at him blankly.

"Because what I'm hearing, at least what I think I'm hearing, is that you want to give up."

I thought he must be proud of his active listening bullshit skills.

"No, I didn't say that I wanted to give up. I said I didn't think we have what we need to get our marriage back. The basic tenet of 'don't fuck anybody else' has been broken by both of us and it can't be..." I grew exasperated. "Jeffrey, it's not like we suddenly proclaim, 'Okay, now, we go back and it's time to trust each other again.'"

"But, Sara, it sounds like you don't even want to try." He got up and moved away from me, standing in the doorway that led into the den.

I looked up at him. "You know what, I'll be honest—ever since you told me about the woman in Austin, I've imagined that this woman was your token confession to me."

Jeffrey looked confused, unsure of what I meant. I thought, *You know exactly what I mean.*

I leaned forward in the chair. "Kind of like a little grain of truth to make you feel better. But since you told me, I imagine you've probably been sleeping with lots of anonymous women. For years."

Jeffrey's mouth dropped opened, and he stared at me in disbelief. He started to come towards me then stopped. I stared at him and didn't move.

Coming back to the couch, he was adamant. "I swear to you, it was only that time, only that one time."

Now he sat, and his face changed again, this time to a sneer. "What about my trust in you, Sara? You totally took what we had and threw it away. With some asshole."

"What we had, Jeffrey? What we had? It was a sham. Austin was eleven years ago. Eleven years!" I couldn't believe how loud I said this and caught myself.

Lowering my voice, I continued, "Our baby was seven years old. My God, we were so happy then, and you did that?" I shook my head and looked at him intently. "I can't imagine how you were able to go on, day in and day out with me. Didn't it even bother you?"

Jeffrey said nothing at first and picked at a piece of lint on his pant leg. Then he whispered, "Of course it did."

In a cold voice, I enunciated my words slowly. "The affair I had wasn't really so bad then, was it? Since it was on shaky, shitty ground to begin with."

I got up and left him, going through the kitchen and out onto the porch. I wasn't finished though and turned right around and walked back into the living room. I stopped. Jeffrey looked up.

"I cannot live like this anymore." My resolve surprised me.

Jeffrey's words poured out. He was rushing to say all he could. "I know, Sara, I know. I agree. This fall and winter have been brutal on us. I feel like, with some effort, we could get back to what we had. Shouldn't we try, though, shouldn't we?"

"And what was that Jeffrey? Exactly what did we have?" I sat back down and turned to him.

"We had a wonderful life going on, and we had Michael. My God, Michael."

"Michael is gone, Jeffrey. Michael has grown up!" I threw my hands up in the air as if it was the most obvious thing in the world—because it was.

We both turned away from each other and sat. The house moved on, slowly making its small noises: the washer in the basement went into the spin cycle, the furnace kicked on for a few minutes, and outside, the mail truck slowed down and parked. It was Evie, signaling 10:00 a.m., the time she did our street's daily delivery. Eventually I got up and went into the kitchen. I reached for a Snapple from the bottom shelf of the fridge. I called to Jeffrey, "Do you want something to drink?"

He got up and came into the kitchen. Leaning against the side of the refrigerator, he quietly said, "People survive things like this in their marriage, Sara."

Jeffrey saw our infidelities as our only problem, but I knew there was more than just that. It was a loss of identity, and, to some extent, a loss of purpose in our marriage. But I focused in on this one statement.

"Don't you see? Every trip you've taken and every trip you'll take from now on will be suspect. And, you'll worry constantly about me, and what I'm doing."

"I'll end the consulting firm. I'll look for positions around here. I can change gears, Sara." Jeffrey moved closer to me, adding, "We can go to counseling."

I opened my drink and took a long sip. I held it out to him. He shook his head.

We returned to the living room and sat quietly. I heard our neighbor's car beep and some voices outside. Jeffrey moved the sheer curtains aside and looked out.

"I don't want to become that kind of couple where we constantly question each other," I said.

"No, I don't want that either, ever," Jeffrey replied firmly.

"Here's what you have to know." I moved, kneeling down before him on the floor in front of the couch. "I'm running on empty."

"What does that even mean, Sara?" he asked, perplexed.

I began to cry and reached for his hand. "I've got nothing left." I didn't have the heart to tell him that I had stopped caring, that it didn't matter what he did from now on when he traveled. That this was the real cause for my tears.

The bafflement I saw weeks ago returned. He started to speak and then stopped. He looked around the room, finally resting his eyes back on me. "You really mean that?"

"Yes," I whispered.

Jeffrey sat and didn't move, his hand resting in mine.

I got up and went into the bathroom to get the box of Kleenexes.

"All this shit? How did we blow it?" he asked as I handed him a tissue.

"When I started the affair..."

He cut me off, his voice suddenly sharp, "Do not talk about that, absolutely not one fucking word to me on that." Jeffrey's face was red, and he stared at me. "I don't want to hear one thing about that. Ever again."

"Okay, I won't." I stood up. "I think it's time we took a breather."

Jeffrey looked out the window and said, "Yeah." He didn't move.

I walked outside, down into the backyard. I breathed in the fresh air and felt guilty for the joy the weather brought to me. It was a stark contrast to the disillusionment and sadness that the house held. I felt the first of something I couldn't quite name. It was like feeling what the definition of the word 'possibility' meant to me: big change mixed in with a hefty dose of uncertainty.

Now, what do we do, Jeffrey?" I asked when we were almost done eating our dinner. It had been hours since our earlier, morning talk. He had washed and dried the window screens, propping them up along the side of the garage. I had washed all our bedding, including in the spare bedroom.

"Oh, you know, we'll figure out how to dissolve all this." He waved his hands, taking in the kitchen, the house in general. He was tired and said this with little emotion, although I could tell he was masking what he was truly feeling.

"I'm the one who's going to leave. You stay here, keep the house for you and Michael."

He looked at me, surprised. "What are you saying?"

"I went from my mother and stepfather's house to college in Keene and then to you. I need the space and time to figure out the rest. With all the Larson shit, Langdon is not my favorite place anymore. As for telling our Michael, we'll have to figure that out, but we've got time."

I got up and put the plates in the sink. I didn't want to fight, talk, or cry anymore. Jeffrey helped load the dishwasher, and we went our separate ways—he to the den and I upstairs.

A kind of peace descended on us. Jeffrey didn't ask me to reconsider staying or going to counseling. I wondered if he too was feeling a strange sense of relief that we had made a decision. I moved into the spare bedroom that evening and filled its closet with my clothes. When I asked Jeffrey if I could have the bench at the bottom of our bed, he immediately moved it into the room.

Upon leaving, he turned to me. "I'm not going to be an asshole in any of this, Sara. I will make sure you have what you need and what's yours. You came to this marriage with a nest egg; it made buying this house possible. I'll call our financial advisor soon and we can sit down with all the numbers. Alright?"

Placing clothes in the dresser, I stopped and replied, "Alright."

One April morning, the Larsons pulled into the driveway. I came down off the porch and greeted Jane with a big hug. They were headed to Hartford to catch a flight to Orlando that early evening. It was nearly a year to the day that I'd seen Jamie with Rice.

All three of the boys climbed out of the Jeep, and I waved to the kid behind the wheel. I didn't know him, but Jackson explained, "Dylan's driving us down; I'm giving him my rig."

I hugged each boy and smiled at them as they straightened up. Jamie was uncomfortable, but I couldn't help myself, I hugged him the longest.

To Jackson, I said, "I'm so proud of you. Remember, most people aren't assholes, okay?"

He smiled and did a little salute. "Aye, Aye, Captain."

I laughed.

Jason motioned for me to take a walk out towards the backyard. He used a cane now. "Funny, luck of the draw." He glanced back to make sure he wasn't being overheard. "You get a mother who struggles or you get a mother who has all her shit together. Michael's the lucky one in all of this."

I stopped walking. "Believe me, Jason, I don't have it all together, far from it." I said this with emphasis.

"I know what you did for us, Mrs. Scott, I know. And my life, and their lives—" he motioned to his family now leaning on the Jeep, waiting for us—"will forever be changed because of you."

I put my hand on Jason's arm. "You're the brave one Jason—you told."

"Oh, I don't know about that. I think I just told the right person."

I hugged him for the second time. We made our way back to everyone else.

I had told Jeffrey that the Larsons were on their way over to say goodbye. He'd remained inside until Jason and I came back from our walk. Now Jeffrey came out to the porch and walked down the stairs onto the driveway. I introduced him to everyone, but when it was Jason's turn, Jeffrey extended his hand and said, "It's been awhile, uh, Jason?"

"That it has, Mr. Scott."

As the boys climbed back in, I went over to the passenger side where Jane sat. "Hey, where's Callie?"

She smiled. "Maple Farms got her until we close on the house—probably this Wednesday. Then they'll put her on a plane to Orlando."

I had sat beside Jane as she and the boys did virtual tours of properties for sale in and around Orlando. They settled on a sprawling stucco with a large pool, four bedrooms, and an impressive game room. It had beautiful landscaping and sat on a street with similar, well-taken-care-of homes. The boys were excited; it'd be the first time ever that they'd have their own bedrooms.

Another time, without the boys present, I had sat with Jane and suggested family counseling, once they felt ready. "There's so much out there on how to approach trauma.

New ways of treating things like Post Traumatic Stress Disorder—that's if the boys are diagnosed with it."

"You mean like vets coming back from active duty?"

"Yes, I think. Counseling can bring out the trauma and teach the boys mindfulness and acceptance practices to help deal with it. If you were all to go together first, then there'd be strength in numbers and not as scary as going it alone. Your family has suffered, Jane, but there's so much love and resilience in each of you."

She had nodded, writing 'family counseling' down on a pad with 'To Do' at the top, getting ready for the big move. She had underlined it twice.

I'd also given Jane the name of a financial advisor who Sal—Freddy's sister again—knew in Orlando. "I dated him in college, but I let him get away. He's trustworthy, he'll do right by them," she'd said.

"We've done pretty good with Freddy," Jane had said. "So I'll go meet with this new guy once we get all settled." They had a lot of things coming through in the estate settlement; someone needed to guide them to make sound financial decisions.

Dylan started up the Jeep, and all of the Larsons looked at me. I had no words, I had only tears. Tears for each one of them. Jeffrey came up beside me and put his arm around my shoulder. Jane was crying too.

"We'll send you pictures," she called out.

"Lots," I replied. Dylan put the car in reverse. A few honks, and they were gone.

Chapter 45
present

I was driving down a county road, passing the Bristol Community Golf Course, when a man caught my attention. He was on the driving range and his build and stance looked familiar.

I slowed down, realizing it was Peter. It'd been almost two full weeks since we'd last seen one another. I turned in at the entrance and drove down the lane. I parked and sat, watching him.

After what Louise told me, I had thought a lot about him and us. I'd made the decision to stay the course at Morris, signing the contract as a new teacher for the following year. I hoped our relationship would get back on track. I missed him.

I had also arrived at the decision that I would not tell him, at least at this point, about my affair and how that played into my marriage ending—although it wasn't the sole reason. My worries from the night of pacing the loft had receded. I was jumping the gun, assuming we were further along in our relationship than we actually were.

I wanted Peter to get to know me better, to know that I was no longer the woman who was with Craig two years ago. If I told him now, I'd worry that he'd see me in a different light. Louise had alluded to the fact that other people knew of Stacey's infidelity before Peter did. I didn't want to give him a reason to doubt me or worry that I would be unfaithful. I only had to recall my own quick reaction when I saw him with Stacey to know how easily the mind can jump to conclusions. I also thought, *It's that trust, it has to be there.*

I got out of the car and walked across the lot. I stood off to the side, watching him hit from the bucket of balls.

Out on the driving range, distances were marked off in increments of fifty yards—the first marker starting at one hundred, going all the way up to three hundred. Peter's drives were impressive. He barely looked at the ball's landing distance before moving the next ball onto the tee. At one point he tipped the bucket over, the remaining balls rolling onto the tee pad. *If I'm going to say anything, now's the time.*

I cupped my hands around my mouth and called out, "Hey there, Tiger. Great drives."

He turned and looked back at me. For a few, brief seconds, I thought, *He's not going to say a thing, this is very awkward.*

But he smiled briefly and motioned for me to come over. I walked the thirty or so feet to him. When I got there, he wasn't smiling anymore. "You golf?" he asked.

"A little bit," I answered. He was out of sorts, I could tell; he looked tired. Again, there was dead silence. I looked down at the ground, but Peter didn't turn away. He stood watching me.

"I haven't been returning your calls, I'm sorry," I said, now looking at him.

"No shit, Sara. Usually when I get dumped, it's pretty clear cut to me. But you, you're subtle, aren't you? You just don't pick up." He held on to his driver. I had never seen him mad before.

I realized that I'd hurt him by not answering my cell or texting him back.

"I didn't dump you, Peter. I thought, no—I saw you with…I'm sure it was your ex-wife. You were pretty affectionate, both of you. Outside your apartment."

Peter looked at me hard, trying to figure out what I had just said. "Stacey was in town. Her husband's been diagnosed with cancer. It's not good. She did come see me. Why, why didn't you ask me?" he replied, shaking his head.

"I thought what I saw was, you know…that you were still feeling…well, it was—it looked like she's still the love of your life."

Now growing defensive I added, "We really don't know each other, do we?"

He appeared dumbfounded, then walked the distance between us. He swooped me up in his arms and hugged me, paused, then kissed me hard. It was, perhaps, the most dramatic move any man has ever made on me. Breathlessly, I kissed him back. "For fuck's sake, don't assume anything with me, ever again, okay?" he said.

I whispered, "Okay," still feeling the pressure of his kiss on my mouth.

Chapter 46

past

Michael found me getting ready to go to work. I was surprised he was up. "Hey, are you still on your early class schedule? Is that why you're up?" I was eating a piece of toast, standing at the ironing board, waiting for the iron to heat up.

He opened the refrigerator and took out the orange juice. Our grocery bill would double now that he was home for the summer. It was the end of May, and he and Lexi had just gotten home the day before.

I fleetingly thought, as Jeffrey texted me while Michael drove up I-91, en route home, that it was the first time I had ever braced myself for seeing him. Our plan was to tell him about our decision to divorce after he got settled, in a couple of days.

Michael was in a bad mood. As I stood, waiting for his answer, he poured a glass of orange juice and then looked at me and said, "When are you going to cut the crap and tell me how you're involved in all The Mountain shit."

Boom. I didn't have a clue how to respond, so I didn't. Jeffrey walked into the kitchen at that moment and said,

"Hey, Michael, why don't you cut the crap and show your mother a little more respect."

He took us both in with a look of contempt. "So this is how you two are going to play this, huh? Like I'm eight years old, and I'm starting to ask if Santa is real." He put down his glass and went out onto the porch.

I looked at Jeffrey. "Did you tell him anything last night? I thought we had a plan for how to do this."

He came over to me and said, quietly, "He heard that you had something to do with the Larsons. Everybody put it together that the boys are the ones Rice molested. Now you and I are sleeping in separate rooms, and, well, he's got questions. The only thing I said to him last night, after you went up to bed, was that we'd had a tough year and that we needed to talk to him about it."

"Dad, are you coming?" Michael asked impatiently from the kitchen doorway.

"Yeah, just a minute," Jeffrey called out. "We're going for a run. Let me see what I can safely say if he's persistent. But I think our plan to wait until he's had a couple of days back—well, he's not going to wait."

I was tired. I was ready for the last three and a half weeks of the school year to end, for Jeffrey and me to break it to Michael, and for the big decisions to be made about when and where I was moving.

Michael decided to give me the cold shoulder treatment. While he wasn't outright rude, he only answered my questions and comments in a perfunctory way. He gave me just enough in his responses to get by, but our usual comfortable banter was gone. Lexi tried to tamp down his shortness and add to the conversation with the humor and affection Michael was holding back.

The next morning, it was Lexi who greeted me as I was eating breakfast. I smiled and said, "Wow, you're up early, just like Michael yesterday."

"We're going for a run—starting to train for the half-marathon in Colton. Didn't Michael tell you?"

I shook my head. "When is that?" I asked.

Michael came in and once more grabbed the orange juice and poured a glass. He smiled at Lexi and ignored me.

"Michael, why haven't you told your mom about the Colton race? I thought you would have by now."

"What, Lexi? It's just a race, Mom, no big deal. Come on, let's go." His tone was abrupt, and Lexi looked back at me. Michael scooted out the kitchen door.

"Wow, he's in a piss poor mood," Lexi said. "The race is for Peddan, Colton, and Langdon to have food shelves right in the schools, like food pantries for kids who need it. It's the brain-child of Luke and two of his classmates from Castleton. I think it's their big senior graduation project. Michael's helping him out, a lot, in organizing the race. It's the last weekend in July."

"Thanks, Lex. You better get going." I nodded to the door.

Later that evening, Michael asked to use the Subaru. I said, "Sure, where you going?" There was no reply until Lexi smiled at me and said, "To see a movie if Michael doesn't keep being such an ass!"

He did manage to say, "Thanks," when I handed him the keys, but no "Momma Leoni" or other term of endearment. I stood and watched them leave.

Jeffrey and I ate a quiet meal, sitting on the porch, watching the neighborhood walkers and bicyclers go by. Somehow, our peaceful co-existence in the house had continued. We'd met with our lawyers; I hired a divorce lawyer who Jeannie knew from Brattleboro to represent me.

Both welcomed our desire to peacefully iron out all of our finances and items in the house. During the meeting, Jeffrey and I went room-by-room, deciding what stayed and what would come with me. Some of my decisions were based on what had been my parents' and whether or not Michael would miss it.

When we got to the question of who should get the kitchen table, I had started to cry and there was an uncomfortable moment. Jeffrey handed me his hankie and put his hand on my back. I blew my nose. "Of course it stays. I'm okay, we can go on," I'd said, looking at Jeffrey and the lawyers.

My lawyer had walked me out to my car. "He's being very generous, Sara. I think you know that."

"Jeffrey's not an asshole," I had responded.

Now on the porch, Jeffrey looked over at me and said, "We have to tell him, as soon as we can. I feel like we're deceiving him, and he knows it."

So we did. One summer night Michael was upstairs, reading. I was always happy to see him read for enjoyment, but as Jeffrey and I came into his bedroom, I asked him to stop. He put the book—*Fixed*—down. I had overheard him talking with Jeffrey about the story of Boston College Basketball getting mixed up with the mob. Jeffrey wanted to read it after Michael was done.

Michael looked at us both. "Is this when you tell me the truth about Santa, and I learn that the Easter Bunny is bullshit too?"

I sat on the floor, on the braided rug my mother had made for Michael years before. Jeffrey took the chair from the desk and turned it out. Facing us, he sat. We waited for him to begin. I heard loud crickets outside the opened window. It was warm in the upstairs of our house.

"I told you that we've had a tough year while you've been at school. By the way, nice GPA this second semester," Jeffrey said. Michael had received a 3.1.

I smiled tentatively at Michael and said, "Yeah, way to go." He ignored my comment and stared, with no expression on his face, at his father.

"Michael," Jeffrey continued, "your mom and I have decided—both of us—that we no longer want to be 'together as a couple.' That doesn't apply to the 'family' part of us. We still want, very much, to remain members of this family. I know it may seem like a contradiction, but your mom and I still love each other. Just not in the…well, I'm repeating myself…but not in the husband and wife sense."

I glanced at Michael; his face looked impassive, but I watched him swallow and thought, *He's trying to keep it together.* My heart broke for him.

Jeffrey shifted in his chair. "We made this decision weeks ago, and we've been amicable about it. We've got lawyers working on our actual divorce, and, well, Mom is going to tell you more." I thought Jeffrey looked relieved that he was done talking and now it was time to hand it over to me.

We had agreed that I would explain the part about me moving out and getting a place of my own, probably down in Peddan or in nearby Colton. We were at that point now.

But I never got a chance, because Michael stood up and reached for his sneakers. "I know Mom's done something. That's why this is all happening. It involves those losers—those fucking losers, the Larsons."

He stared at me with such venom I was taken aback. But what upset me even more than his expression was his characterization of the Larsons.

I stood up fast and said, in an angry voice I didn't even recognize, "Don't you ever, ever call them losers again, do you hear me? Not ever."

Jeffrey stood up too.

"What'd you do, Mom? Fuck Jackson?—or wait, maybe Jason? Which of the sleaze balls did you do?"

I reached up to slap his face, but he was quicker and caught my hand.

"You spoiled, spoiled brat!" I yelled and turned away from him, running to the bedroom. I slammed the door closed. I was furious and shaking.

I could hear both of them going down the stairs, Michael taking two at a time. Jeffrey was behind him, his voice loud and insistent. "Michael, you are so out of line, stop!" But he didn't, because I heard the kitchen door open. Looking out the window from the upstairs room, I watched as Michael took off on his bike, heading toward Lexi's house. I heard him change gears on his bike as he stood up to pedal harder, to get away faster.

Jeffrey came up and knocked softly on the door. I told him to come in. He asked if I was okay. "Did you know that's what he thought? That I...I, fucked one of them?"

"Jesus, no, we've got to set him straight."

And then came the dawning realization that the personal price I thought I had paid was still there, looming over us.

I replied, "The truth is just as bad."

Chapter 47
present

S ara! Hey, Sara, here!" Turning around, I saw Peter walking down the wharf towards me, waving his hands. I waved back at him. Puzzled, I turned back to the parking lot. *Where is his truck?* I wondered.

He had called me earlier, telling me to "dress in layers and bring sunglasses. I'll pick you up at eleven, give or take a few minutes."

I had hung up and looked out the window. I wasn't sure what Peter had in mind for the day, but he sounded excited. The sky above the harbor was gray, and I thought it might be starting to sprinkle. "Sunglasses? Is he crazy? More like slickers and an umbrella," I said out loud.

He and I were back on, with a new determination to work hard at not jumping to conclusions and asking each other more questions. He'd come over the night of the golf course, and we had talked well into the morning. About Stacey, about her husband's illness, what it may mean for his girls. I talked a little more about how and why I'd come to Bristol. I was cautious though. We'd just gotten our footing back. I didn't want to say anything to jeopardize that.

We made love, and I felt like it was the beginning of some strong emotions for the both of us. In the morning, he told me he was going to put up the bookshelves that very day, come hell or high water. I said, in a straight deadpan voice, "I don't want them now." He had picked me up and thrown me onto the bed, covering me with his kisses.

I counted five cars in the parking lot and made a mental note that I should start locking the Subaru now that there were clearly more people going into the shop. Spring had arrived, though today didn't feel too spring-like.

Reaching me, Peter smiled. "You're not going to need that slicker. In about an hour all this gray is going to lift."

Returning his smile, I asked, "What are you driving today?"

He placed his hands on my shoulders and turned me back, facing the wharf. There were three, maybe four motor-boats docked along the wharf.

Keeping one hand on my shoulder, he pointed with the other. "That second one, the Boston Whaler. It's mine. We're seeing the sights today, the sights you haven't seen yet—or perhaps you have. I shouldn't assume, should I?" he said, smiling.

He was wearing his dark green Carhart jacket with a gray sweatshirt underneath and blue jeans. His sunglasses, hanging from the front pocket of his coat, were Ray-Bans. He hadn't shaved; some stubble was growing. His beard was red, I realized.

The day was brisk, but there was no wind. I wondered if I was up for this. Freezing water, rocky boat, waves, endless gray sky. *It's all unsettling to me,* I thought.

"I'm not sure I'm layered as much as I should be, and—" I didn't know how to say it. "Peter, remember, I'm a land-locked girl. Boats and water..." I stopped speaking. I wasn't smiling.

Seagulls were swarming around the end of the pier. It looked as if someone was throwing scraps of food into the water. Peter stood back and looked at me. Taking my hand, he turned, heading to the wharf. "I can modify those sights, Sara." Holding my hand firmly, we set out.

For the next hour and a half, Peter and I sat on his boat alongside the wharf. It was still docked, and we simply talked. The sun started to peak out from behind the clouds. The foot traffic on the wharf was growing as boats and cars came and went.

"Living in Maine now, you have to learn basic boat vocab, okay?" Peter said.

I listened, enjoying his presentation. He moved easily about the whaler, while I stayed put.

Standing at the pilot seat, Peter asked, "Are you ready to review?"

"Of course I am," I declared with confidence.

Pointing to the right side of the boat he asked, "And what, Sara Scott, is this side of the boat called?"

"The starboard side, sir!" I answered.

"And this?" He touched the gear switcher thing.

"The throttle, and that is the safety latch or hook." I pointed down to the red coil near the key.

"Very good. Now I'm going to go faster, okay? Get ready!"

Peter pointed and I called out, in rapid succession, "Bow, stern, port, aft!"

Raising his eyebrows at me, he motioned to the area around him, encompassing the steering wheel and console.

"That is, um, give me a second, it's on the tip of my tongue...the helm, it's the helm."

"You got it!" he exclaimed.

The sun broke through the clouds, and I took the slicker off and put my sunglasses on. Every surface of the whaler was white and stainless steel. I now understood Peter's earlier request to bring sunglasses and was glad I had polarized lenses.

In his gray sweatshirt and wearing his own sunglasses, Peter moved from around the pilot seat. "Trust me, Sara, okay?"

I watched him untie the ropes, first on the port side and then behind me. He returned to the helm and turned the key. Slowly and expertly, he maneuvered us out of the slip. Moving the throttle forward, we eased away from the wharf. I held my breath.

As soon as we were alongside the first buoy marker—the green one I saw every day as I made my way down the wharf to go to school—Peter cut the engine. He reached into the forward hatch and took out a small anchor, slipping it into the water. Taking hold of the grab rail, he made his way back to me in the stern. We were all of about forty feet from the wharf.

Amused, I watched him slide out a cooler stowed under the pilot seat. Opening it, he called out, "We've got salami and cheese, turkey and bacon, and veggies with pesto, all on whole wheat. Oh, and dill pickles with the finest IPA in town."

Sitting together again in the stern bench seat, we began eating our lunch. The sun was warm, the water still. I smelled the cold, salt air.

I looked up at the big window in the loft and commented, "Wow, I've never seen it from this view."

A man leaving Robert's Tackle and Bait Shop called out to Peter just as I reached up to kiss him. *How did I get so lucky after all the shit I've been through?* I asked myself.

Chapter 48
past

Michael stayed away for several days. "He's got to be eating Marilyn out of house and home—please give him money to give her for groceries," I said to Jeffrey. He had spoken to Michael a few times, driving up the hill to the Rec summer camp swim area. Michael had come home and gotten a duffle bag of clothes while I wasn't there, and he'd told Jeffrey that he couldn't stand me—couldn't stand to see my face or hear my voice.

According to Jeffrey, he had asked Michael," Since when did you get so high and mighty and think you were the judge and jury of your mother?"

Towards the end of July, Jeffrey told Michael that he needed to come home and take care of business. I think there was a possibility that Marilyn was tiring of him and Michael could sense it. Having your daughter's boyfriend move in is very different than inviting him for dinner. I winced thinking of poor Lexi having to pick up after him.

Jeffrey grew firm and told him he needed to complete things before returning to school his sophomore year. He needed to speak with his mother to do that. I had scheduled him a dentist appointment, a physical, and an opportunity to apply for work-study through a grant at one of the elementary schools in State College. He needed to do a conference call with the Langdon Elementary P.E. teacher present as well as the Pennsylvania school staff. I had set all these meetings up before our big blow up. Michael didn't know the dates or the times.

I typed up the list, thinking he was going to blow me off, but early one evening he came home, walking his bike down the driveway, duffle bag slung over his shoulder. I was glad Jeffrey was home; he was our buffer.

"Hey," Michael called out as he moved through the house and up to his room. The next couple of days were touch-and-go—we didn't talk much, and if we did, it was nothing of substance. I told him when his appointments were and left the typed schedule in his room. Jeffrey, though, was growing irritated with Michael and his contin-ued cold shoulder toward me.

"This is too much, Sara. He's gotten away with treating you like shit for too long." And just like that, Michael was back before us, this time at the kitchen table. I wasn't sure I wanted to have this conversation, but Jeffrey was deter-mined to set him straight.

Jeffrey, in his even-measured way, told a scowling Michael that I had helped the Larsons report a decade of sexual abuse at the hands of Gerald Rice. He again repeated that I had not had any improper relationship with any of the boys and had acted as their mandated reporter. "Your mother should be commended for the role she played, Michael, not be condemned by you."

Jeffrey continued, "The Larsons have moved to Florida and it's a chance for them to start fresh. To get away from all the trauma of their past here, because of that man's sexual abuse and horrific predatory actions towards each one of those boys."

Jeffrey looked my way and said, "Your mother helped them navigate the legal system and brought them a bit of justice. Some children aren't born into families that have resources or education. And The Mountain is one formidable entity, Michael. Your mother went up against a multi-million-dollar business."

Michael sat with his shoulders slumped, his arms folded, and replied, "I know what kind of family life they had. I know it sucked. I remember the accident on The Mountain with their dad. I remember playing with Jason, too."

"Okay, then you can understand that they deserved someone to stand up for them and to help them. Your mother was that someone. She guided them to the right people who then took over."

Jeffrey moved to the window and looked out. "It's time for you to stop treating her with such disrespect. I won't have it, anymore. Do you understand? Are you ready to finally apologize to her?"

Michael turned and looked at me. I thought I could detect a slight softening of his hardened stance. I smiled at him. I was ready to accept his apology.

"How did you find out they were being sexually abused?" he asked me.

For a brief moment, I watched Jeffrey shake his head ever so slightly as if to say, "Don't go there." But I felt I had to. Michael was an adult; he was ready to hear the ugliness.

I went through it all, from the time I saw Rice and Jamie at the building lot, to the morning in the Café, to Jason's full disclosure at his house, to Freddy and the significance of his fishing buddies. Michael's face displayed an array of emotions: surprise, uncomfortableness, and, I think, a fleeting look of admiration. I wrapped up and exhaled.

But Michael, always a good listener like his father, asked, "What were you doing at that building lot? That's pretty secluded, we used to drink up there."

Jeffrey moved to the table and forcefully said, "Sara, do not go there."

I looked up at him then across the table at Michael, and I went there. I told him about my own ugliness.

"I was supposed to meet a man there." I started to cry, the tears falling down my face and onto my shirt. I reached up with both my hands, grabbing at my collar. I wiped my nose and my face with the cotton t-shirt. Michael's startled look and initial incomprehension were alarming. Between bouts of crying, I blurted out, "That's when I saw Rice molesting Jamie. It was the day you found me throwing up in the bathroom."

Michael suddenly pushed back in his chair and stood up. Disgust and anger radiated out from him. Turning to Jeffrey, he said loudly, "That's fucking okay with you, Dad? You're okay with this?"

"Michael," I pleaded. "I hate what I did. Please, believe me!" I reached out to touch him.

He shrank back from me. "Don't touch me, you god-damn whore!" Then to Jeffrey, he yelled, "Tell her, Dad, tell her to go." He looked back at me. "Get the fuck out!"

I ran to the upstairs bedroom and threw together clothes as quickly as I could. It was imperative that I leave. I couldn't take seeing or hearing anymore of Michael's wrath. Moments later I came back down through the kitchen. Both he and Jeffrey were sitting there in silence. Michael shifted his chair away from me as I passed him.

I opened the kitchen door, unaware that Jeffrey was following close behind. I walked blindly down the stairs and onto the driveway. "Sara, wait!"

"Call Claire, please. Tell her I'm coming and what's happened with Michael and me. I'll tell her more when I get down there. I don't know when I'll be back. But Jeffrey, make sure he does that conference call. None of this shit should impact his work study, okay?" I was now in my car.

"I'm going to tell him about my own infidelity. This isn't fair to you."

"No, don't, Jeffrey. Please, do not tell him." Now, I was pleading, and my voice took on the urgency I was feeling. "He can't handle that. He can't learn that both his parents are fuck ups. Please, do not tell him. He needs you."

And I left. At times I cried on my way south, at other times I was strangely void of any feelings. A whole lot of thoughts flooded my mind, resting on my biggest fear: that the moral price I paid to stand with the Larsons had just cost me my son.

After many long walks on the beach—crowded as it was—and talks with Jeffrey's sister, Claire, I made three decisions in the two weeks I stayed with her. I was moving out of the house, though not until Michael was back at Penn State; I was resigning from my teaching position at Peddan; and I was leaving Vermont. Claire, whom I loved beyond description, heard my rationale for each of them and understood. She was my rock during this time and told me that, regardless of the fact that I was ending my marriage with her brother—and all the crap that had happened—she would support and be there for me for all of "our days on this earth." Between Jeannie and Claire, I would survive.

I drove back, rested and resolved. I went to Peddan Middle School. I had already called my principal from the Cape to tell her of my resignation. We met for an hour. While I was leaving her and our staff in a bind, she said that they could start the year with a long-term sub, if need be. She had already posted the vacancy and had some decent responses. I hugged Gladys in the parking lot and cried as I pulled out. That building held sixteen years of my life and all of my teaching career.

Jeffrey and Michael were en route to State College. I had the next couple of days to myself in the house. I needed to get busy. I was not devastated, nor sentimental during this time. I made a list and kept my focus. Marilyn stopped by, and I told her my situation—not all of it, but enough for her to know that Jeffrey and I were splitting up. We hugged, and she assured me that Michael would be "okay." We didn't visit long—I was done talking and needed to do more packing.

When I left Langdon for good, Jeffrey had only been home for four hours after getting Michael settled in for his sophomore year at Penn State. He was living in a different place, but he and Jayden were rooming together again, their friendship firmly established. It bothered me that I didn't know what Michael's new residential hall looked like. Jeffrey did his best to describe it to me, but I would be leaving without an accurate picture in my mind.

Jeffrey was tired but made sure the electrical wiring of the trailer I was towing was all set. I had texted Jeannie, *"On my way soon."* I was stopping at her house on the way out of Langdon for our final farewell.

"Make sure you register the Outback in Maine and get an inspection as soon as you can. Have you got your insurance cards?"

"Yes, both: one health, one dental. I'm good, really."

Jeffrey was worried, I could tell, about both my mental state and my finances. After resigning from Peddan, we were going on Obamacare, and he was going to pay both our premiums. He'd bought out my half of the house, at fair market value. I had a cushion. "But only for so long," he cautioned me.

Now, standing in almost the same spot where we had said our goodbyes to the Larson family, Jeffrey said, "Sara, please email soon."

"I will, I promise."

We hugged, but when I started to let go, he pulled me closer, tighter. "Please, please, keep me in the loop. For Michael's sake too."

"Okay."

I backed out of the driveway, glanced at Jeffrey, and waved. I slowly pulled up to the top of Dunsmore Street and looked back. He hadn't moved. I beeped and pulled out.

I didn't make it very far. Passing the Little League fields, I pulled over into the lot. I was crying and needed to stop before I drove any further. I turned off the car.

I leaned in, resting my arms on the steering wheel. "I'm literally leaving my life," I whispered between tears. The finality of this moment hit me hard. The last connection to Michael had just been severed and everything I knew was now gone. I wasn't excited; I was terrified.

I looked out across the ball fields and closed my eyes. A memory of long ago came to me.

It was of Michael, first up to bat. On the very first pitch of the season he had hit a line drive, rounded first, and slid into second base. Standing up, brushing off his pants, he had looked my way.

"Hurray, Michael! Go Pirates!" Jeannie and I were overzealous in our cheering, jumping up and down.

Jeffrey, standing just off third base, had motioned for us to settle down. He had held up his hands, making the 'slow down, brake' motion.

"Oh, come on, the kid's a hitter! He needs an agent!" Jeannie had yelled, amusing Jeffrey. I could tell he was trying not to laugh.

It was opening day for the Little League season, a huge day for Langdon. All the ball players rode fire trucks in a parade through town. Jeffrey was always front and center in the planning, making a schedule of parents to man the concession stand, setting up the PA system, and constantly conferring with the Parks and Recreation Director.

Jeannie and I always looked forward to that day, heralding in spring and all the hours of baseball to come. We'd been coming to opening day since T-ball, when Michael was five.

She and I had moved closer to the fence of the Little League field, watching Michael, now on second base. He was so handsome in his royal blue shirt, black baseball pants, new black socks, and spiffy black cleats. He was wearing number two, his favorite.

"A mini you, Sara, if you were eleven and had a penis!" Jeannie had exclaimed.

That comment had set us off into a fit of giggles. A nearby couple gave us a curious glance.

I had hit Jeannie playfully, calling out, "Sorry!" She motioned that she was 'zipping her lips' and leaned on the fence again.

The next player on Michael's team hit a high pop-up. Jeannie and I screamed, "Run Michael, run!"

Jeffrey yelled, "No, Michael!" and for a split-second Michael had looked confused.

The boy at shortstop called out, "Got it!" and caught the ball. Michael looked down the baseline between second and third, first to his dad and then to us.

Jeffrey nodded at Michael. But then he made his way over to us at the fence. "Ladies, you can't call out like that, okay? That's why I'm here, to tell the players when to run." He was serious, looking commanding in his own Pirates shirt.

Somewhat chastised, we burst out laughing when Jeffrey turned and walked back to his spot. Jeannie looked at me and that time I was the one who made the 'zip it' motion.

The Pirates lost that day, but when Michael walked over to us, he was beaming.

"Did you see all my hits, Mom?" He was already up to my chin.

"I sure did, sweetheart, you were awesome."

"A rock star, buddy!" Jeannie added, high-fiving him.

Not long ago, I had told Jeannie the whole story of why our marriage was ending: Craig and my obsession, the Larson boys and The Mountain, and the trip to Austin, *Sorry folks, Quebec is next week*. Only with Jeannie did I confess my porno spread plans and what I actually saw that day instead. Like a true friend, she never looked aghast. Instead, as I started to really open up about all the shit that had happened, she had come closer and sat on the floor beside me. She cried too, mostly when I got to the Michael part. Jeannie and I had met that first summer of Langdon, when he was just three. She was our first friend here and had become a part of our family. While never married or a mother herself, in some ways Michael was her boy too.

Now, in the car, I stopped crying and blew my nose. I took a big gulp from my water bottle and grabbed a banana from my lunch bag behind the passenger seat. When the highway was completely clear, I pulled out once again. I drove to her house, navigating the trailer, growing more confident. Jeannie was waiting for me, sitting on the steps of her front door. We hugged and looked at each other. We really didn't know what more to say—we were depleted from all our earlier intense talks. As I drove away, I heard her yell, "I love you, Sara Scott!" I was determined not to cry again and kept driving.

There's a spot as you come into town that shows The Mountain in all its full glory. Now, late August, there was no snow. But I could see the wide swaths of trails fanning out and down in my rear-view mirror as I drove away. The tree-lines were green, the expanse of The Mountain beautiful. As I reached the top of Sutter's Gulf, just before it dips down, I lowered my window all the way. I raised my left hand up and out and gave The Mountain the middle finger as its view began to recede. "Fuck you, Gerald Rice, you sick, fucking monster," I said out loud. Satisfied, I brought my hand back in, chose an Adele CD and cranked it up. I almost missed the 'For Sale' sign in front of The Chat and Chew.

Chapter 49
present

O n the morning of my forty-third birthday, I woke with a start. I sat up and then stood. I raised the blinds, but the inlet was still dark. I put my robe on and walked into the kitchen. Then I heard footsteps on the stairs. I went to the door, anticipating a surprise visit from Peter. Before he had a chance to knock, I opened it wide. There, in beautiful disarray and exhaustion, stood Lexi and Michael. My Michael.

I didn't know what to say—I looked from one to the other. Lexi, smiling, tilted her head and said, ever so sweetly, "We've come to wish you a happy birthday, Sara!" Michael looked unsure, standing still and holding Lexi's hand.

I stepped back and said, "Come in, come in."

I moved to Lexi. I'd never seen her look so beautiful. Her skin was pale and her blue eyes had circles under them, but she stood with such an air of grace. Her cheekbones were pronounced, her face in perfect symmetry. *She's not a girl anymore*, I thought. *She's a young woman.* Her long blond hair was pulled back in a baseball cap, and she wore an oversized Penn State sweatshirt. I hugged her tightly.

Michael remained uncomfortable, taking in the loft. I moved into the living room and motioned to them. "Come all the way in, please, both of you." I watched Michael from the corner of my eye. He looked tired, and his dark, almost black hair was the longest I'd ever seen it. He hadn't shaved. They were a picture of contrast, cast in shades of light and dark. Michael was wearing a Bucknell sweatshirt and blue jeans. I looked down and recognized one of the two pairs of sneakers we had bought almost two years ago when he was first heading off to college.

"This is a nice place," he said as I tidied the writing papers on the coffee table and moved them in to my school bag. I tucked the bag behind the rocking chair in front of the picture window.

"Thanks." I smiled, straightening up and feeling the awkwardness between us.

Looking at me, he said, hesitantly, "I've never missed your birthday. At least I've always wished you one. And we brought some things you asked Dad for."

"My books?" I asked hopefully. He nodded. Now that the shelving was done and the gliding ladder was attached, I had emailed Jeffrey asking him when I could come get my boxes stored in the attic. I not only had my own reading books but my parents' collection as well. I read many of my mother's favorite authors now: Anita Shreve, Margaret Atwood, and Jeffrey Lent. My collection was mostly fiction—much to Jeffrey's dismay. His books were centered on education and leadership, although he admitted to loving a good John Grisham novel now and then.

The kids were starved, so I made them a big frying pan of scrambled eggs with grated cheddar cheese and cinnamon raison toast. I also made a pot of coffee, but both shook their heads. They told me they'd already had several cups on the drive here. They'd left Langdon at about 3:00 a.m. but had driven—in Lexi's new, "But used Subbie"—from her place in Lewisburg the night before. Michael had texted Jeffrey that his plan was to go see me but that he wanted to bring me my books. Jeffrey had brought them down from the attic and had helped load them into Lexi's car in the middle of the night.

Lexi smiled and set down her fork. "We're all coffee'd out, Sara. It's what kept us awake as we made our way home and then here."

I wondered whose idea it had been to come. I knew that once Michael had his mind set on something, he was hell bent on getting it done. They had driven almost ten hours straight.

As if Lexi had read my mind, she said, "We were sitting in my place and Michael stood up and said, 'My mother's birthday is tomorrow.' And off we went—or came. Which is it?" Her self-effacement was one of the things I'd always found most endearing about her.

"You should sleep for a bit, then I can show you around. Like where I work."

Lexi looked to Michael, and he smiled. "You sleep, I'm going to get the books."

I quickly threw on a pair of jeans and a sweatshirt and then got Lexi settled on my bed with the afghan. Carrying the cartons from Lexi's Subaru up to the loft, I was thankful for the parking lot lights and the two lamps along the wharf. Michael asked me a lot of questions about Robert's Tackle and Bait Shop, the inlet, and how I'd found the loft. But each time we came up the stairs we grew silent, hoping Lexi had fallen asleep. Our last trip consisted of the two paintings I had asked Diana for, wrapped in newspaper.

When we were done, Michael tiptoed past Lexi and used the bathroom. Coming back out, he decided to have a coffee with me and whispered, "Can we take these outside onto the wharf?" The sun was just starting to come up, lightening the gray sky. To the east a beautiful pink was emerging.

I recited the old adage, "Red sky at night, sailor's delight. Red sky in morning, sailor's take warning."

"What does that mean?" Michael asked.

"Oh, I think it relates to the weather coming in from the west—fair skies or rain, what to expect based on the color of the sky."

He nodded his head and said, "Gotcha."

We leaned against the railings and set our mugs down. We looked at the water swooshing up against the pilings of the dock. The few gulls we saw were loud, and the sea smelled strong, but otherwise it was very quiet. I looked at Michael's profile and was struck by how much older he seemed, his unshaven face casting a shadow of a beard, his eyes dark and tired. A random thought crossed my mind: *When I met Jeffrey in college, he was already turning gray.*

Just then we heard the sound of a boat chugging from around the next cove. It came into full view. Sitting low in the water, the red scallop dragger where I bought my fresh scallops was making its way out. I'd never seen it leave for the day's catch. I'd never been up and out on the wharf this early. Two men were moving about the stern. Suddenly, one of them stood up and waved to me. The owner, Stan, was at the helm and gave a short horn blast. I waved back.

Michael, waving both his arms, looked at me. "That's my friggin' boat, my red boat."

I didn't understand. Michael laughed and raised his eyebrows, "My drawing, on your cup?"

"Oh, wow, I love that cup!" We both watched the dragger move out to sea. They had to go miles out, Stan had once told me.

Michael looked over at me again. "Hey, Mom, I've been a real asshole."

I stopped him, putting my hand over his. "We both said some awful things to each other that we didn't mean. I think you coming to me like this is the best thing that could have happened." And I meant it.

Staring out across the inlet, the red boat growing smaller now, Michael continued as if he hadn't heard what I'd just said. "The whole thing with The Mountain and the Larsons, well, I thought it was dirty, like I was embarrassed that we—you—had any connection to it. I thought they were nothing but lowlifes, and here you were, ready to throw me and Dad away for them."

"Michael, we don't have to go through all this."

But he cut me off and said, "Please, let me talk. I've had hours in the car, thinking about what I want to say."

"Okay, sweetie, I'm sorry." I didn't want to blow this. I turned and faced him.

"Besides the Larsons, Luke told me that he was one of the other two kids who'd also been sexually abused by Rice. He's now being represented by big time lawyers."

I did an audible intake and said, "Oh no, not Luke." But my mind quickly assessed Luke's situation as a little boy. His mom, Cecile, had multiple sclerosis and was in a wheelchair, his father wasn't around anymore, having taken off when Cecile's condition deteriorated. Rice must have seen the perfect situation and zeroed in. Luke, the older friend of Michael's who had taken him in under his wing on the Varsity soccer team when Michael was just a freshman. The boy who lettered in three high school sports and had played both college soccer and baseball at Castleton.

Michael continued, "His time with Rice, that bastard, was only for like a year—no not even, because, according to Luke, his mother figured out the shit that was happening. Literally." Michael looked at me for added emphasis. "You've got to keep this confidential, okay? Luke started to like, wet his pants and even poop 'em. His mom focused in on Rice and how Rice had started taking Luke for rides. She knew something was wrong. She stopped it."

I thought of Cecile who spent years in the wheelchair with people helping out as much as they could. And how most, even me, thought she wasn't able to properly parent her boy. But she'd stopped the abuse, known something wasn't right. Cecile had stood up to Rice.

I then remembered her funeral and Luke's complete breakdown. Jeffrey had insisted he move in with us that spring and helped him apply to colleges, took him up to meet with the Castleton coaches. We had kept our home open to him. Jeffrey and Michael both had enduring relationships with Luke.

My thoughts brought me back to what Michael was saying.

"I'm not proud to admit that it wasn't until I knew what Rice had done to Luke that I started to care."

"That's understandable, Michael—sometimes we can't feel the full impact of something, unless, well, it hits home. Like what you're saying about Luke."

"But, Mom, you cared, even without being close to the Larsons, and you did something big about it. That's what I've come to realize."

We were quiet for a little bit, our coffees all gone.

Michael began talking again. "In one of my classes, we really delved into privilege, 'specially white privilege and class. We did this thing where everybody starts out even like this." Michael now moved from the railing to the middle of the wharf and faced the end of it, looking past the tackle and bait shop.

Standing, with both arms at his side, he went on. "Our prof called out things like, 'Did you have books in your home growing up or parents who went to college, or did you live in areas you felt unsafe in or had ancestors who came to this country not by their own accord?' Lots of questions. For everything that like pertained to you as a kid growing up—or as an adult now—he'd tell you to take a step forwards or backwards. A couple of kids, one girl I've gotten to know pretty well, Carolyn, couldn't even finish it, she was so upset. Me, I was like at the farthest point from where we started, meaning I really had a privileged upbringing. And now I'm realizing how it has 'colored' or affected the way I see my world, and the way the big world sees me."

"I've seen that exercise before, Michael, I think in a social justice documentary. The privilege walk."

"Yeah, it's powerful. The Larsons had all that shit happen to them, awful stuff. Luke too. But Luke, he's done really good."

He came back to stand next to me. "I know how privileged I am, how good I've had it being raised by you and Dad."

I glanced at him but said nothing.

"Did you know they bulldozed the Larson house on Gravelin Road? It's all gone, a big field now."

I thought it was a just ending, the only ending. I needed to put that away for another time.

I hesitated, deciding how best to say what I needed to say. "I'm sorry I hurt you, Michael, that your dad and I couldn't stay married, that I was unfaithful to him. I have no excuse, other than it was a strange time for me."

Sensing he had taken that in, I added, "I shouldn't have told you of my own ugliness that afternoon in the kitchen. Your dad was right when he yelled at me to stop and not go there. You're my son, and I should have shielded you from knowing that. It wasn't—" I shook my head, trying to convey to him what I meant. "It wasn't your place to know that about your mother. I regret so much that I did that to you." This was the realization I'd come to in the many nights I spent here in Bristol, not sleeping and thinking.

"What's the saying, hindsight is twenty-twenty." It was more of a statement from Michael than a question.

He kept his eyes focused out on the water and then glanced down at me. "I know I said my fair share of awful things to you last summer. I'm really sorry too." He then moved his hip sideways, bumping me. It was an old, familiar show of affection between us. I laughed, but then I stopped and said, "I've really missed you."

"There, there, Ma Mere," Michael responded, draping his arm around my shoulders, hugging me.

I took it all in, his close proximity, our apologies, and the return of our relationship without all the anger and awkwardness.

Tentatively I asked, "How's your dad doing?'

"Actually, pretty good. I really like—" he stopped suddenly, looking at me warily.

"Diana? I really like Diana too. When I think about the two of them together, I see how well-suited they are."

"Well, she's nice and funny and easy-going. I think Dad's in a good place."

I smiled. "Good."

"Just so you know, Dad has never talked bad about you, ever, in all this. He says you're a 'doer' and he's a 'thinker' and sometimes a situation calls for one over the other."

I recalled the night I'd marched into his office and went off on him about all his educational bullshit.

"Your courses going well this year?" I asked Michael. "Have you started any in education yet?"

"Yeah, I have 'Issues in Education' now and had 'Social Contexts of Education' last semester. That class was hard. I really liked my general psychology course—I aced it but then bombed 'Evolution and Genetics of Sex.' Well, I got C/D. Lexi is going to make Dean's List again. I'm looking at a three-point-oh, I hope."

"How are you two?" I had never asked him that question before; I had never ventured into their relationship at all. I'd only been an observer, making sure I didn't overstep my boundaries. Besides, they were just kids, and I didn't see their relationship as anything too serious at the time. But now, after our separation, the question seemed natural to me. And here they still were, after four years of dating.

"We've had a few rough patches. You know it's different away at school. I thought she was pulling away and that scared me. Then she kind of thought the same thing of me this past winter. But I think we're good now. Lexi has a lot of drive, you know?"

"Does that concern you?" I asked, sensing there was something there.

"No, I admire it, honestly. If she goes all the way, you know, becomes a doctor, and I'm just a gym teacher..." He didn't finish his sentence.

"Maybe that's a good thing for a life together, Michael. You'll be able to support her best by having more time for what's needed. I know my career really allowed me to be there for you when your dad had to travel weeks on end."

He seemed pensive, looking out across the inlet. Now there was much more activity on the water. Other boats were going out—a man in a dingy was heading to a small sailboat moored not far from where we stood. The morning sun reflected off of the windows of the modest houses nestled around the cove. These were fishermen's homes, and it was time to go to work. We heard dogs barking and voices being carried across the water. It was approaching 6:00 a.m.

"Funny, you sound just like Lexi, but yeah, I know what you mean. Being a teacher definitely has its advantages."

"One thing from me." I hesitated for a second, then continued, "When you take your methods and the courses get steeped in educational theory and rhetoric, please remember, it's always about the relationships you build with your students first. That's key. Nothing else happens without that. You know this from your time working at Rec camp. No theory tells you the right, reassuring words to use for a child who's been picked on, and—" I was on a roll now—"proficiency-based standards don't measure the thoughtfulness of a poor boy who..." I couldn't finish, I was seeing Jason's face as he had looked in our backyard the day he left Langdon.

Michael saw I was upset. "It's okay, Mom, I'll remember."

"Good." I wrapped my arms around myself. "Now, let's go in. I'm freezing. Even the tip of my nose feels cold."

Later in the morning, I asked Lexi how her mother was doing. She told me that Marilyn was working for the Director of the Medical Care Systems in the tri-county area. "She likes it. She says it's a lateral move, whatever that means."

Lexi was walking back from the galley kitchen when she said this. Michael came up behind her and tackled her onto the couch. He started tickling her. "This is a lateral move, missy."

Lexi's sing-song voice called out, "Michael, stop tickling me, Michael, get off me, Michael, stop breathing in my face." It brought music to my ears. How much I had missed them.

"What were your plans for your birthday today, Mom?" Michael asked.

"Actually, a friend of mine, Louise, is having a little get together for me, and now I'll bring you two."

I texted both Peter and Louise the news. To Peter's text I added, *"We'll need to dial our relationship back, okay?"* He instantly replied, *"Got it!"* and then, *"Great surprise for you!"*

Both Louise and Peter understood how much Michael's estrangement had weighed heavily on my heart and affected me in so many ways.

I gave Lexi and Michael towels and the privacy of the alcove and bathroom to wash up and get ready for Louise's little gathering. Listening to them while I sat at the kitchen table, it struck me that so much had happened since our time apart and that maybe we'd never quite catch up. The missed months seemed overwhelming.

But when it was my turn for the bathroom and I was putting on a little makeup before leaving, I thought of Jane and her stints in rehab and then all the years after when she didn't know what was going on with her boys. My lament seemed shallow in comparison.

On the way out of the loft, down the stairs, I caught Lexi's hand. Michael kept walking on down the wharf. "Lex, one of the people...well, there's a man you're going to meet at my friend's, his name is Peter. We're kind of in a little bit of a relationship. We're gonna be subtle, you know, but is it going to throw Michael off if he notices something?"

Lexi looked ahead at Michael, now at the Outback, and then back at me. "Sara, he can handle it. But I may give him a heads-up, okay?" I nodded, suddenly worried.

Louise was a gracious host. I introduced Michael and Lexi to everyone. I'd noticed Lexi talking quietly to Michael, walking past Louise's roses. I didn't discern any pulling back on his part, just the opposite—he shook Peter's hand warmly as well as everyone else at the party. Katie had also come with Peter. It was nice to see Peter with her, their easy-going rapport much different from that uncomfortable afternoon at his apartment weeks ago.

I met Louise near the credenza. "Anthony one and Anthony two?" I whispered, referring to the neighbor and his son who had just arrived.

Louise, looking as lively as ever, said, "His son is visiting from Connecticut, some bigwig with Wells Fargo in New York. They were doing yard work across the way at his house. Then they came and pruned my rose bushes. I thought, 'Why not? The more the merrier!'"

Peter and I exchanged looks, and at one point he leaned into me and asked, "Celebrate tomorrow night?" I nodded at him just as Louise set out a rich, thick, three-layered chocolate cake with one candle on it. "This is Sara's first birthday here, in Bristol, thus the one candle," she said, winking at me.

Right after everyone sang and just before I was about to make a birthday wish and blow out the candle, Michael surprised me by standing up. He asked everyone around the table to raise their glass then tilted his head in my direction. "I'd like to make a toast."

Holding a glass of raspberry lemon iced tea, Michael looked directly at me and said, "A toast to you, Mother of Michael, M'Lady of Critters, Conqueror of Mountains, and Slayer of Monsters. We love you."

I looked up at him and then across the table at Lexi. I smiled, but it was one of sadness. *So much lost,* I thought, unable to articulate, even to myself, what I was feeling. A fleeting image of the Gravelin house, now gone, played out in my mind.

Jacob, in a resounding voice, bellowed, "Cheers to that!" We all drank to the toast.

At least Michael's forgiven me, I thought, as Peter smiled, motioning 'cheers' to me a second time. It lifted my spirits.

I was helping Louise pick up in the kitchen when Katie came over to us.

"Wow, who are you, like Daenerys Targaryen in *Game of Thrones*?" she quipped, possibly looking a little stoned.

"Hi, Katie. Louise and I are trying to decide on our next binge. We'd like another British series after *Last Tango in Halifax*."

"Did you know that the first season of *Tango* wasn't even filmed in Halifax? People came looking for the landmark locations of the show and then got upset. They had to change their locale for later seasons to be more authentic and please their fans."

Louise put down her dish-towel and gave Katie her full attention. "Really?"

"Yeah, really. I took an AP film course online. We covered contemporary British films. *The Fall* is pretty decent if you're okay with a British-Irish crime drama. It's filmed in Ireland and Britain. Oh, but wait, do you live alone?"

We both nodded.

She shrugged. "It's about a serial killer who targets women. Pretty graphic, but it's excellent, even if it is a disturbing look into criminal psychology."

Katie took a bite of the cake on the plate she was carrying and wandered off.

"What just happened?" I asked Louise.

"I think we just unmasked the real Katie O'Brien."

The party broke up early. I was glad. Michael and Lexi were exhausted. I thanked everyone for coming. Louise and I hugged. She whispered, "Your boy is wonderful, and his girlfriend, just lovely, a young Grace Kelly. But that man of yours, well, you'll have to make it up to him, won't you?"

Louise, I thought, was one of the most perceptive people I knew.

As I drove home, the kids quiet in the backseat, I wondered, though, if Louise had noticed Anthony '1' watching her every move as she attended to each of her guests. Jacob might have to step up his game or things could get complicated.

That night, Michael and Lexi fell asleep the moment their heads hit the pillow, but I lay awake in the alcove. I thought about the day, and how my life had changed so much in one short year. My forty-second birthday was hardly a memory at all, other than Jeffrey inviting me to Boston as he finished up a consult, knowing I wouldn't come, the knowledge that our marriage was in trouble hanging over us. Michael had called me from a bar near Bucknell. He and Lexi sang to me over the phone, their voices loud, a ruckus in the background. Such a contrast to their voices this morning, soft and sweet. My child, forever my child, had come to me.

The kids woke up midmorning. The plan was to get back to school at a decent hour; Lexi would drop Michael off first then drive another hour and a half to Lewisburg. It was going to be a long drive again, for both of them. I gave them gas money and packed up granola bars, apples, and drinks.

"Any chocolate cake left?" Michael asked, and I packed that as well. I hugged them both and thanked them for making this my best birthday ever. Michael was starting out as the driver, and I warned him about Maine speed-traps and the rotaries he needed to be mindful of.

"Hey, Mom, instead of going to Ogunquit this summer, Lexi and I should just come here."

"That's a great idea, Michael, we'll talk more about it."

Lexi leaned forward so I could see her and said, "I love you, Sara."

I started to cry, my arms crossed up against my chest. "Oh, you beautiful girl, take care of my beautiful boy."

As Michael started to drive away, I called out to them, "Text me when you get there!"

Michael made an 'okay' sign with his fingers. It was not lost on me that the last image I had of him pulling away was of that. I had wondered for the last eight, almost nine months if he was okay. I stayed outside until I couldn't see Lexi's car anymore.

Once in the loft, I counted seven cartons of books to unpack. I started by unwrapping the two paintings Diana had sent, both wrapped in newspaper. In black sharpie she had written, "Enjoy" and drawn a heart on the outside of each package. But then I noticed a birth announcement in a corner of the *Langdon Shopper* that Diana had used: "Baby Ethan Portman was born March 9, weighing in at a healthy 9lb, 2oz, twenty inches long. Baby Ethan joins big sister Emily and…." *Craig's had another child,* I thought, *a baby boy.* The rest of the announcement was missing. I didn't bother looking for it.

Peter came over that night to celebrate my birthday privately. He brought me a wooden window box he'd made from repurposed gray, weathered barn board. A big, bright green bow was attached to it.

"I thought you'd like to see flowers and dirt, you know, when you do your blinds every morning. Kind of temper all that water and coastal crap." I looked up at him quickly and he smiled. "I'll put it up in a week or so—we're still bound to get a frost or two till early May."

It was not lost on me how much my feelings for the loft, the wharf, the sea, the fog, the gray had changed since last September. *But flowers would be nice,* I thought. *Pink geraniums with some vinca.*

We were low-keyed and happy to be in each other's company. I apologized that there was no more cake, that Michael had taken it all. Standing at my refrigerator, Peter had made a face of exaggerated disappointment and had reached over, pulling me close to his body, my head just below his chin, my bare feet resting on top of his bare feet. We had walked like that, Peter balancing me with his hands clasped around my back, me laughing, knowing we were headed to the alcove. There was no pretense about what we both wanted.

After, laying with my head in the crook of his arm, we talked a bit about work. Peter had just taken on a small design project not far from the wharf. But he was most excited about a conversation he'd had yesterday at the party, and its follow up call with Anthony '2' this morning. "He's interested in a piece of property for sale out on the northern spit. It's a big, old place, kind of a money pit, but I like his vision. We're meeting there tomorrow afternoon."

I whispered, "The pit on the spit."

Peter brought his face down to mine and said playfully, "Aren't you a clever one."

I was sending out letters to my students' parents, asking for donations to the local humane society for an upcoming field trip. I told Peter that I was entertaining the notion of a kitten, the idea having taken hold just that afternoon, once the loft had grown quiet after Michael and Lexi's departure. "I think I'd like the company. I'll check out the kittens when we go as a class."

Just before I dozed off, I thought, *How did we, Jeffrey and I, let this go?* It was a powerful reckoning that he and I had both acknowledged and understood that our relationship was over.

Peter asked, sleepily, "Hey, what was that toast all about, that your son gave you?"

I lifted my head from his arm and turned to face him. "One day, I'll break it all down for you, but we're in no hurry, right?" He had pulled me close, his body's heat enveloping me.

I woke sometime in the middle of the night. I could see the stars from the skylight. I did not turn on the bedside lamp. Peter was snoring softly, and I didn't want to wake him. When I returned from the bathroom to climb into bed, I glanced at the bedside stand. Next to the basket of sand dollars, I had placed the book *The Indian in the Cupboard* after finding it earlier that day in one of the cartons Michael brought.

How it got there, in my and my parents' collection, I'll never know. No other book of Michael's youth had similarly found its way to me from the house in Langdon. Like a lot of things that had happened in the past two and a half years, I wondered about chance and fate.

I chose to place it there, on the night-stand, not as a reminder of Michael or even of Jason. It was there to remind me, that for nineteen, almost twenty years, I had shared my life with a good man and an excellent father to my son. I wished Jeffrey happiness.

The following week, I received two important items in the mail. The first was a little box in an express mail envelope. I looked at the familiar writing and knew it was from Maddie. In the box was a pair of bright orange, feathery, dangling earrings. A note was enclosed. It read, *"Happy Birthday, Mrs. Scott, here's earrings to go with your orange sweater! xoox Maddie."* I wore the sweater and earrings the very next day to school.

The second item that came was a postcard from Disney World, in Orlando, Florida. It was the picture of the iconic castle that every Disney movie starts out with. On the back of the card were five words, written in painstaking cursive: *"Thank you, from Jamie Larson."*

I held Jamie's card. "He's forgiven me too."

Postscript

Sometimes when I leisurely wake up like this, in the light of the morning, the summer day looks so promising from my bed. Gloria, my not-so-little-any-more tabby, is nestled up by my head.

This morning, the harbor is sparkling blue, the sailboats are already out, and splashes of color catch my eye. Memories of other, earlier days wash over me. I recall Michael's ninth birthday. We're at the Cape, on the beach with Claire and the little girls. I see their sweet backs and pigtails; Michael's dark hair is sprinkled with sand. They run to and from the water's edge, filling their buckets. Claire and I sit, she with her hand on the brim of a straw hat, keeping it in place, me with my big JLo sunglasses. We're munching on chips, trying to keep the sand out of the guacamole. I can hear the gulls, like now, outside the loft, and I can feel the warmth of the sun.

I move on to remembering Michael's tenth birthday. Claire and Paul and the girls are in Vermont. The soccer goals are set up in the backyard, and we all run around. Jeffrey is carrying Claire's youngest, Emma, in his arms as he kicks the ball past Michael for a goal. We cheer, we boo, and suddenly the sprinkler is added into the mix, which thrills the girls. Michael is determined to win, but he slips and slides as he tries to kick the ball from out of an imaginary goal box. Later, the kids gallop by, trying to catch fireflies in glass jars, while the four of us sip beer, watching the fire, hearing its crackle. "To our children," I remember saying. We all toast.

I then see—and this breaks me to the core—the Larson boys. Bright-eyed Jackson and thoughtful Jason, already experiencing sexual abuse at the hands, literally, of Gerald Rice. I can't fathom their despair, their little hearts pumping in their chests as the monster reaches for them in his car, parked somewhere on The Mountain. Once home, greeted by a woman they don't know, they run to a hiding place, to try to make sense of what has just happened. The man who tells them that he will save their mother has just put his grotesque mouth on their bodies, shushing them as he grunts and groans. The sorrow I feel for their pain is, at times, overwhelming.

Katherine, my therapist, says that guilt is at the center of my *why*—why I went into exile and left Langdon, why I broke down when Don and Kelly came to take Maddie, and why I am still coming to her, now every other Wednesday.

She asked me one time, "What would have happened to you and Craig, eventually, without all of this?"

I had replied, rather quickly, "Our fling would have run its course, and Jeffrey and I would still be married today." I firmly believed that.

Her next question had been, "What would have happened if you hadn't seen what you did and stood up for the Larsons?" I couldn't talk, I had no answer. I cried as we sat in silence, in the waning daylight of her office.

"You can't hold yourself accountable for something you didn't know, Sara. There's nothing you have to be guilty of and be forgiven for. When you did learn of the sexual abuse you told; you did all you could. It stopped. And you've paid a personal price for it."

I am working on this, the letting go of the guilt and the forgiving myself.

"We're all works in progress," Katherine likes to say.

After a lot of the shit that hit the fan had settled, I went to Freddy's office. I wanted to say goodbye; I was ready to head east to Maine. He and I had grown close in all of this, both wanting the Larsons to have a chance, a fighting chance.

I remember him saying, "Sara, you put an end to it. I know the cost to you and your family is immense. But you rectified it."

I was sitting across from him at his desk. Freddy hadn't disappointed me, or Jane, not once since I knocked on his door that early morning almost a year ago. But I couldn't quite accept this statement of his. I stood up and moved towards the door and then came back. I was troubled.

"Nothing is ever truly made right or rectified, though, is it? You can't make right the wrong already done, can you? The wrong still happened, and from that wrong, it wields and forges and molds you to its force. So, Freddy, rectified is a false concept, isn't it?"

"But, Sara," he had implored, now standing, "that's all we have. Once we know, we have to make attempts to rectify the…" He struggled to find the right words.

"The terrible wrong," I answered.

"Yes, the terrible wrong."

I left his office on that late summer day. I came out and moved down through the corridor to the outside door. The two offices that we had given our depositions in were now occupied. A young woman looked up from her computer and smiled at me. I smiled back. *We all have a story to tell*, I thought as I put on my sunglasses and reached for my keys. *What our parents and the grown-ups in our lives do determines the beginning of that story.* And then, just as quickly, a second thought came. *But it's what we do, as adults, with the terrible wrong, or the wonderful right and all the stuff in between, that determines the rest of our story.*

I opened the door to the afternoon sunlight and felt hopeful for everything still to come.

With Gratitude

With gratitude to my husband, Andy, who took this endeavor of mine to write a book in stride, right along with, "We're getting a puppy." Special thanks to Rachel Carter whose editorial expertise and assistance was invaluable, and to Coleen Lawlor for reading the tough parts for authenticity.

Finally, I am deeply grateful to my sisters, Pamela Jane and Priscilla Adele, and my golf buddies, Susan and Janet. I cherish our history and friendships, filled with love and laughter.

If you or someone you know suspects child abuse please contact your local agencies. In the state of Vermont call 1-800-649-5285, 24/7, to report your suspicion.

What is Child Sexual Abuse?

Vermont's child protection law (33 VSA § 4912) defines sexual abuse as any act or acts by any person involving sexual molestation or exploitation of a child, including but not limited to:

- Incest, prostitution, rape, sodomy;
- Lewd and lascivious conduct involving a child;
- Aiding, abetting, counseling, hiring, or procuring of a child to perform or participate in any photograph, motion picture, exhibition, show, representation, or other presentation which, in whole or in part, depicts sexual conduct, sexual excitement, or sadomasochistic abuse involving a child;
- Viewing, possessing, or transmitting child pornography, with the exclusion of the exchange of images between mutually consenting minors, including the minor whose image is exchanged;
- Human trafficking;
- Sexual assault;
- Voyeurism;
- Luring a child; or
- Obscenity.

For more details, please see FSD Policy 50-Child Abuse and Neglect Definitions.

dcf.vermont.gov/prevention/stepup